W9-AEB-281

Toby's Room

ALSO BY PAT BARKER

Life Class

The Regeneration Trilogy
Regeneration
The Eye in the Door
The Ghost Road

Union Street
Blow Your House Down
Liza's England (*formerly* The Century's Daughter)
The Man Who Wasn't There

Another World
Border Crossing
Double Vision

Toby's Room

A NOVEL

Pat Barker

Doubleday   New York   London   Toronto   Sydney   Auckland

BOCA RATON PUBLIC LIBRARY
BOCA RATON, FLORIDA

This book is a work of fiction. Names, characters, businesses, organizations, places, events, and incidents either are the product of the author's imagination or are used fictitiously. Any resemblance to actual persons, living or dead, events, or locales is entirely coincidental.

Copyright © 2012 by Pat Barker

All rights reserved. Published in the United States by Doubleday, a division of Random House, Inc., New York. Originally published in Great Britain by Hamish Hamilton, an imprint of Penguin Books, London, in 2012. Published by arrangement with Hamish Hamilton.

www.doubleday.com

DOUBLEDAY and the portrayal of an anchor with a dolphin are registered trademarks of Random House, Inc.

Jacket design by Emily Mahon
Pastel artwork © 2012 by Joel Spector

Library of Congress Cataloging-in-Publication Data
Barker, Pat, 1943–
  Toby's room / Pat Barker. — 1st ed.
    p. cm.
  Sequel to Life class.
1. World War, 1914–1918—Fiction.   2. Coming of age—Fiction.
3. Brothers and sisters—Fiction.   I. Title.
PR6052.A6488T63 2012
823'.914—dc23   2012007066

ISBN 978-0-385-52436-0

MANUFACTURED IN THE UNITED STATES OF AMERICA

10 9 8 7 6 5 4 3 2 1

First United States Edition

For David, always

Toby's Room

Part One

1912

1

Elinor arrived home at four o'clock on Friday and went straight to her room. She hung the red dress on the wardrobe door, glancing at it from time to time as she brushed her hair. That neckline seemed to be getting lower by the minute. In the end her nerve failed her. She hunted out her pink dress, the one she used to wear for dancing classes at school, put it on, and stood in front of the cheval mirror. She turned her head from side to side, her hands smoothing down the creases that had gathered round the waist. Oh dear. No, no, she couldn't do it, not this time, not ever again. She wriggled out of it and threw it to the back of the wardrobe. Out of the window would have been more satisfying, but her father and brother-in-law were sitting on the terrace. She pulled the red dress over her head, tugged the neckline up as far as it would go, and went reluctantly downstairs.

Father met her in the hall and hugged her as if he hadn't seen her for a year. Outside the living room, she hesitated, but there was no point wearing a red dress and then creeping along the skirting boards like a mouse, so she flung the door open and swept in. She kissed Rachel, waved at Rachel's husband, Tim, who was at the far side of the room talking to her mother, and then looked around for Toby, but he wasn't there. Perhaps he wasn't coming after all, though he'd said he would. The prospect of his absence darkened the whole evening; she wasn't sure she could face it on her own. But then, a few minutes later, he came in, apologizing profusely, damp hair sticking to his forehead. He must've been for a swim. She wished she'd known; she'd have gone with him. Not much hope of talking to him now; Mother had already beckoned him to her side.

Rachel was asking Elinor question after question about her life in London, who she met, who she went out with, did she have any particular friends? Elinor said as little as possible, looking for an excuse to get away. It was supplied by her mother, who appeared at her side and hissed, "Elinor, go upstairs at once and take that ridiculous dress off."

At that moment the gong sounded. Elinor spread her hands, all injured innocence, though underneath she felt hurt and humiliated. Yet again, she was being treated like a child.

Father came in at the last minute just as they were sitting down. She wondered at the curious mixture of poking and prying and secrecy that ruled their lives. Mother and Father saw very little of each other. *She* needed country air for the sake of her health; *he* lived at his club because it was such a convenient walking distance from the hospital, where he often had to be available late at night. Was that the reason for their weeklong separation? She doubted it. Once, crossing Tottenham Court Road, she'd seen her father with a young woman, younger even than Rachel. They'd just come out of a restaurant. The girl had stood, holding her wrap tightly round her thin shoulders, while Father flagged down a cab and helped her into it, and then they were whirled away into the stream of traffic. Elinor had stood and watched, openmouthed. Father hadn't seen her; she was sure of that. She'd never mentioned that incident to anyone, not even to Toby, though she and Toby were the only members of the family who kept no secrets from each other.

She sat in virtual silence for the first half of the meal—sulking, her mother would have said—though Tim did his clumsy best to tease her out of it. Did she have a young man yet? Was all this moodiness because she was in love?

"There's no time for anything like that," Elinor said, crisply. "They work us too hard."

"Well, you know what they say, don't you? All work and no play . . . ?" He turned to Toby. "Have you seen her with anybody?"

"Not yet, but I'm sure it's only a matter of time."

Toby's joining in the teasing, however reluctantly, was all it took to chafe Elinor's irritation into fury.

"Well, if you must know I have met somebody." She plucked a name from the air. "Kit Neville."

This was not true: she'd hardly spoken to Kit Neville. He was merely the loudest, the most self-confident, the most opinionated, and, in many ways, the most obnoxious male student in her year, and therefore the person she thought of first.

"What does he do?" Mother asked. Predictably.

"He's a student."

"What sort of student?"

"Art. What else would he be doing at the Slade?"

"Have you met his family?"

"Now why on earth would I want to do that?"

"Because that's what people do when—"

"When they're about to get engaged? Well, I'm not. We're just friends. Very good friends, but . . . *friends*."

"You need to be careful, Elinor," Rachel said. "Living in London on your own. You don't want to get a reputation . . ."

"I do want to get a reputation, as it happens. I want to get a reputation as a painter."

"You know what I mean."

"Oh, for heaven's sake."

"Elinor," her father said. "That's enough."

So even Father was turning against her. The last mouthful of cheese and biscuit sticking in her dry throat, Elinor followed her mother and Rachel out of the dining room. They sat over a pot of coffee that nobody wanted, staring at their reflections in the black windows that overlooked the airless terrace. The windows couldn't be opened because of moths. Rachel had a horror of moths.

"So who is this Mr. Neville?" Mother asked.

"Nobody, he's in my year, that's all."

"I thought you said classes weren't mixed?"

"Some are, some aren't." She could barely speak for exasperation; she'd brought this on herself. "Look, it's not as if we're *going out* . . ."

"So why mention him?" Rachel's voice was slurry with tiredness. Tendrils of damp hair stuck to her forehead; she'd eaten scarcely anything. She yawned and stretched her ankles out in front of her. "Look at them. Puddings." She dug her fingers into the swollen flesh as if she hated it.

"You must be worn out in this heat," Mother said. "Why don't you put your feet up?"

Feet up in the drawing room? Unheard of. But then Elinor intercepted a glance between the two women, and understood. She wondered when she was going to be told. What a family they were for not speaking. She wanted to jump on the table and shout out every miserable little secret they possessed, though, apart from the breakdown of her parents' marriage, she couldn't have said what the secrets were. But there was something: a shadow underneath the water. Swim too close and you'd cut your feet. A childhood memory surfaced. On holiday somewhere, she'd cut her foot on a submerged rock; she'd felt no pain, only the shock of seeing her blood smoking into the water. Toby had taken off his shirt and wrapped it round her foot, then helped her back to the promenade. She remembered his pink fingers, wrinkled from the sea, the whorl of hair on the top of his head as he bent down to examine the cut.

Why couldn't they leave her alone? All this nonsense about young men . . . It was just another way of drilling it into you that the real business of a girl's life was to find a husband. Painting was, at best, an accomplishment; at worst, a waste of time. She was trying to hold on to her anger, but she'd suppressed it so long it was threatening to dissipate into depression. As it so often did. Why hadn't Toby spoken up for her? Instead of just sitting there, fiddling with his knife and fork.

She was thoroughly fed up. As soon as possible after the men joined them, she excused herself, saying she needed an early night.

As she closed the door behind her, she heard Father ask, "What's the matter with her?"

"Oh, you know," Mother said. "Girls."

Meaning? Nothing that made her feel better about herself, or them.

———

Next morning after breakfast Toby announced that he was going to walk to the old mill.

"In this heat?" Mother said.

"It's not too bad. Anyway, it'll be cooler by the river."

Elinor followed him into the hall. "Do you mind if I come?"

"It's a long way."

"Toby, I walk all over London."

"Don't let Rachel hear you say that. *Rep-u-tation!*"

They arranged to meet on the terrace. Soon Elinor was

following her brother across the meadow, feeling the silken caress of long grasses against her bare arms and the occasional cool shock of cuckoo spit.

"You know this chap you were talking about last night . . . ?"

"Oh, don't you start."

"I was only asking."

"I only mentioned him because I'm sick of being teased. I just wanted to get Tim off my back. Instead of which, I got Mother onto it."

"And Rachel."

"She's worse than Mother."

"She's jealous, that's all. She settled down a bit too early and . . . Well, she didn't exactly get a bargain, did she?"

"You don't like Tim, do you?"

"He's harmless. I just don't think she's very happy." He turned to face her. "You won't make that mistake, will you?"

"Marrying Tim? Shouldn't think so."

"No-o. Settling down too early."

"I don't intend to 'settle down' at all."

She hoped that was the end of the subject, but a minute later Toby said, "All the same, there has to be a reason you mentioned him—I mean, him, rather than somebody else."

"He's perfectly obnoxious, that's why. He was just the first person who came to mind."

Once they reached the river path, there was some shade at last, though the flashing of sunlight through the leaves and branches was oddly disorientating, and more than once she tripped over a root or jarred herself stepping on air.

"Be easier coming back," Toby said. "We won't have the sun in our eyes."

She didn't want to go on talking. She was content to let images rise and fall in her mind: her lodgings in London, the Antiques Room at the Slade, the friends she was starting to make, the first few spindly shoots of independence, though it all seemed a little unreal here, in this thick heat, with dusty leaves grazing the side of her face and swarms of insects making a constant humming in the green shade.

She was walking along, hardly aware of her surroundings, when a sudden fierce buzzing broke into her trance. Toby caught her arm. Bluebottles, gleaming sapphire and emerald, were glued to a heap of droppings in the center of the path. A few stragglers zoomed drunkenly towards her, fastening on her eyes and lips. She spat, batting them away.

"Here, this way," Toby said. He was holding a branch for her so she could edge past the seething mass.

"Fox?" she asked, meaning the droppings.

"Badger, I think. There's a sett up there."

She peered through the trees, but couldn't see it.

"Do you remember we had a den here once?" he said.

She remembered the den: a small, dark, smelly place under some rhododendron bushes. Tiny black insects crawled over your skin and fell into your hair. "I don't think it was here."

"It was. You could just hear the weir."

She listened, and sure enough, between the trees, barely audible, came the sound of rushing water.

"You're right, I remember now. I thought it was a bit farther on."

She thought he might want to go there, he lingered so long, but then he turned and walked on.

The river was flowing faster now, picking up leaves and twigs and tiny, struggling insects and whirling them away, and the trees were beginning to thin out. More and more light reached the path until, at last, they came out into an open field that sloped gently down towards the weir. A disused mill— the target of their walk—stood at the water's edge, though it was many years since its wheel had turned.

This had been the forbidden place of their childhood.

They were not to go in there, Mother would say. The floor-boards were rotten, the ceilings liable to collapse at any minute . . .

"And don't go near the water," she'd call after them, in a last desperate attempt to keep them safe, as they walked away from her down the drive. "We won't," they'd chorus. "Promise," Toby would add, for good measure, and then they would glance sideways at each other, red-faced from trying not to giggle.

Now, Elinor thought, they probably wouldn't bother going in, but Toby went straight to the side window, prised the boards apart, and hoisted himself over the sill. After a second's hesitation Elinor followed.

Blindness, after the blaze of sunlight. Then, gradually, things became clear: old beams, cobwebs, tracks of children's footprints on the dusty floor. Their own footprints? No, of course not, couldn't be, not after all these years. Other children came here now. She put her foot next to one of the prints, marveling at the difference in size. Toby, meanwhile, was expressing amazement at having to duck to avoid the beams.

Because this place had been the scene of so many forbidden adventures, an air of excitement still clung to it, in spite of the dingy surroundings. She went across to the window and peered out through a hole in the wall. "I wonder what it was like to work here."

Toby came across and stood beside her. "Pretty good hell, I should think. Noise and dust."

He was right, of course; when the wheel turned the whole place must have shook. She turned to him. "What do you think—?"

He grabbed her arms and pulled her towards him. Crushed against his chest, hardly able to breathe, she laughed and struggled, taking this for the start of some childish game, but then his lips fastened onto hers with a groping hunger that shocked her into stillness. His tongue thrust between her lips, a strong, muscular presence. She felt his chin rough against her cheek, the breadth of his chest and shoulders, not that round, androgynous, childish softness that had sometimes made them seem like two halves of a single person. She started to struggle again, really struggle, but his hand came up and cupped her breast and she felt herself softening, flowing towards him, as if something hard and impacted in the pit of her stomach had begun to melt.

And then, abruptly, he pushed her away.

"I'm sorry. I'm sorry. Sorry, sorry . . ."

She couldn't speak. How was it possible that anybody, in a single moment, could stumble into a chasm so deep there was no getting out of it?

"Look, you go back," he said. "I'll come home later."

Automatically, she turned to go, but then remembered the river and turned back.

"No, go on, I'll be all right," he said.

"They'll wonder what's happened if I show up on my own."

"Say you felt ill."

"And you went on and left me? Don't think so. No, come on, we've got to go back together."

He nodded, surrendering the decision to her, and that shocked her almost more than the kiss. He was two years older, and a boy. He had always led.

All the way home, treading in his footsteps, aware, as she'd never been before, of the movement of muscles in his back and legs, she was trying to tame the incident. *Incident.* But it wasn't an incident, it was a catastrophe that had ripped a hole in the middle of her life. But then the flash of honesty passed, and she began again to contain, to minimize, to smooth over, to explain. A brotherly hug, nothing to make a fuss about, a kiss that had somehow gone a tiny bit wrong. That was all. Best forgotten. And as for her reaction: shock, fear, and something else, something she hadn't got a name for; that was best forgotten too.

Her thoughts scrabbled for a footing. All the time, underneath, she was becoming more and more angry. For there was another possible explanation: that Toby had been conducting a rather nasty, schoolboy experiment to find out what it was like to be close, in that way, with a girl. But then, why would he need to do that? She knew perfectly well that young men had access to sexual experiences that girls like her knew nothing about. So why would he need to experiment on her?

She looked back over the last twenty-four hours: saw herself coming downstairs in the red dress, sitting at the dinner table boasting about having an admirer. Had it seemed to him that she was moving away, leaving him? His reaching out for her had felt a bit like that. He'd grabbed her the way a drowning man grabs a log.

By the time they got back to the house, she'd developed a headache, the beginnings of a migraine perhaps. She clutched at the excuse of illness and ran upstairs to her room, passing her mother on the stairs, but not stopping to speak.

"What's the matter with Elinor?" Mother asked Toby.

"Not feeling very well. Bit too much sun, I think."

That made her angry too: the cool, rational, *accepted* explanation which emphasized her weakness, not his. She slammed her bedroom door, stood with her back to it, and then, slowly, as if she had to force a passage through her throat, she began to cry: ugly, wrenching sobs that made her a stranger to herself.

———

Elinor missed lunch, but went downstairs for dinner, because she knew her absence would only arouse curiosity, and perhaps concern. Part of her expected, even hoped, that Toby would have made some excuse to return to London, but no, there he was, laughing and talking, just as he normally did. Though perhaps drinking rather more than usual.

She made an effort, chatting to her father, ignoring her mother and Rachel, flirting outrageously with Tim, no longer the little schoolgirl sister-in-law. *Oh, no.* Looking round the table, she resolved that never again would she impersonate the girl they still thought she was.

Toby didn't look at her from beginning to end of the meal, but she made herself speak to him. Where the children were concerned, her mother was an acute observer, and though she'd never in a million years guess the truth, she'd notice the tension between herself and Toby if they weren't talking and assume they'd argued. She wouldn't rest till she found out what it was about, so a quarrel would have to be invented, and in that imaginary dispute Mother would side with Toby, and once more Elinor would be in the wrong. Somehow or other Elinor was going to have to get through the rest of the evening without arousing suspicion.

After dinner, she suggested cards. She knew Father would back her up: he loved his family but their conversation bored him. So the table was set up, partners chosen and all conversation was thereby at an end. Toby dealt the cards, smiled in her direction once or twice, but without meeting her eyes. Or was she imagining the change in him? Even now a little, niggling worm of doubt remained. Was she being—dread word—hysterical? Her mother had accused her of that often enough in the past. Elinor knew that even if there were any family discussion of the incident she would be made to feel entirely in the wrong. But there would be no discussion.

So the evening dragged on, until ten o'clock, when she was able to plead the remains of a headache and retire early to bed.

Once in her room, she threw the window wide open, but

didn't switch on the lamp. No point inviting moths into the room, though she didn't dislike them, and certainly wasn't terrified of them as Rachel was. She thought she looked a bit like a moth herself, fluttering to and fro in front of the mirror as she undressed and brushed her hair. It was too hot for a nightdress; she needed to feel cool, clean sheets against her skin. Only they didn't stay cool. She threw them off, looked down at the white mounds of her breasts, and pressed her clenched fists hard into the pit of her stomach where she'd felt that treacherous melting. Never again. She would never, *never,* let her body betray her in that way again. A little self-consciously, she began to cry, but almost at once gave up in disgust. What had happened was too awful for tears. She'd been frightened of him and he hadn't cared: Toby, who'd always protected her. She saw his face hanging over her, the glazed eyes, the groping, sea-anemone mouth; he hadn't looked like Toby at all. And then, when he pulled her against him, she'd felt—

Downstairs, a door opened. Voices: people wishing each other good night. Footsteps: coming slowly and heavily, or quickly and lightly, up the stairs. The floorboards grumbled under the pressure of so many feet. Two thuds, seconds apart: one of the men taking his shoes off. Then silence, gradually deepening, until at last the old house curled up around the sleepers, and slept too.

Not a breath of wind. A fringe of ivy leaves—black against the moonlight—surrounded the open window, but not one of them stirred. Normally, even on a still night, there'd be some noise. A susurration of leaves, sounding so like the sea that sometimes she drifted off to sleep pretending she was lying on a beach with nothing above her but the stars. No hope of that tonight. An owl hooted, once, twice, then silence again, except for the whisper of blood in her ears.

Was Toby lying awake like her? No, he'd drunk so much

wine at dinner he'd be straight off to sleep. Imagining his untroubled sleep—Toby's breath hardly moving the sheet that covered him—became a kind of torment. After a while, it became intolerable. She had to do something. Reaching for her nightdress, she got out of bed and let herself quietly out of her room.

On the landing she stopped and listened: a squeal of bed-springs as somebody turned over; her father's fractured snore. She tiptoed along the corridor, avoiding the places where she knew the floorboards creaked. She'd made this groping journey so often in the past: the unimaginably distant past when she and Toby had been best friends as well as brother and sister. He'd shielded her from Mother's constant carping, the comparisons with Rachel that were never in her favor, the chill of their father's absence. And now, for some unfathomable reason, he'd left her to face all that on her own.

Outside his door, she hesitated. There was still time to turn back, only she couldn't, not now, she was too angry. Something had to be done to dent his complacency. She turned the knob and slipped in. Once inside the room, she held her breath. Listened again. Yes, he was asleep, though not snoring: slow, calm, steady breaths. Not a care in the world.

She crossed to the bed and looked down at him. Like her, he'd left the curtains open; his skin in the moonlight had the glitter of salt. Leaning towards him, she felt his breath on her face. She knew there was something she wanted to do, but she didn't know what it was. Jerk him awake? Shock him out of that infuriatingly peaceful, deep sleep? Yes, but how? There was a jug of water on the washstand near the bed. She twined her fingers round the handle, raised it high above her head . . .

And then, just as she was about to pour, he opened his eyes. He didn't move, or speak, or try to get out of the way. He simply lay there, looking up at her. In the dimness, his light-famished pupils flared to twice their normal size, and forever afterwards, when she tried to recapture this moment, she remembered his eyes as black. Neither of them spoke. Slowly, she lowered the jug.

The chink, as she set it down on the marble stand, seemed to release him. He reached out, closed his hand gently round her wrist, and pulled her down towards him.

2

Every window gaped wide, as if the house were gasping for breath. Barely visible above the trees, a small, hard, white sun threatened the heat to come. Mother's precious lawn had turned yellow, with bald patches here and there where the cracked earth showed through.

Elinor chased clumps of pale yellow scrambled egg around her plate. It was absolutely necessary that she should appear to eat, but so far she hadn't managed to force one mouthful down.

"Water?" Mother asked. She topped up her own and Elinor's glass without waiting for a reply.

"Look at Hobbes," Elinor said.

Hearing his name, Hobbes raised his head, fixed his bloodshot eyes on her for a moment, then sank his slobbering jowls onto his paws again.

Her mother's face softened, as it never did when she looked at Elinor. "Poor old thing, he really hates this weather."

"Yes, imagine this in a fur coat." They ate in silence for a while.

"You were very quiet last night," Mother said.

"Headache, I expect. Where is everybody?"

"Rachel's having a lie-in. Your father's in his study, been up since six, and Tim and Toby have gone shooting."

"Toby hates shooting."

Her mother's jaw clicked as she chewed on a triangle of dry toast.

"Well, that's where they've gone."

Conversation wilted in the heat. Soon there was no sound except for a discreet, well-bred scraping of knives on plates. Elinor could feel her mother's gaze heavy on the side of her face. She put her fork down.

"Shall we have coffee outside?" her mother said.

They took their cups onto the terrace, where a table and chairs had been set up overlooking the lawn. The smell of dry grass tightened Elinor's chest; she was finding it difficult to breathe.

"Are you all right?"

"I'm fine. Looks like we're in for another scorcher."

Her mother tested the cushion for dampness before sitting down. "It needs a thunderstorm, freshen things up."

As she spoke, the crack of a rifle sent wood pigeons blundering into the air. Elinor drew a deep breath, or as deep as she could manage, and gazed straight ahead.

"You and Toby haven't quarreled, have you?"

"What makes you think that?"

"I thought I detected a bit of an atmosphere last night."

"No, I was just tired."

Mother sipped her coffee, put the cup down, dabbed her lips on the napkin. "I want to tell you something, Elinor."

This might have sounded like the beginning of a mother-daughter chat, except that she and her mother never had them. That was Rachel's province. The bare minimum of information that had been imparted to Elinor when she reached the age of thirteen had been conveyed by Rachel, in this, as in all other things, their mother's deputy.

"I don't think I've ever told you Toby was a twin?"

This was the last thing she'd expected. "No, I had no idea. Well . . ." She tried to gather her thoughts. "What happened?"

"It died. She. It was a girl."

She swallowed, obviously finding it difficult to go on. She was a reticent woman—or vacant—Elinor had never been sure which, though she was inclined to favor vacancy. "Bland" was the word. It was almost as if her mother's beauty, which even now was remarkable, had taken the place of a personality.

"I never felt really well when I was expecting him, and with Rachel I had—in fact, I felt wonderful; but with Toby, no. I was so breathless by the end I used to sleep sitting up. And then when I went into labor it was . . . Well, it was difficult. A whole day and half the following night."

Elinor winced. "I couldn't do it."

"When you're nine months pregnant, dear, you don't have a lot of choice. Anyway, he was born, *at last,* and of course I felt relief and joy and all the things you do feel, and it actually took me quite a while to realize the midwife was looking worried. She called the doctor—he was downstairs having a drink with your father—and I'll never forget him coming through the door." She cupped a hand over her right eye. "His eyes just bulged. And then there was a great flurry and panic and . . . this *thing* came out."

She was folding her napkin, carefully running her fingers along the creases. "It had died quite late in the pregnancy, six, seven months, something like that. Normally, if a baby dies, labor starts straightaway, but for some reason it hadn't. And so Toby went on growing and, as he grew, he'd flattened it against the side of the womb. They didn't want me to see it, but I said, 'No, I've got to.' I said if they didn't let me see it, I'd only imagine far worse things . . ." She glanced at Elinor, then quickly away. "I don't know what the worse things would've been. It had turned into a kind of scroll. You know the parchment things the Romans used to write on? A bit like that, but with features, everything. You could tell it was a girl."

What to say? "That's awful, I'm so sorry."

"It's called a papyrus twin, when that happens. Apparently, it's very rare. The doctor and your father got quite excited."

"I'm sure Father didn't."

Her mother smiled.

"Does Toby know?"

"I've never told him. Your father might have mentioned it, I don't know."

Another burst of gunfire from the wood. Rooks, crows, and pigeons were circling over the treetops now, the air full of their cries.

"When he was little, Toby, he had this imaginary friend. I suppose a lot of children do, but this one was very real; I mean, we had to set a place for her at the table, and everything. I wasn't worried, I thought it would all disappear as soon as he started playing with other children and made some real friends. But it didn't. I used to lie awake at night sometimes and listen to him talking to her. I think I almost started to believe in her myself."

"Did she have a name?"

"D'you know, I can't remember."

"So what happened? Well, she's not still here, is she?"

Another, slightly acid, smile.

"You. You happened. As soon as you could walk, you followed Toby round like a little dog. I used to think he'd get tired of it, but he never did. And the girl vanished. He didn't need her anymore, you see. He had you."

Elinor was trying to read her mother's expression. Jealousy? Yes. Resentment of their closeness, hers and Toby's? Yes. But something else too. It occurred to her, for the first time, that perhaps Toby had formed so effective a barrier between herself and the rest of the family, that her mother might actually feel some grief for the loss of *her*.

No, no. She was being overanalytical, or just plain stupid. Her mother wouldn't feel anything for the loss of her, except, quite possibly, relief.

And yet, if things had been different, she might have taken the place of the lost girl. In many families, that's exactly what would have happened, but not in this one.

She said, stiffly: "Thank you for telling me."

"I thought it might help . . . You're getting to know a lot of new people and that's good, of course, but sometimes I think perhaps Toby's a bit afraid of losing you. He hasn't been happy recently, and I don't know why."

"No, but then we don't know very much about him, do we?"

She would have gone on, but her mother held up a hand. Toby and Tim were striding up the lawn.

Elinor felt as though she was watching them from a great height, almost as if she were one of the birds that their guns had startled into the air. Two young men in shooting jackets and cord breeches, squinting into the sun, while on the terrace a woman and a girl, both in white dresses, rose to meet them. A jarring of two worlds, or so it seemed to her, looking down.

Suddenly, she was hurtling to the ground. Back in her body, she stared at the thing that dangled from Toby's hand: a gleam of white bone in a mess of blood-spiked fur, eyes filmed over. The silence gathered.

"It's a hare," she said.

"Ye-es?"

"It's bad luck to kill a hare."

"Won't stop you eating it, though, will it?" Tim said, with an attempt at jocularity. He was no fool, he sensed the atmosphere; he just didn't know what to do about it.

"I thought it was a rabbit," Toby said.

She could see how he hated it, the limp, lifeless thing in his hand. Looking through his eyes, from his brain outwards, she saw the hare come over the hill, flowing like water through the long grasses. Oh, he'd have called the bullet back if he could, she didn't doubt that, but it was too late. Flies were already laying their eggs inside the bloody hole.

"Elinor—"

Refusing even to look at him, she turned and went back into the house.

3

Climbing the stairs to her lodgings, Elinor felt vulnerable; an animal leaving a trail of blood behind in the snow. Even with the door locked, the gas ring lit, and the kettle boiling, she still didn't feel safe.

She forced herself to butter a slice of stale bread, but her stomach rose at the sight of it. Although it was still early she went into the bedroom and undressed, wrapped a robe tightly round her, and then sat down at the dressing table to brush her hair. The nightly ritual: she'd done this every night since she was four or five years old. The face in the mirror stared back at her with no sign of recognition.

Suddenly, she was rummaging through the top drawer searching for her scissors. As soon as she found them, she began hacking away at her hair. The blades weren't sharp enough; they mouthed thick clumps of hair like a snake struggling to ingest a rat. Still, she persevered. Floating between her and the glass, she saw the flattened, scroll-like body of the little female thing Toby had killed. Oh, what nonsense, of course he hadn't killed it; he hadn't *killed* anybody. It had died, that was all, it had died, and he went on growing, as he was bound to do, taking up more and more room until there was no space left for her.

How quiet it was in these rooms. She'd not yet learned to live alone, though she'd been excited at the prospect, not nervous at all. She had close friends nearby, Catherine and Ruthie, so she knew she wouldn't be lonely. Now, she realized that silence has a sound; well, this kind of silence did anyway: toxic silence. Somewhere between a hum and a buzz. Only the crunching of the scissors through her hair interrupted it. When she'd finished cutting, she raised both hands to the nape of her neck, feeling the dangerous freedom of the shorn ends. Her hair lay in coils and question marks around her feet. She scooped it up and put it in the bin.

Lying between the sheets, she felt different; her body had turned into bread dough, dough that's been kneaded and pounded till it's gray, lumpen, no yeast in it, no lightness, no prospect of rising. Her arms lay stiff by her sides. When, finally, she drifted off to sleep, she dreamt she was on her knees in a corner of the room, trying to vomit without attracting the attention of the person who was asleep on the bed. Her eyes wide open in the darkness, she tried to cast off the dream, but it stayed with her till morning.

———

At seven, she forced herself out of bed, determined to go into the Slade at her usual time. Everything was normal, she was normal, she wasn't even going to think about it. Though she'd need to keep her hat on in the studio; she didn't normally, but she just couldn't face the inevitable comments on her hair.

In the ground-floor cloakroom, she bumped into Catherine, who asked about her weekend. Fine, she said, a really nice break. Then, quickly, she asked about the dressmaking session. It was a hoot, Catherine said. She should have seen them, giggling and sticking pins into each other. They were doing it again, next Saturday. Would she be able to come?

"Yes," Elinor said.

"Really? But you always go home."

"Not this weekend."

She let Catherine go on ahead, pretending she had to look for something in her bag. As soon as she was alone, she took off her hat and stared into the brown-spotted mirror behind the washbasins. Huge, frightened eyes looked back at her. The cropped hair revealed the shape of her head, which was remarkably like Toby's. All that chopping and hacking and all she'd succeeded in doing was to make herself look even more like him.

Impatient with herself, she turned away. She had to face people; there was nothing to be gained by putting it off. At least in her baggy, ankle-length smock she hardly looked like a woman at all. And that was a comfort: any exposed skin felt dangerous. Resisting the temptation to tuck her hands into her sleeves, she walked along the corridor to the life class. Even her hands looked different as she was signing the register: longer, thinner, with prominent tendons and raised veins. Her signature too, usually so sprawling and self-confident, seemed to have crumpled and folded in on itself, like a spider in the bath when the first swirl of hot water reaches it.

Professor Tonks had arrived early and was leaning against the wall at the far end of the room: a tall, formally dressed, thin, ascetic man with the face of a Roman emperor, or a fish eagle. Behind him, the wall was covered in palette-knife scrapings, the colors canceling each other out, so that his black-suited figure was outlined in swirls of shimmering gray. Like birds' feathers. It was actually rather a remarkable sight.

You wouldn't need a plumb line to draw Tonks: his body was a plumb line. How tall would he be? Six five? Something like that. She remembered coming to the Slade for her admittance interview, how intimidated she'd been, by his height, by his manner; and his reception of her drawings had done nothing to make her feel less silly, less immature. Her school-teachers had praised her work so highly; she'd won prizes, for heaven's sake, and not piddling little local prizes either, *proper* prizes, *national* prizes. Tonks held those same drawings up to the light, and winced. It was like having a bucket of icy water thrown in your face. She'd come up gasping, shocked out of her complacency, and more alive than she'd ever felt.

Some of the other students had already started drawing. Reluctantly, she sat down and looked at the model. Slack breasts, belly wrinkled from decades of childbearing, and a grayish pallor to the skin, as if she'd kept herself going for years on doorsteps of bread and dripping and mugs of stewed tea. Not all the models looked like that; some of the younger ones were really beautiful. She'd overheard two male students laughing about Tonks and one particularly attractive model, insinuating that she was his mistress. Elinor hadn't believed it, not for a second. But now, suddenly, she did.

She knew that some of the women students waited out-side Tonks's house for him to set off on his evening walk. So many Héloïses and only one Abelard: no wonder the atmo-sphere was fraught. Not that he'd be stupid enough to do any-thing with a female student. Flirtation, yes; never more. He'd go for models and married women, working, as so many men did, on the well-tried and oft-tested principle that a slice off a cut cake won't be missed. She remembered Father helping the dark-haired girl into the cab, his face, as he looked down at her, almost unrecognizable. All her life, Elinor had been brought up not to know things, but not knowing didn't keep you safe.

She forced herself to pick up a pencil and at once, almost involuntarily, she began to draw Tonks, working with a sure-ness of touch she'd never experienced in this room before. All those things Tonks tried to drill into them, day after day:

look for the line, try to see the direction, no such thing as a contour in nature—suddenly it all made sense. And it was easy, so easy: every mark the pencil made seemed to be the only mark possible. But then, Tonks moved away from the wall, breaking the pose and with it her concentration.

Reaching for a fresh piece of paper, she started work on the model. She knew before she started that the foreshortening of the pose was beyond her, but still she scraped away until, after forty minutes of dibbling and dabbling about, she sat back and contemplated her work.

"God, that's awful," she said, shocked into speaking aloud.

"Hmm. Certainly isn't your best."

She hadn't heard him approach. He bent forward, his sleeve a black wing brushing her face, and picked up the drawing. But in so doing he revealed the portrait of himself underneath.

She waited for the explosion of anger, one of his rare, white-lipped rages that she'd heard about but never witnessed.

Instead, he burst out laughing. "Really, Miss Brooke, you flatter me."

Without further comment, he took her drawing of the model and began making quick, anatomical sketches in the margin, each of them better than anything she'd managed to achieve. Tonks's skeletons had more life than her nudes. She tried to concentrate on what he was saying, but it was hopeless: she was too aware of whispers spreading round the room. By the end of the session, everybody knew what she'd done.

No sooner had Tonks left the room than her friends clustered round her. "Oh, Elinor, you *didn't*." "What did he *say*?" "Come on, let's see it." "Don't be such a spoilsport." Finally, a gasp of sheer horror: "It wasn't *nude*, was it?"

She escaped as soon as she could. Outside the quad gates, she hesitated. If she went back to her lodgings now, she might well spend the rest of the day in bed with the covers pulled over her head. No, somehow or other, she had to keep going, and she had to get away from the Slade.

Russell Square was the nearest green space. She often came here, though not usually at lunchtime. The benches were crowded with people eating soggy sandwiches from greaseproof-paper bags. She found herself a place on the grass and lay down, lifting her face to the sun. Somewhere near-by a fountain played, though the sound of trickling water brought no relief. God, it was hot. She could barely swallow, her throat was so dry. At the far end of the square was a hut with a few tables outside, where you could buy lemonade, but there was a long queue. Not worth it, she decided. Not in this heat.

Thoughts floated to the surface of her mind and burst like bubbles. I should have brought a drawing pad. You never really felt alone if you were drawing; it formed a sort of cocoon around you. And why didn't I wear a thinner dress? That queue's quite a bit shorter now. And why, *why,* wasn't she wearing a straw hat? She had one—well, it was there somewhere—only that morning she'd been in such a state she'd grabbed the first thing she could lay her hands on. Black felt, oh God, far too hot in this weather, although at least she could pull it down and hide her cropped hair. But now her scalp itched. A bead of sweat ran down into her eye, burning like acid, and suddenly it was all too much. She tore the hat off, leaned forward and shook her fingers through her hair.

At the same moment, a shadow fell across her. Peering up through the mess of jagged ends, she saw Kit Neville, in a baggy, creased suit, looking down at her.

"Miss Brooke, you look rather hot, I wonder if you'd like some lemonade?"

"There's a queue."

"It's not so bad now. Shall I get us some?"

She nodded, trying to think of something slightly more gracious to say, but he'd already turned away. He'd startled her, appearing in front of her so suddenly. When he vanished behind a clump of bushes, she was half inclined to think he'd been a mirage, but no, minutes later, there he was again, his burly figure making great strides across the grass, a ragged shadow snatching at his heels.

He handed her a glass. "Don't know how cool it is, mind."

Cautiously, with an audible clicking of the knees, he lowered himself to sit beside her, risking grass stains on his obviously expensive suit. That was one of the things you noticed about Kit Neville. He wore extremely well-tailored suits, and he looked a mess. She didn't particularly like the man—or, rather, she didn't like what she'd heard about him. He was a bully, people said. But now, looking at him, she saw none of the swaggering self-confidence he projected so expertly at the Slade. He seemed, if anything, distinctly shy, afraid of rejection.

He took a sip of lemonade. "Ugh! Warm."

"Least it's wet. And thank you for getting it, I just couldn't face the queue."

They drank in silence for a moment. Then: "Are you going back to college?" he asked. "Only if you're not, we could go on the river."

The idea of playing truant for the whole afternoon shocked her.

"No, I've got to get back."

He was tempted to skip the men's life class, he said. Couldn't face another dose of Tonks. He seemed to have developed almost a feud with Tonks, whose excoriating comments on his work were passed from mouth to mouth, losing nothing in the repetition. "Did you hear what Tonks said to Neville?" "Oh, he didn't, did he?" "I think if anybody said that to me, I'd leave." Suddenly, it all seemed rather immature to Elinor: the relish, the furtive excitement, children wetting themselves with glee because somebody else was in trouble. She had been guilty of it herself, more than once, but she wouldn't do it again, because, in the length of time it took to drink a glass of lemonade, Kit had become a friend.

Getting up was difficult. She'd got pins and needles from sitting in the same position too long; she rested a hand, briefly, on his arm to steady herself and caught a glance of such open admiration that she blushed. He'd made no comment on her hair, but he hadn't taken his eyes off it either. Perhaps short hair wasn't such a disaster, after all.

They walked back to the Slade together. At the entrance to the quad, they paused. Groups of art students were chatting in circles on the grass, while on the steps of the medical school rows of young men were lined up side by side, looking, in their black suits, like swallows waiting to migrate.

"Perhaps we should go in separately?" he said. Male and female students were not supposed to mix.

"No, I think we should have the courage of our convictions."

She took his arm and, conscious of heads turning to follow them, they marched across the lawn, through the double doors, and into the entrance hall, where a single glance from a disapproving receptionist was enough to make them collapse into giggles.

Suddenly serious, Kit said, "I enjoyed that. I hope we can do it again."

"Yes, I hope so too."

They parted at the foot of the stairs. The last hour seemed extraordinary to Elinor, though they'd done nothing special. Only, for those few minutes, in spite of everything, she'd been happy.

———

Every afternoon, when Elinor left the Slade, she looked up at the steps of the medical school, half expecting to see Toby there, waiting for her, as he so often had in the past; but it was a week before she saw him again, and then he came to her lodgings.

She was sitting at her dressing table, getting ready to go out, when she heard footsteps running up the last—uncarpeted—flight of stairs. The door was unlocked. Toby called to her from the living room, briefly darkened the bedroom doorway, and came to stand behind her. She didn't turn round, merely looked at his reflection in the glass.

He was staring at her hair. "My God, sis, what have you done?"

Sis?

"What do you think? Do you like it?"

"No, well, it's a bit of a shock . . . No, no, it's good, it suits you." His eyes skittered round the room. "When did you do it?"

"When I got back."

He sat on the bed, big hands clasped between his thighs, bulky, helpless. It made her angry.

"I was surprised you left so early," she said.

"Dad gave me a lift. No point hanging around."

"Mother was a bit put out." She waited. "We had quite a long chat, you know, Mother and me. While you and Tim were out shooting." Was that fleeting change of expression one of fear? "Did you know you were a twin?"

"Yes."

She was taken aback. "So why didn't you tell me?"

"Didn't seem important."

She thought of the boy in the garden playing with a girl whom nobody else could see. "Mother doesn't even know where she's buried."

"Buried?"

"Well, yes. They wouldn't—"

"It's in a museum, a *medical* museum. Edinburgh, I think." His eyes slid away. "They are quite rare."

"So what happened? The doctor gave her to a museum?"

He looked down.

"No. Dad wouldn't do that," she said. "His own flesh and blood?"

"Oh, listen to yourself: 'His own flesh and blood.' He's a scientist, for God's sake."

"I can see it mightn't be much of a barrier to you."

They'd got there, by a rather circular route, but there, nevertheless. She watched the Adam's apple jerking in his throat. Like everything else about him, it seemed to be trying to escape.

"You came to me," he said. "I'll take ninety percent of the blame, but I won't take it all."

It was impossible to speak without crying, and she was determined not to cry. So she said nothing, sitting there with her face in her hands and her eyes closed. After a moment, she felt him get up and come to stand behind her again. He reached out, but stopped just short of touching her shoulder, though close enough for her to feel the heat of his fingertips. She remembered the sea-anemone groping of his mouth, the shock of his harsh bristles on her skin.

"If you like, I'll stay away from you," he said. "You won't have to see me again."

Christmas? Birthdays?

She put up a hand and twined her fingers round his. "You know I don't want that."

"Neither do I."

They looked at each other in the glass, then for the first time she turned to face him directly. He touched the side of her face, lowered his head . . . With his mouth less than an inch away from hers, he recoiled violently, almost as if some external force had grabbed him by the hair and pulled him off. Breathing heavily, he said, "We've got to get back to the way things were."

"I don't know how they were."

"We were friends."

She shook her head. "No. If we'd been friends it would never have happened."

"We've got to try. Sis?"

"Yes, I suppose we do. *Bro*."

He took a short step back. Released.

"I've brought my anatomy textbooks. You must be starting the course soon."

How easily he'd returned to "normal." She felt a spasm of anger, but relief too. A minute ago, she'd thought it was starting again, and she wasn't sure she could have stopped him, or herself. Because he was right, she'd gone to him, gone in bewilderment and ignorance, nursing vague childish schemes of revenge, yes, but had that been her only motivation? The more she thought about that night the more . . . complicit she felt.

Now, she followed him through into the living room; they sat on the sofa, side by side, and talked about the anatomy course she'd be starting on Monday. And after a while, things did begin to seem normal, almost normal, though she noticed he sat a few feet away from her, about as far away as he could get. Even so, there seemed to be no space between them. If she closed her eyes for a second, she could feel the prickle of their shared sweat on her thigh.

Anatomy was Toby's favorite subject, his passion, and he was a good teacher. As he talked, she forgot to feel distaste for the scurf of human skin on his notes, and simply marveled, as he did, at the beauty and complexity of what lay beneath.

"You'll enjoy it, sis, honestly you will. Bit of a shock at first, but you soon get over that. I'm sure once you get the hang of it, it'll really help your drawing, and then, *wow*—the next Michelangelo."

"I don't like muscly men."

"Oh, well, never mind . . ."

He stayed for exactly one hour. It was like a tutorial. When he got up to go, she accompanied him to the front door, not wanting to be left, too abruptly, in a room that would still be full of his presence. He called her "sis" again as he said good-bye. She watched him walk off down the street, unloading guilt behind him, step by step.

With his departure, her anger returned. All that stuff about bringing his anatomy textbooks . . . He'd come to say one word, no, not even that, the stupid, amputated stump of a word: *sis*. That was his pledge that what had happened between them would never happen again, that it would, in time, be forgotten.

And it was all lies. At one point, back there in the bedroom, they'd been on the verge of starting all over again. She'd felt it; she didn't believe he hadn't felt it too. How could he come as close as that, and then tell her to forget?

She mustn't let herself slide into hating him. He was doing his clumsy best to repair the damage. And he did love her, she was sure of that. But in declaring that the events of that night must be forgotten, he'd left her, in effect, to face the memory alone. And that just wasn't fair.

She watched him turn the corner into Bedford Square, but for many minutes, after he disappeared, she remained standing in the doorway, staring at the space where he'd been, feeling the empty air close around his absence.

4

ELINOR BROOKE'S DIARY

7 October 1912

The Indian summer's well and truly gone. Today was cold and windy with bursts of torrential rain. I was almost blown into the hospital, dripping wet, and late, of course. I got up early, but then wasted time trying to decide what to wear. Don't know why I bothered. I arrived looking like a drowned rat anyway.

The other girls were all waiting outside the lecture theater. I must say my heart sank when I saw them—scrubbed faces, scraped-back hair, sensible shoes and suits. The jackets were cut exactly like men's and the skirts swept the floor—so you got the worst of both worlds. Hats, of course. One or two of them were actually wearing ties. I've never seen that on a young woman before. Everybody had a good look at my hair. I stared back at them. At least my hair's clean. I never noticed till the last few days how dirty most women's hair smells. No wonder, when you think of the palaver of washing it—it used to take me an entire evening. I look back on that and I just think: what a complete waste of time.

The lecturer, Dr. Angus Brodie, positively bounced on to the platform—short, red-haired, bristling with authority, skin speckled like a thrush's egg. He took one look at me—I was sitting by myself right at the end of the third row—and said, "Miss Brooke, I presume?" Then he made a concertina movement with his very small, neat hands. I shuffled along to join the others—blushing like mad and cursing myself for it— and he beamed. "There," he said. "Art and medicine reunited."

Crime and medicine more like. Really, I had no idea. Leonardo was fascinating, of course, but there was a lot of boring stuff after that. Until he got on to Burke and Hare, that awful killing spree they went on, supplying cadavers to the Edinburgh medical schools, especially to Dr. Robert Knox, who used to give public demonstrations of dissection. The last—second to last? Can't remember—victim was a retarded boy known as Daft Jamie. He was a well-known figure on the streets, so when he turned up on Knox's slab several of the students recognized him. He was known to be missing, his mother was doing the rounds asking if anybody had seen him. Knox must have heard the whispers because he changed his usual routine and started by dissecting the face.

Within minutes, Daft Jamie's mother wouldn't have known him. It horrified me, that. The cold-bloodedness of it. I seemed to hear Toby's voice saying, "He's a scientist, for God's sake."

Burke and Hare were caught not long after that. Knox got off scot-free, at least as far as the law was concerned, though the Edinburgh mob attacked his house. Hare turned King's evidence; Burke was hanged. His death mask's in the medical museum, in Edinburgh.

I lost interest after that. I kept seeing Toby's twin, in a glass jar on a shelf. Why can't he see how horrible that is?

At the end of the lecture, Dr. Brodie offered us a way out. Dissection was not for everybody, he said. Women, in particular, found the long hours of standing difficult. Any young lady who discovered she'd been mistaken in her aptitudes should come to him at once—there'd be no disgrace in this, mind, none whatsoever—and he'd arrange for her to transfer to a more suitable course: biology or chemistry or—his face brightened—botany.

Ah, yes. Girls and flowers.

I don't know what effect it had on the others, but it made me more determined to stick it out, no matter how hard it is. Anyway, by this time tomorrow, we'll know what we're in for. Toby says I'll enjoy it, but I can't see how that's possible.

Well, I'm off to bed—an hour early!—hoping not to receive any visits from Daft Jamie and his ruined face.

———

Next day, in the changing room, the smells were of wet wool, hair, and rubber. A cold wind was blowing: everybody's eyelids and nose were a bright, unbecoming pink. One girl stifled a yawn and immediately an epidemic of yawns spread around the room. There was a good deal of nervous giggling as they helped each other tuck strands of hair inside the green rubber caps that were obviously designed to be worn by men. Rubber boots, gloves, and aprons completed the garb. They looked and smelled unfamiliar to themselves. Every time they moved they either rustled or squeaked.

"Hurry up, ladies," said a bored male voice from behind the door. "We haven't got all day."

Miss Cunningham, whom Elinor had spoken to briefly the previous day, looked around to check that everyone was ready, then pushed open the door. They filed into a long room where white-sheeted cadavers seemed to float like huge, dead fish in the subaqueous light. A fluttering sound was just perceptible above the squeaking of rubber-soled boots on the tiles. Elinor raised her eyes to the ceiling and saw that a small, colorless moth had become trapped inside the skylight and was fumbling against the glass, no doubt mistaking a watery sun for the moon.

Lowering her gaze, she saw that a thin young man had appeared in front of them. His name, he said, was Smailes, and it was his job to guide them through the process of dissection. He didn't seem to be looking forward to it much. In fact, he sounded thoroughly bored and fed up. He kept scratching at a red patch on one side of his chin, pimples or a shaving rash or eczema, perhaps. Elinor was briefly curious about this yawning male presence, but nothing could distract her for long from what lay underneath the sheets.

She was directed, along with four other students, to the nearest cadaver. Miss Duffy and Miss Cunningham, who seemed to be friends, faced each other across the shoulders. Two other girls took up positions on either side of the torso. Elinor, in this, as in so much else, the odd one out, stood alone by the feet.

"I think I'm going to faint," Miss Duffy said.

"Don't you *dare*," Miss Cunningham replied.

She sounded so fierce that the other girls immediately put all thoughts of fainting out of their heads, though the smell of formaldehyde and disinfectant—and another, nameless, smell—lay heavy on their stomachs.

"All right," Mr. Smailes continued. "Let's unwrap the parcel."

Miss Duffy and Miss Cunningham glanced at each other and then, with the determined calm of housemaids dealing with an unexpected death in the family, removed the sheet.

Mantegna's *Dead Christ*. From where Elinor stood at the foot of the slab, the feet appeared huge, out of all proportion to the body. His face was dark, the eyes shuttered; nobody could have mistaken this stillness for sleep. Freed from the apprehension of an answering gaze, she let her eyes slide down, across the soaring chancel arch of his rib cage, along the flat nave of his belly to where his penis lay, a shriveled seahorse on an outcrop of wrinkled and sagging skin.

Miss Duffy produced a sound midway between a giggle and a gasp. Of course, this would almost certainly be her first sight of a naked man. Elinor glanced at the other girls and saw from the slithering away of their eyes that the same was true of them. Mr. Smailes smirked and suddenly, fiercely, Elinor hated him. But then at once she was back with the dead man. His skin glowed like a lit lampshade. Tiny moles and scars seemed to float on the surface where one quick flick of a palette knife would sweep them all away. She took a step back, and this movement seemed to break the stillness that had descended on them all.

"Well, now," Mr. Smailes said. "The first thing is to open the chest."

A suture line ran along the base of the neck and down the center of the chest. Under Mr. Smailes's direction, Miss Duffy wormed her fingers into the incision and pulled the chest wall back. Miss Cunningham did the same on the other side. The halves lay across his upper arms, almost casually, as if he'd done this to himself, removing his chest wall as nonchalantly as he might a shirt. It was rather horrible. But then they got their first glimpse of what lay beneath: the pectoral muscles, glistening under a translucent layer of connective tissue, fanning out in two huge wings to cover the ribs. It reminded Elinor of the roof of King's College Chapel, though she had enough sense not to confide this thought to Mr. Smailes, who would certainly have thought her mad.

Somebody had to make the first incision. "Miss Brooke."

He was holding out a scalpel. She looked from him to the other girls, all of them training to be doctors, for God's sake; she was an artist, no, not even that, an art *student,* she couldn't be expected to—

Fumbling, she took the scalpel from him.

"Careful! You could have your finger off with that."

He placed his two index fingers on the cadaver's chest, indicating the length and direction of the cut. *Look for the line,* she heard Tonks say. Oh, my God, how did he get in here? Evidently the honor of the Slade was at stake. Well, then. She positioned the scalpel, took a deep breath, and began the cut.

"No, too hard. You don't need to press."

He was right there. She'd never encountered a knife as sharp as this. Flakes of putty-colored flesh rose on either side of the blade as easily as water round the prow of a boat. When the incision was long enough and—she hoped—deep enough, but not too deep, she straightened up and immediately her hand began to shake.

She heard the other girls breathe out. Only one of them had held the scalpel, but all of them had followed its progress, inch by painful inch, and now they felt, with a great rush of blood to their faces: *Yes, we can do this.*

By the end of the session Elinor's brain was aching almost as much as her back. She was too tired to follow Mr. Smailes's summing-up of what they'd learned and merely pretended to listen while gazing around the room. There were three cadavers. She worked out that the one on the next table was that of a very old man, though the fatty deposits around his nipples looked exactly like breasts. Perhaps that was what happened in extreme old age, the two sexes growing to resemble each other more and more, so that finally, in death, the body became androgynous again, as it had been in infancy? But the cadaver farthest away from her was no more than middle-aged and definitely female, despite the shaved head and sunken breasts. The width of the pelvis alone . . . Whatever tricks the flesh may play in death, the bones don't lie.

Instantly, she wanted to transfer to that group, to work on the female body. She knew, without being able to say how or why, that her business as an artist was with women. Women's bodies held a meaning for her, a spark, which the male body lacked. Might it be possible to switch groups? After all, they'd only done one session. Why not? But then, none of the other girls had requested a transfer, and they'd all, in their professional lives, be mainly concerned with women's health, if only because no right-thinking man would let a lady doctor anywhere near him. If it made sense for her to work on a female cadaver, it made even more sense for them.

Still, it couldn't hurt to ask . . .

After the other girls had gone, she lingered in the changing room, hearing their excited, chattering voices recede along the corridor. They knew one another now, were well on the way to becoming friends. When everything was quiet, she went in search of Mr. Smailes.

She didn't have far to look: he was standing by the lift, wearing his overcoat and hat. Divested of the rubber cap and apron, he looked more, rather than less, strange. For a moment, it crossed her mind that he might have been waiting for her, but she didn't let the idea settle. His face, as he turned towards her, wore its usual slight sneer. He gave every indication of disliking her intensely, and she didn't understand why. It couldn't be anything personal: he didn't know her. Of course, unlike the other students, she didn't have the cloak of serious professional intent to hide her femaleness. Perhaps that was it. She could easily imagine what Mr. Smailes would make of lady artists studying anatomy.

They got into the lift together. He pulled the door across with a clang and at once she felt trapped behind the iron grille as the lift began its slow descent. Neither of them spoke, and with every second of silence the awkwardness increased.

"Mr. Smailes?"

He turned to look at her, his eyes snot-green behind pinky-beige lashes.

"I was wondering if it might be possible for me to transfer to the female cadaver?"

"Now, why on earth would you want to do that?"

"Well, you know, I suppose, I draw mainly women—well, nearly all women—and so I just think it would be more . . ."

She was gabbling, but it hardly mattered: he was already shaking his head.

"Believe me, Miss Brooke, you do not want to work on a female cadaver. The fat gets under your fingernails and however hard you scrub you can never quite get it out."

But surely he would always wear gloves? She looked down at his hands. The nails were neatly trimmed and immaculately clean, but the cuticles had been picked raw. She found it disturbing: the carefully tended nails embedded in half-moons of bleeding flesh; and she knew he'd enjoyed telling her about the fat on female cadavers, how repulsive it was.

The jolt of the lift arriving on the ground floor saved her from the need to reply. He pulled the gates open and stood aside to let her pass, but even that small courtesy struck her as sarcastic. She held her head high as she swept past him, but she felt her cheeks burn.

5

At first, Elinor thought she'd never get used to the sight, sounds, and smells of the Dissecting Room, but gradually, as the weeks passed, she became accustomed to them. As all the girls did. The cathedral hush of that first session had been replaced by chattering, even giggling. Left to herself for a moment, Elinor would slip into daydreaming, and at such times her thoughts invariably turned to Toby.

We've got to get back to the way things were.

I don't know how they were.

Compulsively, now, she scrutinized the past, searching for the moment when it had gone wrong. She saw them walking through the woods together, watched them as if she were actually a third party present at the scene, a ghost from the future. They were off to the pond to collect minnows and frog spawn and they were taking it in turns to carry the big jar. At the pond, they took off their clothes, because the spawn was at the far side among the reeds. They looked like little albino tadpoles themselves, stirring up clouds of milky sludge as they walked around the edge. At the center there was supposed to be a deep well, hundreds of feet deep, though perhaps their mother had told them that to stop them going so far in.

On the way home, Toby insisted he should carry the jar,

which was heavy now, full to the brim with murky water that slopped over onto his chest with every step. They'd got masses and masses of frog spawn, and minnows too, *and* they'd remembered to put in a clump of reeds for food and shelter. They didn't know that lurking in the reeds was a dragonfly larva, the most voracious of all pond creatures. Over the next few days it had devoured every other living creature in the jar.

"Don't they get on well together?" one of the aunties said, watching them walk up the drive.

They did. They were about as close as any brother and sister could be. Dragging herself back to the present, Elinor found herself staring at the cadaver's shrunken genitals, feeling again a spatter as of hot candle wax on the back of her hand. When had it become the wrong kind of love?

"Miss Brooke, if we could have your attention, please?"

They were about to remove the lungs. Despite their increasing skill with the scalpel, this rapidly degenerated into an undignified tug of war. So much for treating the cadaver with respect. The chest cavity just wasn't big enough to get the lungs out. Elinor gritted her teeth, tried not to think too hard about what she was doing, and pulled. At last they were out, lying side by side on the still-intact abdomen, like stillborn twins. Stillborn, *black* twins.

"Why are they black?" Miss Duffy asked.

"I expect he was a miner," Mr. Smailes said. "You might like to think about that the next time you're toasting your toes in front of the fire."

Elinor needed no urging to think about the cadaver away from the Dissecting Room. After a night out with Kit Neville, dancing or at a music hall, she'd return to her lodgings and lie in the darkness, sniffing the tips of her fingers, where, mysteriously, the smell of formaldehyde lingered. Gloves, scrubbing: nothing seemed to help. Sometimes she dreamt about him, hearing a hiss of indrawn breath as she made that first incision. Always, in the dreams, she avoided looking at his face, because she knew his eyes would be open. Even by day, he followed her. She didn't know how to leave him behind in the Dissecting Room, where, session after session, the slim girls swarmed over him like coffin beetles, reducing him to the final elegance of bone.

————

She and Kit Neville had become close friends and spent a lot of time together. Kit was London born and bred, and he enjoyed showing her his native city. They went to Speakers' Corner on Sunday mornings, sat in the gods at the music hall, danced the turkey trot till sometimes well past midnight, or simply wandered along the Strand, tossing roasted chestnuts from hand to hand till they were cool enough to eat.

Away from the studio and the Dissecting Room, she lived a life almost obsessively devoted to triviality. She'd turned into a pond skater, not because she didn't know what lay beneath the surface, but precisely because she did.

At the end of their evenings, Kit would escort her back to her lodgings, but he never tried to kiss her good night and he never asked to come in. They were both rather proud of their platonic friendship. She knew he had a life apart from her, that he was having an affair—if you could call it that—with one of the models, in fact with the same girl whose name had been linked with Tonks.

Laura, her name was. When she sat for the women's life class, Elinor settled down to draw her with a painful sense of invading Kit's privacy. Laura was beautiful: she had the milky white skin that sometimes goes with dark red hair. She was a wonderful subject. And yet Elinor produced a bad, weak, timid, insipid drawing, far below the standard of her recent work. She couldn't seem to grasp the pose at all.

That night, when she'd finished undressing, she tilted the

mirror to show the bed and lay down in the same pose. She told herself that an attempt at a self-portrait might serve, in Tonks's words, "to explicate the form," but she didn't pick up the pencil. Instead, she cupped her breasts, feeling the warm, white weight of them, and then spread her fingers lightly over the curved flesh of her belly. After that, she simply lay and stared at herself, before, suddenly, jumping off the bed and pushing the mirror away.

Sometimes, like this morning when she'd looked at Laura on the dais, trying not to imagine her in bed with Kit, she felt . . . No, there was no point saying what she felt.

She felt spayed.

————

She saw Toby once or twice a week, never for very long, and he never again came to her rooms. The idea they'd once had that he would teach her anatomy was quietly dropped. Sometimes they'd meet for tea in a restaurant and then they'd talk at greater length, but this was a Toby who painstakingly called her "sis" and teased her in a ghastly imitation of brotherly affection. He had nothing in common with the other Toby, whose weight on her chest in the darkness cut off her breath.

Once, she and Kit Neville were having tea in Lockhart's, when Toby came in with a group of friends. Seeing her sitting there by the window, he came across to join them. As she introduced Kit she was aware of Toby's eyes flaring: he'd recognized the name. He sat down; they talked, Toby drawing Kit out on the inadequacies of Tonks as a teacher. Not a particularly difficult subject to get Kit started on.

"To hear Elinor talk you'd think he was God," Toby said.

"Huh. To hear Tonks talk you'd think he was God."

And then he was off, on the uselessness of drawing from the Antique, the blind worship of the past, the failure to engage in any meaningful way with the realities of modern life and, above all, Tonks's deplorable tendency to devote too much time to teaching women and useless men.

"Do you think time spent teaching women is wasted?" Toby said, with a sidelong glance at Elinor.

"Present company excepted, yes. Well. Largely."

"I don't think Elinor wants to be that kind of exception, do you, sis?"

She could feel Toby walking round Kit, sniffing him, assessing him as a rival, rather than meeting him as his sister's friend. It was a relief, to her at least, when he got up and went to rejoin his friends.

"Nice chap, your brother," Kit said, later.

"Hmm."

Even now, she still craved Toby's approval. When one of her drawings won a prize—an exceedingly small prize, but a prize nevertheless—her first thought was, I must tell Toby. It had been like this ever since she could remember; nothing really happened to her until she confided it in him.

She waited for him at the foot of the medical school steps. Students came and went in a steady stream. She was frozen by the time he appeared, muffled in a long coat with its collar turned up against the wind. He was coughing badly and stopped to get his breath, one arm resting on the plinth of the huge bronze male nude that towered above him. Somehow the statue's heavily muscled torso served to emphasize how thin he'd become. She hadn't noticed the change in him till now and the sudden perception produced a tweak of fear. When she ran up the steps to meet him, he waved her away.

"You don't want this."

"You should be in bed."

Another fit of coughing. "Can't. Exams."

"Toby, you look awful. Come on, let's get you back to my rooms, I'll make you a cup of tea."

"No, got to revise."

"Just for a few minutes; I'll put the fire on."

Did he hesitate? She thought he did, but then he fell into step beside her. For once, she was the one who had to slow her pace so they could keep in step. By the time they'd reached the top floor of her lodgings, he was gasping for breath and almost fell into a chair beside the fire.

Tight-lipped, she bent down to light it.

"Seriously, Toby, you need to be in bed."

"No, if I miss the last two exams I'll have to repeat the entire year—"

Again, a spasm of coughing cut off his breath.

"Does Mother know you're like this?"

"No—and you're not to tell her either."

The room warmed up quickly; by the time she'd made the tea he was starting to breathe more easily. But he was sweating heavily, and when he took the cup from her his fingers felt clammy. He wouldn't look at her.

"There's no reason to go putting the wind up people. It's just a cold, everybody's got it."

"Hmm. Have they all got it as bad as you?"

He shook his head. There was nothing to be gained by nagging him; he'd made up his mind. She sat in the other armchair. "Oh, one bit of good news: I've won a prize."

"That's wonderful. Oh, I am so pleased."

He was genuinely, unaffectedly delighted for her. Of course he'd been the one who'd fought for her to go to the Slade in the first place, when her mother and Rachel had been so resolutely opposed. Toby had badgered their father until suddenly the impossible had become possible. He was a good brother. She felt a sudden pang of grief for everything they'd lost.

"What did you get it for?"

"A female nude. Not very good."

He raised his eyebrows.

"No, no, *really* not very good. I only won because Tonks was the judge and the anatomy was spot on."

"So this course is helping?"

"Well, I'm not sure it is, actually. My nudes used to look like blancmanges, now they look like prizefighters."

As she chattered on, she was watching him intently, alert to every catch in his breath.

"Where've you got to in the dissection?" he asked.

"The face. And I'm not sure I can face it." She winced. "Sorry, not intended."

"Why can't you?"

"The face is the person, I suppose. Cutting into that, it's . . . I don't know. Different. I keep thinking about Daft Jamie, which is . . ."

"Daft?"

"Well, yes, I suppose so. How did that dreadful man get away with it?"

"Hare?"

"No, Knox."

"He didn't, I don't think he ever practiced medicine again."

"He didn't die though, did he?"

"No, but it might have felt like it—to him."

Toby was breathing more easily now and some of his color had returned.

"The other girls call him George; the cadaver, I mean. One of them said she thought it was more respectful, to give him a name. I don't know, I don't see it like that. The fact is, he's got a name. It's just that we don't know it."

"Ours was called Albert. It's nearly always the royal family. Though I think one of the other tables called theirs Herbert. Asquith."

She hoped he might stay for a while, perhaps even have

something to eat, but as soon as he'd finished drinking the tea he was on his feet.

"Can't you stay? I've got some soup, I could—"

"No, thanks all the same, but I need an early night. The first exam's at nine . . ."

He touched her hand as he said good-bye, his fingertips as cold and slippery as a dead fish. He stood looking at her for a moment. "Don't worry, I'll be all right."

But the cold air tightened his chest and he was coughing again before he reached the bottom step.

6

December was unusually cold and foggy even by the standards of London in winter. Day after day went by with no glimpse of the sun and it never became really light, not even at midday. Whenever someone came through the doors of the London Hospital, wisps and coils of sulfurous smoke followed them in. The air on the ground-floor corridors tasted metallic.

These mornings Elinor went straight to the cupboard where the heads were kept. By now, in this final stage of dissection, the face had become unrecognizable. She identified him only by the name tag clipped to his right ear. Not his name, of course—officially he had no name—but hers. At the start of each session she looked into the pallid eyes, still in place inside the dissected orbits, and once again became possessed by the desire to know who he was. The need to name him, to understand how and why he'd come to this, grew in her with each stage of his disintegration.

As soon as she started work, however, this obsession with his identity fell away. Under Mr. Smailes's appraising eye, they teased out layers of muscle and exposed nerves and tendons to the light. He encouraged them to explore their own and one another's faces: to feel the skull beneath the skin. It made sense to test what they'd learned against the living reality. All the same . . . Elinor couldn't help noticing how Smailes's lips parted as he watched their fingers probe and delve.

She hated these sessions of "living anatomy," but they were probably more useful to her as an artist than the actual dissection. Certainly, she felt her growing knowledge was now feeding into her drawing, though for a long time she'd been unable to make a connection. The cadaver hadn't helped her see the model on the dais more clearly. If anything, the dissection had become linked in her mind to the passion, bewilderment, and pain of that night in Toby's room. As if it were his body on the slab: familiar, frightening, unknown.

And then, one morning, it was over. Elinor left the Dissecting Room determined she would never go back. Next term the other girls would start work on another cadaver, the second in a long line, but for her there would only ever be this one. She lingered for a moment in the doorway, trying to squeeze out the appropriate emotion, whatever that might be.

As she closed the door behind her, one of the attendants was sluicing down the slab.

It was snowing when she left the hospital, as it had been, on and off, for the past two days; the sky above the rooftops had a jaundiced look that suggested more was on the way. The pavements had been trodden to a gray sludge. She stopped outside the main entrance to watch the flakes whirling down. Before the end of term—and that wasn't far away now—she'd have to see Tonks and explain that she didn't want to go on with dissection. She'd say she'd learned a lot and she was very grateful to have had the opportunity, but . . . *But*. Still planning what she'd say to Tonks, she set off to catch the bus home, walking fast, head down, arms swinging, away, away, away . . .

And then, just as she reached the bus stop, she realized she'd left her bag behind.

It was Friday afternoon, and the Dissecting Room would be locked up over the weekend. It was no use: she'd have to go back. She ran most of the way, a blundering, impeded canter through slush and icy puddles, slipping and slithering across patches of black ice. As she pushed the doors open, cold air rushed after her into the building. She waited impatiently for the lift and then ran all the way down the top-floor corridor.

The Dissecting Room smelled different: less formaldehyde, but enough bleach to make your eyes sting. The lights were still on, so somebody must be around. In the harsh glare, the organs in their display jars glittered like jewels. Forgetting her lost bag, she stood at the foot of the slab where she'd worked and slowly re-created the man who'd lain there, surrendering himself to their scalpels through the long hours of dissection. She remembered the shock she'd felt when the covers first came off; the glow of his uncut skin. Now, when there was nothing of him left, the full force of her desire to know who he was, who he'd been, returned.

The door at the far end of the room had been left ajar. Normally, it was kept locked. This was where the mortuary attendants disappeared to at the end of each session; access to students was strictly forbidden. She walked across the room, hesitated, then pushed the door farther open. Nobody spoke, nobody demanded to know what on earth she thought she was doing, so she went in.

To her left, a trestle table ran the full length of the room. On it were three bundles of bones, each with a label attached. With a thud of the heart, she guessed the labels would have names on, and walked across to read them, but no, there were only numbers. Number three was hers, the little that was left of him. He looked like a Christmas turkey the day after Boxing Day, when all the bones have been picked clean.

She looked around for solace, for something, anything, to make this bearable, and her eye fell on a green ledger. The corners were furry with use and so smeared by greasy fingerprints they looked black. *Of course:* they'd have to keep records because these pitiable piles of bones had to be given a proper burial—and presumably they'd be kept under the names they'd borne in life. She picked up the book and, fully aware that she was breaking every conceivable rule, began shuffling through the pages. The last entry should give her three names, one of them female. That would still leave two possibilities, but, irrationally perhaps, she felt she'd know his name when she saw it.

"Miss Brooke! Can I help you?" The usual sneer.

"I was looking for my bag."

"Well, you're not likely to find it in here, are you?"

She tried to push past him, but he wouldn't step aside. She was totally in the wrong, she knew that, but she didn't take kindly to being bullied, and instinctively she went on the attack. "Why do you dislike me so much?" she asked.

"Because you think you're the lily on the dungheap."

So direct, so uncompromisingly contemptuous, it shocked her. "Well, somebody has to be and it's never going to be you." How childish that sounded. How embarrassingly childish. "I just wanted to know who he was."

He took the ledger away from her. "I think you'll find your bag's in the changing room."

He waited till she reached the door. "It wouldn't have done you any good anyway," he said, holding up the ledger. "He was one of the unclaimed. Nobody knows who he was."

"The unclaimed?"

"Found in a shop doorway, I expect."

She nodded, took one last look at the heap of bones, and went in search of her bag.

7

That evening Elinor sat alone in her lodgings. She'd had a bath, washed her hair, put on her dressing gown, and curled up in front of the fire. Only now, when it was over, did she realize how much the work of dissection had taken out of her. She stared at the blue buds of the fire, listening to its hissing and popping, but saw only the nameless man as he'd been on that first morning: the huge, yellow-soled feet and the flat plane of the body stretching out beyond them. What a dreadful end. Even Daft Jamie had had a name.

She ought to make the effort to go out, if only round the corner to Catherine's. A few of the girls had started to meet and do life drawing away from the college, taking it in turns to pose. They were supposed to be meeting tonight, but nobody would show up in this weather. Still, an evening alone with Catherine—the little German girl, as Kit Neville rather patronizingly called her—would be good too. Cocoa and gossip, that's what she needed. But how bad was the snow? The way it was falling when she came in, it might be impossible to get out.

She couldn't see much from the window, so she went downstairs and looked out into the street. Snow was still coming down fast, six inches at least had piled up against the door; it must have been falling steadily ever since she got home. Looking up into the circle of light around the street-lamp, she could see how big the flakes were. Whirling down from the sky, each flake cast a shadow onto the snow, like big, fat, gray moths fluttering. She'd never noticed shadows like that before. Mesmerized, she stood and watched, trying to follow first one flake and then another, until she felt dizzy, and had to stop.

When she looked up again, she realized she wasn't alone. A man was standing at the foot of the steps, only five or six feet away from her. The snow must have muffled the sound of his approach. She took an involuntary step back.

Instantly, he took off his hat. "Miss Brooke?"

"Ye-es?"

"My name's Andrew Martin. I'm a friend of Toby's."

Yes, she remembered seeing him on the steps of the medical school with Toby. "Is he all right?"

"Well, no, not really, that's why I'm here."

Fear slipped into her mind so easily, it might always have been there. "How bad is it?"

"I think you should come."

"I'll get dressed. You get back to him."

"No, it's all right, I'll wait."

She stepped back. "Well, at least wait inside."

He brushed past her. She closed the door, shutting out the dervish dance of flakes and shadows. He stood awkwardly, snow coating his shoulders as if he were a statue. Big, raw, red hands—he'd come out without gloves—a long nose with a dewdrop trembling on the tip, and a terrible, intractable, gauche shyness coming off him like a bad smell.

"I won't be a minute," she said.

She ran upstairs, burst into her bedroom, snatched up the first clothes that came to hand, put on her coat, and wound a scarf round her neck, all the time trying to think what she would need to take. She'd be staying all night; she might have to stay longer than that. Nightdress, then: soap, flannel, toothbrush, toothpaste, brush, comb. What else? She snapped the lock shut and carried the case downstairs.

The snow on his boots had melted to a puddle on the floor.

"Can we get a cab?"

"No, I tried on my way here but they said they're not taking fares."

London had become a silent city. For Elinor the stillness added to the strangeness of this walk through deserted streets with a man she didn't know to a place she'd never been. How secretive Toby was, really. She hadn't realized till now. He always seemed so laughing and open, so uncomplicated, and yet he'd never once invited her to his lodgings or offered to introduce her to his friends.

"Has he seen a doctor?"

"Two days ago, he said go home and go to bed."

"Which of course he didn't."

"No, well, he had to go into college; he had an appointment with his tutor. And he didn't seem to be too bad. But then last night his temperature absolutely shot up."

"What's his breathing like?"

"Quite bad, I think it might be pneumonia."

"Is there a telephone?"

"I think the landlady has one, but she lives next door."

"It's just I'll have to tell my parents."

"No, you mustn't, he doesn't want them to know. He's afraid if your mother comes she'll get it herself."

"They've got a right to know."

"You talk to him then, he might listen to you."

Mother *would* come and nurse him. Surprising, perhaps, in such an indolent woman, but she'd have been on the next train.

"Is term over?"

"Finished yesterday. That's why he wouldn't give in, you see. He won't take time off."

She caught the note of hero worship in his voice. When Toby was at school, he'd always had hero-worshipping younger boys trailing round after him, coming to stay in the holidays, taking him away from her. This Andrew might think he was special but he was merely the latest in a long line.

They were climbing a steep hill now, which at least allowed her to stop talking for a while. The smell of sulfur that had hung over the city for weeks had gone; the air tasted crisp and sweet. With each step she pressed her foot down hard, relishing the squeak of her boots on the impacted snow. Odd, to be able to feel pleasure at such a time. She didn't, even now, believe Toby was really sick, or in any danger. He never had been. Apart from the usual childhood things that everybody gets, she couldn't remember a time when he'd been ill.

The houses on either side were more imposing now, set well back from the road and screened by trees. She bumped into a low-hanging branch that sent snow cascading over her head and shoulders. Taking off her hat, she beat it against the side of her coat.

Andrew was staring, as if he'd only just seen her. "You're awfully like him, aren't you? I didn't think boy-girl twins could be identical."

"They can't," she said. "One's a boy, one's a girl." He was supposed to be a medical student, for God's sake. "Anyway, we're not twins."

"Oh. I'm sure Toby said—"

"I think I'd know." That verged on the sharp. "Toby was a twin, the other one died."

"Sorry, I must've got it wrong."

He was still looking puzzled: Toby *had* said they were twins. She didn't understand any of this, but there was no time to think about it now. "Is there anybody in the house who can help look after him?"

"No, not really. I live at home, I can come in during the day, but I couldn't stay overnight."

"I meant the landlady, somebody like that."

"I'm afraid she's much too grand for anything like that. And I don't think he knows any of the other tenants."

The walk took a lot longer in the snow than it would normally have done. By the time they reached Toby's lodgings Elinor was gasping for breath, in no state to face four flights of stairs, or brace herself for what she might find when she reached the top.

Andrew pushed open the door, called out a cheerful greeting, and then stood aside to let her go in first. Her nostrils caught the usual sickroom fug of camphor and stale sweat. The room was in darkness except for a circle of firelight flickering on the hearth rug. She couldn't see where she was going, but then Andrew stepped in front of her and lit the lamp. A bristle of meaningless detail: clothes, shoes, socks, furniture, books, dirty dishes piled up in a sink. None of it registered. She saw only Toby's face.

"Elinor."

Three quick strides took her to the bed. "It's all right," she was saying. "It's all right."

He gazed up at her, and a thick, pasty-white tongue came out and licked his cracked lips.

"Don't try to talk."

As she spoke, she was pulling off her coat and scarf. She tossed them onto a chair and stamped her feet to shake off the curds of snow. The room filled with the smell of wet wool and the cold air they'd brought in on their skins.

Elinor glanced round. The fire was burning low, but there was a basket full of logs, presumably carried up by Andrew. There was a jug of water by the bed. As for food, well . . . She doubted if Toby could eat anything and she certainly didn't want to.

"You won't tell Mother, will you?"

"She's got a right to know. *And* Father."

"Honestly, Elinor, this is a terrible thing . . ." He was struggling to sit up. "Don't let—"

He'd always been like this about Mother. Nothing must be allowed to upset or disturb her at all. It made Elinor actually quite angry: so much concern for Mother, so little for her. It obviously didn't matter if *she* got ill. And Father, where was Father in all this? Nowhere. Rachel, not even mentioned. But she could see he was becoming more and more agitated.

"All right," she said, at last. "I promise."

He closed his eyes then and let her settle him onto the pillows, which were damp with his sweat.

When she'd made him as comfortable as she could, she turned to Andrew, who'd been hovering, awkward and clumsy, by the door, his gaze fixed on Toby's flushed and sweating face.

"I'll be all right now, if you want to get off."

He glanced at the clock on the mantelpiece. "I don't want to, but I think perhaps I'd better."

He went to stand by the bed. For some extraordinary reason she felt she ought to look away, but then, deliberately, didn't. She watched him wrap one big red hand round Toby's twitching fingertips.

"Right, then, I'll see you in the morning."

"What time?"

"Nine-ish."

"Oh. Not till then?"

"All right, I'll try to get in for eight."

Toby seemed about to say something else, but then shook his head.

She followed Andrew out onto the landing.

"Look," he said, "here's my telephone number. You will let me know, won't you, if he gets worse?"

"Yes, of course," she said, automatically, though she thought: *I've just promised not to tell my mother and father. Why on earth would I tell you?*

She stood in the darkness, listening to his footsteps going down the stairs, until she heard the click of the front door closing behind him. When she got back to the room, Toby's eyes were shut, though she didn't think he was asleep. Perhaps he wanted to avoid the rawness of undiluted contact with her, now that his friend had gone and they were alone. She looked down at him. There was a gray tinge to his complexion now, except for two patches of dark red on his cheeks that seemed to get more intense as she watched. The effect was ridiculous and even slightly sinister; he looked like a broken doll.

He'd thrust the bedclothes down below his waist. She tried to pull them up again, but he resisted. "No, I'm too hot."

"You've got a temperature."

When she touched his forehead the heat frightened her, but a few minutes later he'd started to shiver and complained of feeling cold. She tucked the coverlet up around his chin, but almost immediately he started tugging at it, fighting to get it off. He opened his eyes and looked at her.

"Has Andrew gone?"

"Yes, just now."

He nodded, but kept glancing towards the door.

"He left me his telephone number."

"You won't ring him, will you? He lives at home."

"No, I won't ring."

The port-wine stains on his cheeks turned him into a stranger. She sat by the bed, suddenly frightened, dreading the long night ahead.

"I don't know what to do," he said.

Bizarrely, he'd voiced her thoughts. "I think the best thing you can do is get some sleep."

He lapsed into silence then, his eyes fluttering upwards behind his half-closed lids. Perhaps he would sleep. She sat back in the chair and gazed around the room. It was very much a student's lodgings, right down to the cheap prints tacked on the walls. Books were stacked on every available surface, sometimes spilling over onto the floor. In one corner, wedged between the wardrobe and the window, was a skeleton, wearing Toby's hat.

A carriage clock on the mantelpiece ticked out the slow minutes. She felt lonely, and she hadn't expected that. She'd thought they'd be in this together, but they weren't. Toby had vanished into his illness, leaving her to face the night alone.

As his temperature rose, he began to mutter, a jumble of words that made no sense. He seemed to think he was back at home, in his own room. Once, he even called her "Mother."

She touched his hand. "It's Elinor."

"Oh, yes." He managed a smile. "I'm glad it's you."

But then he started rambling and the muttering got louder. He seemed to be saying one word over and over again. She bent closer, getting the full blast of his rancid breath.

"Toby, I can't hear you."

"Sorry. Sorry sorry sorry sorry . . ."

"*Shush.*"

She put a hand over his mouth, but the sorries kept streaming out of him. He must be apologizing for what had happened between them, at the old mill and later in his room. What else could it be? Without warning he threw the covers off and swung his legs over the side of the bed. She pushed him back, knowing if it came to a fight he was almost certainly, in spite of his illness, stronger than her. She couldn't make out what he was trying to do. He seemed to be staring at something, not at her, something or somebody behind her.

"Sorry, I am so sorry."

"Go to sleep, Toby. Please."

Sleep was what he needed, but she wanted him unconscious as much for her sake as his. He lay back, defeated, and closed his eyes. At first, he simply tossed and turned, made restless by the tightness of his breathing, but then, at last, he slipped into a deep sleep, and she was able to relax, a little.

A sulky fire burnt in the grate, spitting whenever a flake of snow found its way down the chimney and hit the hot coals. The room was beginning to feel cold. She pressed a log down hard onto the embers, but the flames that licked round it would take an hour or more to get a hold. The chair she was sitting in had springs sticking through the cushions. She twisted and turned, trying to get comfortable, but nothing worked, and the coat she'd wrapped round herself was still wet from the long walk through the snow. Toby was clinging to the edge of the bed, leaving plenty of space on the other side. Without undressing, or even loosening her belt, she climbed across him, and curled up in the narrow space between his spine and the wall.

She pulled the damp sheet over her, convinced she wouldn't sleep, not with those dreadful rattling breaths beside her, but after a while she did manage to doze off, though she was aware, all the time, of the other body beside her, kicking, turning, never still, not for a moment, always wanting more room, more room. Without waking, he rolled over towards her. She wriggled away, but he seemed to be following her, pressing in on her, until her face was only a few inches from the wall. And he was pouring out sweat. At last, she gave up, and went back to sitting in the chair, trying to persuade herself that the curtains were beginning to let in a little more light. Though the clock said it was only twenty past three: the dead of night, the hour when the grip on life weakens.

She lit the lamp and brought it closer to his face so she could see the color of his skin. The extent of his deterioration was frightening. While she'd been dozing, he'd turned from a doll into a clown. She put a hand on his chest and felt the huge, dark muscle of the heart laboring away in its cage of bone. Somehow or other she had to get his temperature down. She looked around for something to put water in, but all she could see was the jug by the bed. There had to be bowls somewhere. She found one in a cupboard beside the sink, and another in the bathroom across the landing. She filled them with tepid water and carried them to the marble washstand beside the bed.

As she brought the wet flannel close to his face, he said, "No!" loudly, almost shouting, and reared away from her.

"We've got to get your temperature down."

He withdrew from her then, from his own body almost, straining his neck and head back as if to disassociate himself from the sweating bulk on the bed. She began to wash him down, singing little snatches of songs: *Daisy, Daisy, give me your answer do, I'm half crazy . . .* How different this body was from that other one on the slab, and yet how alike too. The glow of his wet skin in the lamplight . . . *All for the love of you.*

She worked rapidly, drying and covering him again as she went, so that he wouldn't get chilled. Nursing was the only part of her education that hadn't been neglected, until she'd gone to the Slade and met Tonks. At the end, she soaked the flannel in cold water and laid it across his eyes. She felt the darkness on her own lids, the cold weight, like the pennies they used to put on the eyes of the dead. As soon as the thought occurred she wanted to snatch the flannel away, but no, he was making little grunts and murmurs of pleasure, so she left it there, wetting it again to cool it down whenever it warmed through.

After that he slept for almost three hours. But then, gradually, inexorably, his temperature rose again, until he was twisting and flailing about, trying to escape from the bedclothes, even, it seemed, from his own body. And the muttering started again, but this time she couldn't make out the words. Something about a train, was it?

"You don't need to go anywhere, Toby. Lie down."

He gripped her by the upper arms so tightly it was an effort not to cry out.

"Elinor?"

"I'm here."

He looked puzzled. Obviously he'd no idea where he was, or why she was here, but he let her plump up his pillows and straighten the sheets.

When she was sure he'd stopped struggling, she stepped away from the bed. Looking down at him, rubbing her arms, thinking: *That'll bruise.* The fight seemed to have gone out of him. She didn't know whether that was a good thing or a bad thing, and she was almost too tired to care. She sank back into the chair, pulled the coat over her again, and slept.

———

She woke an hour later with dry lips and a dry tongue; she must have been sleeping with her mouth open. Toby was awake, watching her. She was so stiff it was a struggle to get out of the chair, but she managed to hobble the few steps to the bed and touch his hand. She was amazed to find it as cool as her own.

"You look a lot better."

"Yes, I think I am."

"Do you think you could eat something?"

He was staring up at her, dazed by his recovery, but then suddenly his expression darkened. "I must have talked an awful lot of rubbish last night."

She busied herself straightening the sheets. "No, you rambled on a bit, but I couldn't make any of it out."

His gaze wandered round the room, no longer with the confusion of high fever, but with a baby's indiscriminate curiosity.

"Have you been here all night?"

"Yes."

"I hope to God you don't get it."

She shrugged. "Lap of the gods. Do you think you could manage a cup of tea?"

As she searched for cups and saucers she felt his gaze heavy between her shoulder blades, but he said nothing and before the kettle boiled he'd drifted off to sleep.

She went to the window and looked out onto the garden far below. Snow, snow everywhere. Every roof, every gable, every branch of every tree had changed shape overnight. Big white birds circled over the gardens searching for scraps, finding none, until the back door of one of the houses opened and a woman carrying a blue-and-white serving dish came out. She threw a chicken carcass onto the lawn, and then stood scraping small bones and scraps of fat off the plate with the side of her hand. The minute she turned to go back in, the birds swooped down, fighting over the carcass in a great flurry of wings and snow.

How close had Toby come to dying last night? Easy, sitting here in broad daylight, to think she must have exaggerated the danger. He was, after all, young and strong, and strong young men don't die.

What would her life have been like if he had? She couldn't bear to think about it, not now, not while the fear was still present. But perhaps, after this illness, it would always be there? For a few hours last night, the unthinkable had become entirely possible, and from a realization like that there's no going back.

She turned and looked at him. His mouth had slackened in sleep; each breath puckered the upper lip. But his color was so much better; he would get over this. And the separation, the distance, that had grown up between them in the last few months, that had to end. *Now.* Toby had been right all along. Somehow or other they had to get back to the way things were. What had happened was not something that could be talked about, or explained, or analyzed, or in any other way resolved. It could only be forgotten.

She stood at the window, timing her breaths to match the rise and fall of his. After a while, out of a white sky, more snow began to fall, tentatively, at first, then thick and fast, covering up the signs of battle on the lawn.

8

A few days later Elinor was sitting under the tall window outside Tonks's room. There was a row of five chairs, but she was the only person waiting. She was nervous, as she always was before meeting Tonks, and the bright light from the window hurt her eyes. She hadn't had much sleep the last few days. Toby had now gone home to recuperate, but worrying about him still kept her awake. Silly, really, because he was getting better.

She was here to tell Tonks that she didn't want to continue with the anatomy course, and she didn't know how he'd respond to that. He'd gone to a lot of trouble to get her into it. She looked at her watch: five minutes past the time of her appointment, but there was no sound from behind his door.

Tonight, she was going to the end-of-term Christmas party: one of the social highlights of the Slade year. Normally, she loved parties, she loved dressing up, but this particular one aroused mixed feelings because it marked the end of Kit Neville's time at the Slade. Tonks had told him he was wasting his time, he'd never make an artist, and Kit had said, "That's it, then, I'm off." His leaving wouldn't make any difference to their friendship, they'd still see each other, but all the same . . . The last few days she'd had a constant sense of change, of movement, gears shifting, life taking a new shape, a new direction. Asking to see Tonks, taking the initiative, rather than waiting, passively, for him to send for her, was part of that. She was beginning to feel she belonged here: this was her place.

She looked up. A man was coming down the long corridor towards her. At first, he was merely a dark, indistinct shape, moving between patches of light and shade as he crossed in front of the windows. As he came closer, she could see he was wearing a black overcoat so long it nearly reached the floor, and so shabby it must surely be secondhand. He sat down, three chairs away from her, clutching a battered portfolio to his chest. A prospective student, God help him. She felt a stab of sympathy, remembering the day she'd come to the Slade to show her drawings to Tonks. How totally crushed she'd been. She wanted to reach out to him, to say something encouraging, but she couldn't catch his eye. He had one of the most, if not *the* most, remarkable profiles she'd ever seen. She wondered if he knew.

The door opened. Tonks appeared and waved her to a chair in front of his desk. All her carefully prepared speeches crumbled into dust. She sat there, in the light from the window behind him, gobbling like a turkey that's just realized why it's been invited to Christmas dinner. At last she dribbled into silence.

"You've had enough?" Tonks said.

"Yes."

"All right. Though I hope you don't feel it was a waste of time—?"

"Oh, no, not in the—"

"Because, actually, your work's come on leaps and bounds this term. After"—he smiled, delicately—"a somewhat shaky start."

Oh, God. He hadn't forgotten the drawing.

"It's been very useful," she said.

Was that it? Evidently it was. Tonks was on his feet, escorting her to the door, saying he hoped to see her at the party that night. "Oh, if there's a young man out there, could you ask him to wait a few more minutes? There's just something I need to do . . ."

She left the room, thinking: *Leaps and bounds? Leaps and bounds?* Praise from Tonks was so rare she could've leapt and bounded all the way along the corridor. But there was the young man, head down, picking at a ragged cuticle on his right thumb. He looked up, startled, when she approached.

"Professor Tonks says he'll see you in a moment. He's just got something he has to do."

He was struggling to his feet. She'd noticed before how surprised men were when girls spoke directly or behaved confidently. Almost as if they were so used to simpering and giggling they didn't know how to react.

She held out her hand. "Elinor Brooke."

"Paul Tarrant."

"Are you coming to the Slade?"

"Don't know. Doubt it."

The northern working-class accent came as a bit of a shock. "Well, don't let Tonks put you off, his bark's worse than his bite."

Liar. She smiled and walked off, already thinking about the dress she was going to wear to the party that night, but at the end of the corridor, she turned and looked back. He was still on his feet, watching her. She gave him a little wave, before leaping and bounding down the stairs.

Part Two

_1917_

9

The heat on the hospital train, as it crawled through the fields of Kent, was almost unendurable. Nobody came to open the windows and none of the four men in the compartment could get off their bunks. The air was tainted with the smell of gangrene coming from the shoulder wound of the lad opposite Paul. Young, red-haired, his face streaked with blood and oil, wildly excited because he was going home. What time is it? he kept asking. Are we there yet? God, he was like a child on an outing to the seaside. He couldn't stop talking, the people he was going to see, the things he was going to do: Mam, Dad, booze, football, girls, more girls, booze, girls . . .

SHUT UP! Paul wanted to shout, but he didn't. All that talk about girls made him think about Elinor, how soon she would come to see him, whether she would come to see him. After her silence of the last two months, perhaps not . . . By the time they reached Charing Cross, the chattering had died away to a low mumble, followed by a succession of loud snores.

Unloading the train took the best part of an hour. At last, though, Paul was lying, strapped to a stretcher, staring up at the station roof where hundreds of bright-eyed pigeons cocked their heads at the noise and confusion below.

A crowd of well-wishers had gathered, but the police were keeping them back. An elderly man with a white mustache and a soldierly bearing did not so much break through the cordon as ignore it. He bent over Paul, his face reddening with effort, and thrust a leaflet into his hand, followed by a bag of sweets. The leaflet was headed: JESUS SAVES. Paul looked down at the sweets, thought about unwrapping one and decided not to bother.

A stretcher carrying the red-haired young man, still asleep or possibly unconscious, had been set down beside him. Minutes passed; how many, he didn't know. After a while, a nurse came up to him, asked him how he felt and lifted the blanket to check the dressing on his leg.

"Wasting your time on that one, love. It's in splints," a passing soldier said.

She actually blushed. It was rather nice, seeing that. He decided he would have a sweet after all.

By the time he'd unwrapped one and popped it into his mouth, she'd moved round to the other stretcher and was kneeling by the red-haired man, looking rather concerned. She put two fingers to his neck. Waited. Then, carefully expressionless, she pulled the blanket up over his face.

Looking up, she caught Paul watching her. "Is that nice?" she asked.

He rolled the sweet from side to side. Tears gathered at the corners of his eyes and trickled into his hair. "Lovely."

"Shouldn't be long now. Soon have you on the ambulance."

Standing up, she dusted down the skirt of her uniform and left him alone with the dead.

ELINOR BROOKE'S DIARY

3 August 1917

Arrived in Lewes not even knowing if I was going to be met or not. In the event: not. *I'd brought a really heavy suitcase so stood there pinned to the wretched thing while the heat crept into the station from the dazzling street outside and everything started to prickle. Scalp, arms, back, chest. In the end I surrendered my case to the stationmaster—who seemed to be familiar with the problem—and he said he'd send it up on the milk float in the morning. I thought about my evening dress— such as it is!—trapped inside. Well, that couldn't be helped, but I decided I needed my sketch pads and pencils. He watched me, looking rather amused, while I scrabbled about. Oh, they're well known, the Charleston crew. Without needing to be asked, he pointed out the path and soon I was swinging along between the harvest fields. It was unpleasantly hot, but beautiful too. I stopped to rest under some trees and the shade was full of the humming of insects. A heap of horse manure, still steaming, was covered in butterflies, which rose up in a great blue cloud as I approached.*

VB was in the drawing room when I arrived, with her sister, Mrs. Woolf. I've met her more than once, though I don't think she remembered me and gave me a lukewarm welcome. Doesn't like young women, I suspect. I thought the talk would be well above my head, but they were quite relaxed and gossipy and we chatted on easily enough. Or they did. I was too nervous to say much. It was like listening to an old married couple. They've got that habit of completing each other's sentences, and yet VB seems . . . I don't know. Wary? Something.

The men came in from the fields, brick red from the sun, hands covered in stubble scratches, and no doubt their ankles too—stubble gets through anything. They went off to wash,

*and came down more civilized, better-tempered. Meanwhile,
a woman appeared with a tray of bread and butter, not home-
made, of course—nobody can get the ingredients—which seems
mad in the country, but there you are—and jam. The jam was
marrow and ginger, the ginger's supposed to counteract the
blandness of the marrow. Hmm. We chewed valiantly and
talked, mainly about painting. Which pleased me—I was so
afraid it would be terribly intellectual, but I've decided I like
the way artists talk, it's so* practical *most of the time.*

*And I like VB a lot, though she paid hardly any attention
to me after the men arrived. She is superbly casual with her
painter's smock and her slipping hair and her rather fine but
obviously capable hands. That's what I like about her, I think,
her ability to* do things. *You feel she can stretch a canvas,
decorate a room, soothe a fractious baby, sew, knit, grow plants,
even cook, I suspect, if she had to. And, of course, paint. I like
people who can do things. And I have less and less patience with
those who can't. At Garsington, some of the conchies make
no effort to acquire the skills they need to do farm work. Oh,
I know it's compulsory, they haven't* chosen *to do it, but I do
think, in their place, I'd make a bit more of an effort. But then,
I never shall be in their place so oughtn't to criticize, I suppose.*

*Later. Between tea and dinner I walked in the garden. I
didn't have any unpacking or changing to do and I'm beginning
to suspect I shan't have tomorrow, either. Apparently the man
who drives the milk float is trying to dodge conscription, so if
he sees the police, or even thinks he sees them, he abandons the
float and takes off into the Downs. I'd been hoping the evening
would bring some relief from the fierce heat, but it didn't. The
walled garden was particularly hot. I stood still for a long time
surrounded by tall flowers—sunflowers, hollyhocks, foxgloves—
they always make me feel I'm five years old again, I have such
a vivid memory of what it was like to poke my finger down*

*their speckled throats—and everything seemed to be stunned
by the heat. Few birds now, they've all gone quiet, just the hum
of insects and a frenzy of midges around my bare arms, little
frantic things, as if the air had turned to glass and they were
trying to get out. I sat and sketched, though I'm not good at
doing that in strange places—you'd think the unfamiliarity
of the landscape would help you to see it more clearly, but it
doesn't seem to work that way.*

*The midges were a nuisance, particularly near the pond,
where there was a punt tethered—all rather romantic. And of
course I went off into a daydream, bending over the water, as
if I were going to kiss my own reflection—and judging from the
glimpse I had of the conscientious young men at tea I think I
may have to. There was a shoal of fish, quite small, striped green
and gold, very pretty, until you looked more closely and saw
their malevolent grins.*

*When I looked up again, I'd been joined by two entirely
naked young boys. The elder—about twelve, I suppose—had that
finished look of late childhood, confident, even arrogant, a little
prince in his wild kingdom. The other was still soft and round
and vulnerable. They were employed in blowing up toads.
Apparently you insert a straw into their rear ends and blow
and—Well! I just refuse to think about it.*

*Over dinner we talked about the war. What the men will
do in winter when work on the land isn't needed, though they'll
still have to do something, work in a factory or a hospital,
I suppose. The boys didn't appear, though through the open
windows you could hear them fighting a battle of some sort, lots
of blood-curdling yells and screams; and inside there were the
adults being so seriously, conscientiously, determinedly opposed
to it all. But it's the little wild savages in the garden who'll win,
I think.*

*Now I'm sitting in my bedroom listening to an owl hooting
and wishing I could talk to Toby. Or Paul. Paul's in hospital*

in London, badly wounded, and I haven't even been to see
him yet, so what does it mean when I say I want to talk to
him? It's not even a conscious decision, not going to see him;
I mean, I just can't seem to make myself do it. Ever since he
volunteered to fight, we've been drifting further and further
apart. Sometimes I wonder if there'll be anything left when
we do, finally, meet. And then I feel terrible because while he
was out there I virtually stopped writing to him altogether. Just
couldn't do it anymore, couldn't bear to spin out the trivialities
of my life. And now there he is in hospital with a lump of
shrapnel in his leg—though I suppose they'll have got that out
by now—and here I sit in a cozy little bedroom in a borrowed
nightie, and . . . And none of it is my fault.

   And yet there's so much guilt: always another letter needing
to be written. And when you do write you can't say any of
the things you want to say—I can't, anyway—because it might
be the last thing they read. So you have to be nice, you have to
be cheerful, you aren't to mention anything that might upset
them. It's horrible for them, but it's horrible for us as well.

   Only it can't be just that; I mean, the reason I stopped
writing to Paul, because all that applies to Toby too, and I write
to him twice a week.

4 August 1917

   I think my heyday's over. This came to me very clearly
walking in the garden this morning after breakfast. Everybody
else had gone off to work, or almost everybody. The boys had
vanished, but I could feel them tracking me. I think all visitors
are German spies in their eyes, needing to be watched. You hear
them rather than see them, a twig cracking or the rustling of a
leaf. Anyway, there I was, "alone" in the garden, thinking, I'm
past my prime.

   Oh, what nonsense, Catherine would say. At least I hope

*she would! I've lost touch with all my other Slade friends, so I
don't suppose they'd have an opinion. No, my best time was at
the Slade before the war, I was happy then. Pursued by men,
especially after I cut my hair off. (So much for Mother's fears
that I'd become a nun.) And let's face it, being pursued is always
rather nice, however little one may wish to be caught.*

*And then I saw Michael Stoddart, one of the conscientiously
objecting young men, standing by the pond smoking a cigarette,
so I went up to him, suggested a walk through the fields, and off
we went.*

*Intolerable heat, really intolerable. Generally there's a
breeze on the Downs, so you know you're going to be cool up
there, however hot it is elsewhere, but these last few days even
the breeze has been hot. Something very un-English about
it—the Sirocco, one of those peculiar winds I used to know the
names of, which are supposed to drive people mad. So anyway,
we walked and observed an aeroplane flying over us towards
the coast, and countless butterflies. It's been a fantastic year for
butterflies, silver fritillaries, peacocks, blues—clouds of blues—
but the conversation limped along. I did my Jane Austen–ish
best with the weather—how strange it's been, so hot and dry
in Kent, absolutely pouring down everywhere else—and the
farmhouse, how beautiful it is, and the very convenient ease
of the train journey from London, I almost asked after the
health of his family, but then I thought, No, for goodness' sake,
I haven't met them.* Your turn. *And to give him his due, he did
his best.*

Him. *Tall, lean, floppy blond hair, blue eyes—very striking
at the moment because he's suntanned from all that working
on the farm—slightly stuttering speech, a rather modest, self-
deprecating air, which I always think conceals arrogance, but
then I'm getting cynical in my old age.*

We carried on walking across the fields. The heat of the

sun seemed to have contracted to a single point that was boring into my head like a bottle opener being screwed into a cork. Great blasts of hot wind coming off the Downs—a furnace door opening and shutting. He didn't say much, just glanced at me sidelong now and then. I think girls must be a rarity in his life because he certainly seemed to think I was some kind of exotic creature. He asked about my painting, and obviously expected me to ask about his, but I hadn't heard of him, so I didn't, and then he asked if I had anybody Out There. So of course I told him about Toby and Kit Neville, and the others. Sometimes it seems as if every young man I've ever known is in France. (Or under it.) I could see him waiting for me to ask why he wasn't Out There too, but I didn't. I never do. When he pushed, I said it didn't concern me. As a woman, it didn't concern me. To be honest, I was copying something I'd heard Mrs. Woolf say last night after dinner, about how women are outside the political process and therefore the war's got nothing to do with them. It sounded clever when she said it, and stupid when I repeated it. And immediately I started thinking about women in Deptford hurling bricks through the windows of "German" shopkeepers— they aren't German, they're Polish or Russian or something, but the name's foreign and that's enough—and about the girls who handed white feathers to Toby when he was called back to London to complete his studies. All the medical students got white feathers, that's why in the end they had to let them wear army uniform. And I thought, No, it's not true, women aren't more peaceful than men. It pains me to say it, but the one thing this war has shown conclusively is how amazingly and repulsively belligerent women are. Some *women.*

Anyway, he didn't have the temerity to disagree with me. No doubt Mrs. W's views are sacrosanct.

We were walking down a lane between two fields. In the one on the right German prisoners were cutting the corn with hooks, guarded by a soldier with a gun, though he was cradling it in his arms like a baby and seemed half asleep. The prisoners were joking and laughing as they worked, though they looked up as we walked past. Farther on was a field reduced to its last stand of corn, the grain heads heaving and turbulent with the wild life trapped inside. With every turn of the harvester the cutting blades moved nearer. We stopped to watch. Men like charred sticks stood around—I mean, they were black against the burning gold of the field—everything seemed to be on the point of bursting into flame, like one of Van Gogh's landscapes, and the air burnt the back of your throat. Dogs leaping up and down on the end of their leashes like black scribbles on the air. Then first one rabbit broke cover, then another, and another. Almost leisurely it seemed, the guns were raised, one smooth fluid movement, and a rabbit leapt off the stubble, fell, ran on again, limping and falling, until a second shot put an end to it. It lay there twitching for a few seconds, then went still, a bundle of dusty fur, looking suddenly much smaller than it had in life.

I turned to say something to Michael, who was breathing rather heavily, but suddenly he grabbed me by the arms and kissed me. Not very expertly, it has to be said. Our teeth clashed. My mouth fell open in surprise. Perhaps he mistook this for feminine yielding—at any rate, he stuck a surprisingly long tongue down my throat. I got both hands between our chests and pushed him away. I don't know why I wasn't flattered—as I say, my heyday's over and we old maids must take what we can get—but I wasn't. As quickly as possible, I started off to walk back. The sun on my back seemed to push me along. I was sweating, thoroughly out of sorts; it was easier to blame the weather than think seriously about bloody Michael.

His friend Philip Bannister was waiting on the lawn when we got back. Michael kept darting little defiant glances at him, very daring, very naughty-boy, and suddenly I knew why I wasn't flattered. I nodded to Philip, and went straight upstairs to my room. I hope *without a flounce, but I can't be sure of that.*

Later. *What a silly trivial little incident—and yet it's opened a door into a room I never thought to visit again. I keep thinking about that walk to the old mill with Toby and the night that followed. I resent having it dragged out into the daylight like this—by nonsense. Toby and I put it behind us so successfully, we built a different, in many ways deeper, relationship, on that patch of burnt earth. And now I feel I'm being dragged back to the beginning again. Well, I won't go. Michael bloody Stoddart doesn't have the power to do that.*

After dinner, there was rum punch. I drank a bit too much of it and ended up with a bursting head and a short fuse. At some point—I can't really remember—the talk turned to who was likely to be commissioned as a war artist. And of course Kit Neville's name came up—and then Paul's.

"You know both of them, don't you?" VB said.

Glances across the table. Immediately I felt my relationship with Paul—possibly even with Kit, not that there ever was one—had been a topic of discussion, and I hated the idea. So I just said yes, I'd overlapped with both of them at the Slade, Kit Neville in my first and second year, Paul in my third.

Then Michael said he didn't know what he thought about war artists. Wasn't it just propaganda? And then Philip said, "At least it'll get them out of the war."

Now that is a perfectly innocuous remark, if you're not on your fourth glass of rum punch.

I said I was sure that was the last thing on either of their minds. And I pointed out that Paul was back home wounded so getting out of it wasn't an issue for him, and then I said, "They did both volunteer."

What a thing to say in a room full of conchies. A hole

*opened up in the conversation and we all stared into it, until
several people at once rushed in to fill the silence.*

*After dinner, we walked in the garden, the moths fluttering
round a lamp, the women in their pale dresses looking like
ghosts. VB came up and sort of semiapologized for Philip's
behavior at dinner. "I don't think he realized how close you
are to Paul Tarrant." I just muttered something and changed
the subject. I couldn't be doing with it all, and besides my
headache was getting worse by the minute. I could hear a steady
thump, thump, thump and I really didn't know if it was inside
my head, but then I thought, No, it's thunder. I said, "Thank
goodness"—something like that anyway—and everybody looked
amused. And then Philip said, "No, it's the guns."*

*I don't know what's the matter with me. You can hear
the guns in south London sometimes—teaspoons rattling in
saucers, that sort of thing—so they're bound to be audible here.
But, surely, not as loud as that? It must mean something's going
on—a "show" they call it, bloody stupid word—and I'd really
rather not know. It only deepens the fear that's there beneath
the surface anyway.*

*When everybody else went inside, I stayed in the garden
saying I had a headache and thought the fresh air would do me
good. I had the feeling that my relationship with Paul was being
gossiped about, fingered, passed round, pawed at, the way the
Bloomsbury crowd always do, and that made me think about
it: the fact I haven't been to see him, didn't write. I don't know
how much is left—if anything. Probably not very much. I threw
it away—and I did throw it away, we didn't "drift apart," as
people say. I ought to have written more regularly when he
was in France, and I didn't. I ought to have been to see him in
hospital, and I haven't.*

*And when I ask myself what went wrong the only answer
I can come up with is the war. In those first weeks it seemed to
throw us together—and then there was that mad weekend in*

*Ypres, in the room with the big shiny brass bed and the view
over the rooftops—which aren't there anymore. Apparently, you
can look from one end of the city to the other and there's hardly
a wall left standing that's above knee height. But Paul and I
became lovers there in that doomed city, the first bombardment
started while I was there, and somehow the war has always
followed us. It made us and then it unmade us.*

*Because late in 1915, Paul enlisted—and not for medical
work this time—no, he volunteered to fight. And I know he
says he volunteered because everybody knew conscription was
coming anyway and he didn't want to be dragged, kicking
and screaming, to the front—but still he did it, and from that
moment on things began to unravel between us. It became
harder and harder to know what to write.*

*So that's the truth, I think, or as close as I can get to it. The
war brought us together; the war tore us apart.*

*At least he's back home now, and that's one less to worry
about. I'm so frightened for Toby. Of course I'm worried about
Kit Neville too, he's in the same unit, facing the same dangers,
but fear has an awful way of revealing the truth. Toby's the one
I couldn't bear to lose. Nobody else, not even Paul—certainly
not Kit, though I'd be terribly upset, of course, if anything
happened to him.*

*I sat on a bench for a full hour and listened to the night
sounds. The soft explosive hooting of an owl seemed to be
compounded of blood and fear. And I thought, nothing's safe
anymore.*

5 August 1917

*I knew I wouldn't sleep and I didn't. The room was too hot
so I had to leave the window open, and the thud-thud of the
guns went on all night. I tried to cry; I've never found it easy
and it seems almost impossible now. I manage a couple of sobs,
and then give up in disgust. And, of course, I tell myself there's*

nothing to cry about. Yet. Only, as the night hours pass, that belief starts to wear thin.

This is difficult to write. Just before dawn I got dressed, walked down through the sleeping house, across the garden, and into the fields beyond. I was trudging uphill, feeling spikes of stubble jab my ankles, and then, just as I reached the top, the sun rose—huge, molten-red—and at that moment I knew—not thought, not feared, knew—*that Toby wasn't coming back. Not that he was dead, I didn't think he was dead, it was quite precise: he wasn't coming home.*

10

Days went by before she stood at her bedroom window and watched the telegraph boy—"boy" you called him, though he was a middle-aged, even elderly, man; all the boys were in France—dismount from his bicycle and push it up the hill.

At one point his head disappeared behind the hawthorn hedge—the lane dipped sharply there—and she convinced herself, standing motionless at the window, that he would never reappear. She had willed him away; even when, slowly, his peaked cap reappeared and then his head and shoulders and he stopped to mount his bicycle, even then, she knew it was in her power to prevent the telegram being delivered. There were other farmhouses, other families, farther down the lane. The Smeddles had three sons; they could afford to lose one of them. She'd have swept all three Smeddle boys off the face of the earth without a second thought if by so doing she could have prevented Dodds coming through the gate and crunching up the gravel drive. Listening to the doorbell chime, she almost shouted out: *Don't answer it, he'll give up, he'll go away.* If he went away it wouldn't have happened. Only by now she was halfway down the stairs. She looked over the banisters at Mrs. Robinson, drying her hands on her white apron as she hurried to answer the door. Then Elinor's mother came out of the breakfast room, her face blank, but fearing the worst because these days no telegram was innocent. She, too, disappeared into the porch and, a minute later, Elinor heard a thin, despairing cry. *That doesn't sound like Mother.* Elinor's hands gripped the banisters. *Doesn't sound like her at all.*

———

Mother became a white slug lying on the sofa in the living room. Rachel, with her two boys and their nurse, moved into the house and was in constant attendance, though after the first week she began to get resentful. She had a husband working in the War Office, resigned to staying at his club all week, but expecting home comforts at the weekend and deserving them too. She had a house to run, two small children, who were so much easier to manage at home with their own toys and beds and a garden to run around in, this garden wasn't even fenced in, and the pond, for God's sake, ten feet deep at the center if it was an inch ... And what did Elinor do? Go off and see her friends in London, and not just there and back in a day, either. No, she stayed away two or three nights at a time. It was perfectly plain what should happen. Elinor should stay at home and look after Mother, freeing her, Rachel, to see to her husband and children, who were, after all, her primary responsibility. Elinor could go on painting—if she really felt she had to—but it was absolutely clear where her first duty lay, and it was jolly well high time she started doing it too.

Elinor refused.

"You are so selfish," Rachel said. "I don't think I've ever met anybody as selfish as you."

"Yes, I am selfish. I need to be."

Their father said very little, but Elinor knew he agreed with Rachel. Everybody—the aunts, the uncles, the second cousins twice removed, Mrs. Robinson, the village, the farmer, the farmer's wife, for all she knew, the farmer's dog— agreed with Rachel, but it was only her father's opinion that hurt.

It made no difference. She went back to London on the next train and forced herself to paint. She had very little contact with other people. She seemed to be surrounded by a great white silence, long echoing corridors, doors opening into empty rooms. On the rare occasions when she had to meet people, she barely coped. A solitary visit to the Café Royal lasted a mere twenty minutes, before she began to feel anxious to get away.

Round about this time, she went to see Paul Tarrant in the Third London General Hospital because really there was no alternative: she had to go. As she walked down the center of a long ward she kept her eyes fixed on the bed at the end, afraid of the injuries she might see if she looked to either side. She wasn't good with hospitals at the best of times and some of the war wounds were so dreadful she couldn't bear to look at them. Paul was sitting up in bed chatting to a middle-aged couple. His eyes widened with surprise when he saw her; her letters had become so infrequent he may well not have expected her to come.

The man beside the bed stood up and Paul introduced him as his father. He had Paul's way of ducking his head when he shook hands, but not Paul's looks. The woman was Paul's stepmother. To Elinor's dismay, they showed every sign of leaving her alone with Paul though they'd traveled three hundred miles for this visit. She could see they were slightly in awe of the nice middle-class young lady their son was walking out with. She supposed some such term as "walking out" would be the one they'd choose.

"No, please," she said. "Don't leave on my account. I can only stay a few minutes anyway."

And it was a few minutes. Afterwards she thought she might have done better not to have gone at all, since she and Paul had not managed to have any real conversation. The surgeon was pleased with him; he might get quite a bit more movement in the knee, probably not the full amount, but enough to get around. No, crutches, then? No, no crutches. He thought perhaps a nice stick with a swan on the handle. Out of hospital, probably by the end of the week, then a convalescent home in Dorset for a month after that. Looking forward to that, never seen Dorset. Had she ever been? And so it went on, until she was able to take her leave. After a second's hesitation, she bent to kiss him, and felt his father and stepmother exchange a glance. Then she was off down the ward as if all the fiends in hell were after her. She might have deceived his parents about the warmth of her regard, but she was under no illusion that she'd deceived Paul.

––––––––

Not long after the telegram arrived, Elinor was standing on the terrace when once again a postman turned into the drive. This time he was carrying a big brown-paper parcel entwined with thick, hairy string. It was addressed to her parents. Already fearful of what it might contain, she took it into the conservatory, where Rachel sat by their mother, who lay stretched out on the sofa. She'd hardly moved since the news of Toby's death. Her skin seemed to have slackened, as if she'd shrunk away inside it. Until recently, she'd still been considered a beautiful woman, though nobody would think so now. Again, the image of a moist white slug came into Elinor's mind. It filled her with guilt, but then, almost at once, her impatience returned. She couldn't bear the weeping and wailing that punctuated her mother's long silences. Elinor was determined not to grieve, and particularly not to grieve *like that*. Her own first reaction to the news had been a blaze of euphoria; immediately her fingers itched to grab a brush and paint. Grief was for the dead, and Toby would never be dead while she was alive and able to hold a brush.

But now here the three of them were. They looked at the parcel, trying to decipher the postmark, and then at one another.

"Well," Rachel said.

Suddenly sick of the suspense, Elinor began trying to unfasten the knots, but her fingers felt swollen and stiff.

"Ring for Mrs. Robinson," Mother said. "She'll have some scissors."

Mrs. Robinson's eyes widened when she saw the parcel. She looked, rather shamefacedly, excited, as indeed she had when the telegram arrived. She'd been genuinely fond of Toby, but still, his death was drama in a humdrum life. She'd talk about him in the village post office; no doubt the family's bereavement had enhanced her status there.

"It'll be his things," she said. "They send them back. They did with Mrs. Jenkins's lad."

The scissors were duly fetched and the string cut, but even before the first layers of brown paper had been stripped away something entirely unexpected entered the room: the smell of the front line. Filthy water, chlorine gas, decomposition—and because it was a smell, and not a sight, Elinor was defense-less against it. She walked, stiff-legged, to the window, where she looked out over the lawn and trees, not seeing anything, every nerve and muscle in her body fighting to repudiate that smell.

When she turned back into the room they'd got the par-cel unwrapped. Tunic, belt, a periscope, breeches, peaked cap, puttees, boots—all reeking of the same yellow-brown stench. Elinor's mother touched the tunic, timidly, stroking the sleeve nearest to her. At first, she seemed entirely calm, but then her mouth twisted, a crease appeared between her eyebrows and she began to cry. Not like an adult; no, this was the dreadful, square-mouthed wail of an abandoned baby.

Rachel gathered the things together and thrust the bundle into Elinor's hands. "Take it away."

"Where shall I put it?"

"How do I know? Just get rid of it, for God's sake."

Elinor backed out of the room—bumping into Mrs. Robinson, who'd heard the cry and was rushing in to help—and took the parcel upstairs to her own room, then along to Toby's room, but then she remembered that her mother often came up here and sat in the window, for hours on end sometimes, looking down the road into the village, to the train station, where she'd seen him for the last time. He wouldn't let anybody go to London with him.

Nowhere seemed to be the right place. In the end, she wrapped everything up again as best she could and took the parcel up into the attic, where she pushed it deep into a recess under the eaves. Right at the back, out of sight. Then she piled old blankets and a rug in front of it, anything to fend off the smell. Closing the door at the top of the stairs, she felt as if she'd disposed of a corpse. Out of sight, out of mind, she told herself.

Only it never was, quite. That smell broke the last numbness of shock. The following day Elinor's mother left for Rachel's house; Elinor was left alone, and glad to be alone. The parcel containing Toby's clothes remained in her mind, but separated from her waking consciousness, like a nightmare whose every detail is forgotten, though the fear survives, poisoning the day.

Now that she could work at home, there was no need to go back to London. She spent all the hours of daylight painting in the barn across the yard, creeping back into the house at dusk, often forgetting to eat at all. At night, she slept in Toby's room.

Painting numbed the pain; nothing else did. In the evenings, when she was too exhausted to work, she sat in front
of the fire, trying to read. Usually, she had to abandon the
attempt because nothing stayed in her head. She could read
the same paragraph half a dozen times and still not be able
to remember what it said. Above her head the floorboards
creaked as if somebody were pacing up and down in the corridor outside his room. She paid no attention to this. It was a
trivial manifestation of her state of mind; no more.

For long stretches of time he might not have died at all.
He wasn't present, but then he hadn't been present for most
of the past two years. There was no body. No grave. No cere-
mony. Only his spare clothes, the stuff he'd left behind when
he went into the line for the last time, and they'd been pushed
out of sight.

At first, this limbo state didn't bother her, but then, as the
days and weeks went by, not knowing how he'd died became
a torment. She had to make his death real; otherwise this half-
life could go on forever. She knew there were people who
cherished the malignant hope that their sons or husbands
were still alive, prisoners of war perhaps, or mad, wandering
the French countryside with no memory of who they were,
or lying in a hospital bed too badly wounded to communicate
at all. These were hardly consoling thoughts, and yet people
clung to them. Anything, rather than face up to the finality of
death. But it was finality that she'd begun to crave.

She knew so little. What did "Missing, Believed Killed"
actually mean? What degree of certainty did it imply? Apart
from the telegram and the official letter that followed, there
were only two brief notes, one from Toby's CO, another
from the Chaplain. She read them again and again. How
short they were, how grudging. She'd been puzzled by that
at the time, though nobody else seemed to notice anything
amiss. And there was another thing: Kit Neville, who was in

the Royal Army Medical Corps and had served with Toby, hadn't written.

The more she thought about that, the more extraordinary it seemed. She wrote to him, asking if he knew anything about Toby's death. No reply. Thinking he might not have got the letter, she wrote again. Still no reply. She bought the *Times* and searched the columns of wounded and dead for Kit's name, convinced that something dreadful must have happened to him—nothing short of serious injury or death could excuse his silence—but his name wasn't in the lists. Of course, it might have been in previous issues, but no, if he were back in London she'd have heard.

She was left with nothing to fill the gap but her own imagination, and even imagination needs some facts to work on. Now, when it was too late, she'd have liked to know the details of Toby's life out there, but her long insistence on ignoring the war worked against her. When she tried to picture his final hours, her mind was blank.

One morning she began to paint Toby's portrait, wondering why it had taken her so long to think of doing it. As she worked, she kept stepping back from the easel and closing her eyes. She could see him more clearly like this: the shape of his head, the way his hair sprang from his temples, the blue eyes so like her own, but with a fleck of brown near the right pupil, his ears, the lobes extravagantly long and full; and then down across his body: the wart an inch away from his left nipple, the appendicitis scar . . .

It was about this time she became aware that the smell of his clothes had begun to invade the lower rooms.

At first she thought she must be imagining it. She was reminded of how the smell of the cadaver had pursued her even when she was miles away from the Dissecting Room. How strange: she hadn't thought about that for years. But now, she remembered lying in bed at night, sniffing her fingers, always catching the whiff of formaldehyde though it couldn't possibly have been there. Warily, she lifted her fingers to her nose, relieved to find only the familiar smells of oil and turps. No, the smell was just her imagination running away with her. She had to get a grip, stop thinking about the uniform, thrust it away again out of sight. And for a time she succeeded: the smell did seem to go away, only to return, a few days later, even more pungent than before.

She couldn't finish the portrait, or rather she couldn't trust herself to recognize the moment when it was finished. Her judgment had deserted her. A morning came when she hardly managed to work at all. Toby's features eluded her; his face seemed to be sliding in and out of focus. She took a short break and tried again, but it was no use. Tiredness; she'd been working too hard. This time, she gave herself several days off, only to find, when she returned to the studio, that she couldn't paint at all.

The clothes in the attic drew her to them. For days the smell had been particularly strong, especially in the corridor outside his room. At last, early one morning when it was no more than half light, she steeled herself to go upstairs to the attic. Madly, she managed to convince herself there would be nothing there. Rats and mice would have eaten them. So it was a shock to grope behind the old rug and the blankets she'd piled in front of them and find them still there, instantly recognizable to her probing fingertips by the cardboard stiffness of the cloth. She pulled the tunic clear of the wrapping and shook it, producing such a cloud of dust she started to cough. Then she wrapped the paper round the clothes again and carried them down the narrow stairs, clinging to the banisters with an old woman's fear of falling. If she fell now she could lie here for days.

At the foot of the stairs she hesitated, cradling the lifeless bundle in her arms, wondering where to take it, but these were his things: they belonged in his room.

She dropped the parcel on the floor beside the bed, and knelt down to look at the clothes. The smell was still there, but fainter now. This was hardly reassuring, since it meant she must have been imagining it, in part at least. On a sudden impulse, she began laying out the garments on the bed: the peaked cap, the tunic, the Sam Browne belt and revolver case, breeches, putties, boots . . . And there he was, his body shaped by the clothes he'd worn in life.

The smell was getting stronger again. Nothing else, nothing, could have made her want to imagine how he'd died. No words, no photographs, would have been powerful enough to break the taboo she'd imposed on herself: that the war was not to be acknowledged. But now smell, the most primitive of the senses, the one most closely linked to memory and desire, had swept all that away.

Bullet wound, bayonet wound, shrapnel? She saw him staggering on a few paces before collapsing, lying under the patient stars, alone. Only that was nonsense, of course; if he'd died like that there'd have been a body. A grave. Even the cadaver she'd worked on all those years ago had been buried in the end. What she couldn't grasp was the idea of a human being disintegrating; *nothing* left, not even a pile of greasy bones. And in only a second. Painless, everybody said. Yes, but also inhuman. Outside the natural order of things.

She knelt beside the bed and pressed her face against the tunic, feeling the rough cloth scrape her cheek: the slight shock of it, like the roughness of his chin in life. Close up, like this, she caught the faint smell of his body underneath all the other smells. A giant hand got hold of her heart and squeezed. She stroked the cloth, the skin of her fingertips clicking on the threads, and then heard, or felt, something else: a crackle of paper from the lower-left pocket. She delved into it as deep as she could and found a hole in the lining, big enough to get two fingers through. There was a piece of paper there. Grasping it in a scissor movement, she maneuvred it up into the light.

Some sort of list—medical supplies. She could have wept with disappointment, but then she turned the page over and saw her own name.

Elinor—I've had two goes at this already, so this is
it, has to be, because we're moving forward soon and
there'll be no time for writing after that. There's no
way of saying this without sounding melodramatic,
and I really don't think I am. In fact, I feel rather
down-to-earth and matter-of-fact about it all. I don't
think I would even mind very much, except I know it's
going to be a shock to you—and I can't think of any
way of softening the blow.

I won't be coming back this time. This isn't a
premonition or anything like that. I can't even explain
why. I used to think officers' letters weren't censored,
but they are sometimes, not by the people here, but
back at base. They do random checks or something,
and I can't afford to risk that. I hate not being able to
tell you. If you ever want to know more, I suggest you
ask your friend Kit Neville—assuming he survives, and
I'm sure he will. ~~He's been no friend to me~~. I know
you'll take care of Mother as best you can. Father'll be
all right, I think—he's got his work. And Rachel's got
Tim and the boys. I don't know what to say to you.
Remember

Nothing else. One word: "Remember," and then nothing else. She knew at once it was impossible to go on living without knowing what had happened to him, but beyond writing to Kit again . . . She would write, though she knew it was useless. What else could she do? All the years she'd pushed the war out of her mind, refusing to admit it had any significance, and now her ignorance was an impassable barrier between her and what she needed to know. She had no useful contacts; her friends were almost all pacifists. When she tried to think of somebody who might be able to help, the only person she could come up with was Paul. He had contacts in the army, and might know how to set about getting more information. And he and Kit were friends—rather prickly, competitive friends, it was true, but friends nevertheless. Only, after the grudging ten minutes she'd spent at his bedside in hospital, how could she possibly ask him for help?

But Paul was Paul: he wouldn't hold that against her. And however little was left of love between them she knew she could rely on his kindness. Paul, then, it must be.

11

Paul landed heavily on the platform and had to stand still for a moment, clenching his teeth against the pain. His fellow passengers stared down at him until, with a cough and wheeze, the train pulled away and their pale faces were replaced by reflections of sky. He drew a deep breath, waiting for the pain to subside, and then looked around him. The station was deserted. The blue paint on the waiting-room door was cracked and blistered; grass grew between the flagstones in the small yard. The last time he'd been here was with Kit Neville, August Bank Holiday weekend, 1914, the last few days and hours of peace. They'd been met, then, by a pony and trap. Not much hope of that now. He shouldered his kitbag and set off to walk.

As he pushed open the gate, the first thin blowing of rain met him and, before he'd gone a hundred yards, it was pelting down. On either side of the lane, the plowed fields had become a waste of mud; black, leafless trees were stenciled onto a white sky. Everything he saw, everything he felt, seemed to be filtered through his memories of the front line, as if a thin wash had been laid over his perceptions of this scene. Columns of sleety rain marched across the fields while, in the distance, gray clouds massed for another attack. Somehow or other, he had to connect with the present, but he found it almost impossible. Turning to look back down the lane, he saw the pony and trap of that prewar visit turn the corner and come towards him, the fat, chestnut pony twitching its skin against the flies. And there, on the left-hand side of the trap, was his younger self, staring up into the green canopy above his head. There'd been a smell of hot tar, of warm dust on nettles. A bluebottle had zoomed drunkenly about, trying to settle on his upper lip. He remembered it all so vividly, and yet he couldn't get back inside the mind of that young man. Boy, really, though *he* would not have said so. He'd been recovering from a love affair with one of the models at the Slade; no doubt he'd thought his heart was broken, though actually he'd been more than ready to fall in love again. And there in the farmhouse, waiting for them, was Elinor; and beside him, in the trap, was Kit Neville, who also loved her.

Three years and many lifetimes later, Paul watched the trap carrying two raw, hopeful young men reach the crest of the hill and dip into the hollow beyond it, and then, forcing his stiffening leg to move, he turned and limped after it.

It had become a preoccupation of his—almost an obsession—working out how the war had changed him; other people too, of course. He never managed to talk openly about it, not even to men he'd served with, perhaps because, for him, the changes had been mainly sexual. The young man in the trap had been a romantic: deferential, almost timid, in his approach to women. Three years later, he'd become coarser, less scrupulous; his behavior verged, at times, on the predatory. For two years, his relationship with Elinor had protected him, but then her letters had become shorter, colder, until eventually she'd stopped writing altogether; after that, he'd regarded himself as free to take what he wanted.

Ahead of him, the farmhouse appeared and disappeared behind waves of rain, like an outcrop of rocks at low tide.

The last hundred yards was up a steep hill. When, at last, he reached the gate he paused, not wanting to arrive breathless and in pain from the cramping of his leg. It was a full five minutes before he was ready to go on, and then he was aware, as he trudged up the drive, of a face looking down at him from an upstairs window. Elinor. A girl's face at an upstairs window, framed by ivy leaves. It seemed like the beginning of a story, though after her silence of the last few months their story must surely be drawing to a close. One visit to the hospital. *One.* People he hardly knew had visited more often than that. And then, during his stay in a convalescent home in Dorset, when he'd been bored almost to distraction: no letters, no card, nothing. Right, he'd thought. That was that. Over.

And then, out of the blue, this invitation to spend a weekend at the farmhouse. Not with her parents either; the note had made it clear they'd be alone. But no warmth in the note, no expression of love or longing, no hint that she continued to feel for him what he still felt for her. He'd found the tone chilling—and yet it hadn't occurred to him not to accept.

Outside the door, he paused again. He was just raising his hand to knock when the door opened and there stood a tall, thin girl dressed in black. It took him a second to recognize her. "Elinor."

"Paul."

A moment's uncertainty, then she raised her face for him to kiss. Her lips were as dry and cracked as baked mud and she pulled away from him immediately.

"You sound surprised," he said. "I haven't got the day wrong, have I?"

"No, of course not, come in."

The porch was exactly as he remembered it: a jumble of muddy boots, umbrellas, mackintoshes. A powerful smell of wet dog hung over everything, though it was a while before a springer spaniel appeared, his claws clicking on the stone flags: old, milky-eyed, but still going through the motions of defending his mistress and his home.

Paul knelt down and rubbed behind the dog's ears, producing grunts of contentment. "Hello, boy."

"Oh, he'll take any amount of that."

"I don't remember him."

"He'd have been in the kitchen; he used to live there more or less. Nowadays, he's got the run of the house." She led the way into the hall. "I expect you'd like to freshen up before tea?"

He followed her upstairs, watching the sway of her hips under the narrow skirt, hearing the whisper of silk as her thighs brushed together. Suddenly, he was aroused, impatient to hold her. He'd have liked to reach out now, but knew he had to be careful. She seemed so . . . friable, as if one rough movement might break her. He'd never seen her like this before.

"I've put you in Toby's room."

She opened the door and stood aside to let him pass. He swung his kitbag onto the nearest chair. When he looked round she was standing by the bed, stroking the jade-green counterpane. He heard the click of silk threads as they snagged on the palms of her hands.

"I'm afraid I'm not very well organized these days." She didn't meet his eyes, wouldn't look at him, kept chafing her arms as if she were cold. "I paint till my head spins and then there's no time left for anything else." An attempt at a smile. "Anyway. Come down when you're ready."

He moved towards her, but she slipped past him.

"I'll be in the kitchen. Give me a shout if there's anything you want."

I want you.

She'd gone. He heard her footsteps running downstairs.

Left alone, he poured tepid water into a bowl and splashed his face and as much of his neck and chest as he could easily reach. Still dripping, he went to stand in front of the mirror. The face looking back at him had a pink, excited, slightly furtive look. Behind his reflection, he could see one side of the double bed; he didn't intend to sleep in it alone. The house creaked and sighed all around him. How long had she been living here by herself ? Painting, she said, till her head spun, and obviously neglecting herself: she was stick thin. The house, too, seemed bereft. He'd glimpsed dust sheets shrouding the furniture in some of the downstairs rooms. She was not so much living here as camping out, and he felt a stab of pity for her, mingled with curiosity. What on earth possessed her, to shut herself away like this? Of course, her brother's death must have been devastating, but for a few weeks after it, she'd been seen frequently in town. But then—and nobody seemed to know why—her trips to London had ceased, and she'd walled herself up here, alone.

Well, no doubt she'd tell him, sooner or later. He dried his hands and face and went downstairs.

She was making a cup of tea. "I've forgotten if you take sugar."

"Two, please."

It mattered, that she'd forgotten. When they first became lovers "sugar" had been their private word for sex. One weekend they'd stayed in a boardinghouse on the coast—Eastbourne, was it? No, Brighton. Elinor was wearing a wedding ring he'd bought in Woolworth's. Over tea, sitting in a prim, chintzy lounge on a fat, overstuffed sofa, she'd leaned towards him and said, in a stagey whisper, "Darling, I can't remember, do you take sugar in your tea?"

They'd collapsed in giggles while, at the next table, a

middle-aged couple, puzzled and slightly scandalized, had pretended not to listen.

He sat at the kitchen table, his bad leg stretched out in front of him, and watched her pour boiling water into the teapot.

"How is it? Your leg."

"Still attached. I'm one of the lucky ones."

"Do you feel lucky?"

"We-ell. No; yes, I do really."

"I'll let you put the milk in, you know how you like it."

"Do you remember the night I proposed to you, I couldn't kneel down?"

"I don't recall you trying very hard."

"Oh, I'm sure I did, I was very romantic. Then."

"Well, go on, what about it?"

"It's the same knee."

"That's it, is it? I was expecting another proposal, at least."

"It's interesting, that's all. Wounded twice in exactly the same place."

"What do you think God's trying to tell you, Paul? Leave the Church of England? Become a Methodist? They don't kneel."

She came and sat opposite him. With her thin arms crossed over her chest, she seemed wary, almost nervous. There was something dried up about her, old-maidish, even. A flare of hope he'd experienced upstairs, when he watched her stroke the counterpane, faded. He thought, sadly, of the house in Ypres where the brass bedstead had seemed to grow till it filled the whole room. And that night, the first night they'd ever spent together, that bed had been the whole world.

"I kept expecting to see you in London," he said.

"I don't get up to town much these days."

He glanced round the room. It was a farmhouse kitchen, designed to be lived in rather than set apart for cooking. A fire burnt in the small grate; there was a scent of pine cones. On a table by the door, a vase of dried hogweed cast dramatic shadows across the whitewashed wall.

"It's nice here, but doesn't it get a bit lonely?"

"Not really. And I certainly don't miss London. You get so much more work done down here."

"So you are managing to work?"

"Nonstop. How about you?"

He hesitated. "I've been commissioned as a war artist."

"Yes, I heard."

He waited for her to congratulate him.

"Pay's good. Five pounds a week."

"That *is* good. Have you started anything yet?"

"I've done a couple of landscapes. Well, you know me, what else would I paint?"

"Corpses?"

"Not allowed."

"Ah."

"You don't approve."

"It's got nothing to do with me."

The conversation was sticky, punctuated by long silences, though not from any lack of things to say. They were tiptoe-ing round each other, each aware of the possibility of a sudden flare-up. If nothing else was left of their long, fractious love affair, a willingness to speak hurtful truths, and a fear of hearing them, remained.

"I'm actually working at the Slade," Paul said. "I bumped into Tonks and he said I could have a room."

"Doesn't five pounds a week run to a studio?"

"Yes, but I need a lot of space. Some of the paintings are going to be quite big."

"How big?"

He spread his arms wide.

"Hmm. Mind you don't fall off the scaffold."

He laughed, but he was nettled by her sarcasm. This was exactly the kind of prickly, competitive exchange he was used to having with Kit Neville, and one or two other of his male contemporaries. But then, Elinor had always been more like a brilliant, egotistical boy than a girl. He remembered a fancy-dress party at the Slade—the end of his first term—and coming into the hall and seeing a figure dressed as Harlequin, wearing a mask. He hadn't known, at first glance, whether it was a man or a woman. Later, when he danced with her, her body against his had felt slim and muscular, but very far from masculine. The mask, the anonymity, had excited him, especially when he realized there was a second Harlequin figure, also female. He didn't know, to this day, which girl he'd danced with first.

With an effort, he dragged himself back to the present. He'd feel more bones than curves if he danced with her now.

"I was so sorry to hear about Toby."

He'd already offered his condolences twice, once by letter and once, in person, at the hospital, but he felt it needed to be said again. She nodded; her eyes were bright though he suspected she was past crying. He wondered if she'd ever really cried at all.

"You know, at first I thought 'Missing, Believed Killed' meant there was a tiny bit of hope, but Father says they don't say that unless they're sure. It just means there's nothing left, nothing identifiable."

She was looking at him, perhaps even now cherishing a small, flickering hope that he might say something different.

"Your father's right, I'm afraid."

"But surely they'd find the identity disk?"

"Not necessarily, not if it was a direct hit." He groped for something to soften the brutal reality. "It would be very quick, no pain, he wouldn't even have known."

God, the platitude count was mounting. He hated visiting bereaved relatives; you always ended up saying something utterly banal. Or, worse still, telling lies.

"Did you know Kit was one of Toby's stretcher bearers?"

"No, I didn't," he said. "Actually, I haven't heard from Kit for quite a while."

"Nor me." She took a deep, unsteady breath. "After Toby—after we got the telegram—I wrote to Kit to ask him if he knew anything, but I didn't get a reply. I thought it was a bit odd, really. I mean, you'd expect a letter of condolence, wouldn't you? I mean, he knew Toby, they served together. Only for two or three months, but . . . Well, I suppose that's not very long."

"Out there it is."

"But no, nothing. Not a word. I thought, he can't have got the letter, so I wrote again." She shrugged. "Still nothing."

"Perhaps he just didn't know what to say."

A weak explanation, and not one he accepted for a moment. It was extraordinary that Neville hadn't written. Why hadn't he? Because he knew how Toby had died and for some reason couldn't bring himself to trot out the usual consoling platitudes? But that didn't excuse ignoring her letters. In fact, Paul couldn't think of a single acceptable excuse.

"You must have heard from Toby's CO?"

"A couple of sentences. Quite . . . I don't know. Grudging."

"You could always try the Padre."

"Oh, he wrote too, same sort of thing. 'Very gallant officer'—so on and so forth. I could've told them that."

"They mightn't know anything."

"No, I suppose not." She wiped her hand across her eyes. "Do you think it's too early for a glass of wine?"

"I think it's a marvelous idea."

She fetched a bottle from the dresser. "Here, you open it. I get into a muddle with that corkscrew."

He drew the cork, poured wine into two glasses, and handed one to her. "Well," he said, at a loss for words. "Absent friends."

They moved closer to the fire. He was glad not to have the expanse of the table between them, though she chose an armchair and left him to occupy the sofa alone. For a moment the only sound was the crackle and hiss of flames.

"You know, you said once if Toby died you'd come back here and paint the countryside he grew up in. You said you'd want to paint what made him, not what destroyed him."

She smiled. "That's exactly what I've done."

"Does it help?"

"No, nothing helps."

He waited, but she was not to be trapped into a line of conversation that might end in tears.

"Come on, I'll show you."

They walked across the yard, where a few white hens pecked in a desultory way at the dust. A cockerel stalked towards them, shaking his bloodred comb, the last rays of the setting sun waking an emerald gleam in his black neck feathers.

"I work in the barn now. I find it helps to leave the house in the morning, you know? To actually *go to work*."

"I'm just the same, I thought at first I'd hate getting up in the mornings and going to the Slade, but actually I prefer it."

The barn was dark at first, so dark he almost stumbled, but there was a door immediately ahead. Once that was open, he saw that the interior was flooded with light: oblique, amber light at this hour of the afternoon, but the windows faced north. The morning light must be wonderful.

Facing the door was an easel, partially draped in a paint-daubed white cloth. Instinctively, he looked away; work in progress was always private. The completed canvases were stacked against a wall.

She waved him over to them. "Go on, have a look."

He took his time. To be brutally honest, he'd expected nostalgia: scenes from rural life, happy children, impossibly long, golden summer days. Instead, he found himself looking at a series of winter landscapes, empty of people. Well, that was his first impression. When he looked more closely, he realized that every painting contained the shadowy figure of a man, always on the edge of the composition, facing away from the center, as if he might be about to step outside the frame. Many of these figures were so lightly delineated they might have been no more than an accidental confluence of light and shade. He stood back, trying to pin down his response. At one level these were firmly traditional landscape paintings, but there was something unsettling about them. Uncanny. Oddly enough, he recognized the feeling. It was the paradox of the front line: an apparently empty landscape that is actually full of men. How on earth had she managed to get that?

"They're very good," he said, at last.

"It's not about that."

"No."

He held up a canvas, one of the few she'd had framed. It showed the hill behind the house; under the trees, at the edge of the painting, was a patch of deeper shadow that might, or might not, be the head and shoulders of a man. Paul intended to say how much he admired it. Instead, he said, "He looks as if he's trying to get out."

Her eyes flared. "It's interesting you should say that. I had a lot of trouble with that one. I thought I'd got it and . . . and then when I came down the next morning the figure had moved." She caught his expression. "Of course, I don't mean actually moved. I must have remembered it wrong."

"He's in every painting. Toby."

"A male figure." She couldn't meet his eyes. "Oh, all right,

Toby. But I'm not running away from it, you know. It's not like you and your corpseless war."

"Don't let's argue. They are very, *very* good." Clearly, Toby had become her muse. Her talent flourished on his death, like Isabella's pot of basil growing out of a murdered man's brains. Elinor wasn't flourishing, though. When he turned to look at her, he noticed again the shadows under her eyes. "You must be pleased."

"Ye-es. Only I don't seem to know where I'm going anymore." She pointed to the easel. "I've been trying to finish that for . . . Oh, I don't know, feels like forever."

"Perhaps you need a break. Why don't you come to London?"

"Yes, I will, I do need a break, but it can't be next weekend, I've got to go to my sister's. It would've been Toby's twenty-eighth on Saturday. I can't not be there for that."

He took a last look round. The sunlight was almost gone and there was a distinct chill in the air.

"Come on," she said, touching his arm. "Let's go and eat."

————

Dinner was rabbit stew with herbs and vegetables from the garden: better food than you'd easily find in London these days. At first they ate in silence. Fastidiously, he removed a slug from his cabbage and set it down carefully on the side of his plate.

"Protein," she said, drily. "Don't waste it."

"I'll stick to the rabbit, if you don't mind."

After they'd finished eating, they returned to sit by the fire. She was drinking quickly, always an encouraging sign, and as she drank some color returned to her cheeks and her cheekbones looked a little less sharp, but she was much too thin. Her breasts hardly lifted the cotton blouse, though he caught the shadows of her nipples as she leaned forward to refill his glass.

"Do you know," he said, "I was trying to remember the first time I saw you."

"It would've been in the Antiques Room, surely?"

"No, I mean, *really* saw you. *Saw you,* saw you. You were running down Gower Street with the girls—"

Her lips curved. "Oh, the wild girls—"

"And you must've got a stone in your shoe or something because you suddenly stopped and took it off, and you had these black stockings on, and there was a great big hole in the heel and all this pink skin peeping out. I thought it was the most erotic thing I'd ever seen."

She burst out laughing. "Paul, that is *pathetic.*"

"No, it's not—"

"You were drawing naked women every day."

"Nudity's not all that interesting. Your heel—that was the thing."

Self-consciously, she tucked her feet under the chair. She sipped her wine, not looking at him, but she was aware of him now, and, more importantly, she was aware of herself, of her nipples rubbing against the rough cotton of her blouse, of the tops of her thighs pressed moistly together under the thick woolen skirt. Feeling his gaze on her, she put a hand up to the nape of her neck.

"You're growing it again."

"Not really, I just can't be bothered to get it cut."

He began deliberately to talk about the past. The weekend war broke out they'd all been together in this house: Elinor, Toby, Kit, and himself. Blazing hot, he remembered it, and as the dusty, late-summer days passed, the news from London had become grimmer.

"I remember," she said. "I looked out of the window and you and Dad were on the terrace talking about it."

"Oh, and Toby's friend was staying too—what was his name?"

"Andrew? He was killed in 1915. It changed Toby, there was always a kind of sadness about him after that."

"They were revising, weren't they? And the rest of us all went off to see a church. The Doom. And on the way back Kit fell off his bike. Do you remember?"

"Yes—he asked me to marry him."

"Then?"

"Lying on the ground like a wounded hero."

"I didn't know that. The slithy tove."

"Did you ever see him out there?"

"Once, in Ypres. That was back in—oh, I don't know. December '14? He was incredibly drunk, and we spent the entire evening talking about you."

"Hmm, did you? I'm glad I wasn't a fly on that wall."

"All very flattering." Though it hadn't been. Our Lady of Triangles, Neville had called her, and he certainly hadn't meant it as a compliment. Well, no triangles now: just a strange, solitary woman obsessively painting her dead brother. "This is good," he said, taking another sip of the wine.

She'd eaten well, and the food seemed to have lightened her mood. She sat more easily, smiled more naturally. He wasn't absolutely sure, but he thought she might have run a comb through her hair.

After coffee, they spent a few minutes walking in the garden. A full moon threw their linked shadows across the lawn, but the temperature was falling rapidly and he was glad when she suggested they should go back inside. In the doorway, he paused, looking at the room they were about to enter: shadows flickering on the walls, pools of golden light around the lamps, two wine glasses side by side on the table. Whatever else happened tonight, he would remember this.

And what was going to happen was agonizingly difficult

to predict. They took their glasses through to the drawing room. She sat at the piano, he joined her there, their hips and thighs almost, but not quite, touching. He could hardly play at all and she was by no means the accomplished young lady her mother had no doubt wished to produce, but together they managed to cobble together a medley of music-hall favorites, improvised, talked, laughed, sang, drank, before finally sinking into two armchairs. Suddenly, neither of them could think of anything to say. In the silence, he heard the clock ticking towards midnight.

He reached out and took her hand, feeling her finger bones crunch as he tightened his grip. "How long have you been here on your own?"

"I don't know, I've lost track. Mother's staying with Rachel."

"How is she?"

"Not good. To begin with she just seemed . . . dazed. Lay on the sofa all day, didn't get dressed . . . They all thought I ought to stay and look after her, but . . ." She shook her head. "We'd have killed each other in a week."

That hardness in her. It was growing, he thought.

"Anyway, she's happier there. She's got the grandchildren. Children help because they don't understand, they live in the present. Animals too. *He*'s been wonderful." She nodded at Hobbes, who raised his head, then lowered it again with a groan, keeping his bloodshot eyes fixed on her. "Never says the wrong thing because he never says anything."

"Doesn't it help to talk?"

"Well, you know. You must've lost people . . . ?"

"It's not the same out there."

She was waiting for him to go on, and that was new. For the first time ever she'd asked him a question about the war.

"Chap out there—Barnes, he was called, *Titus* Barnes. God knows why his parents thought they had the right to inflict that on him. Anyway, he got hit in the head, one side blown off. It was a couple of days before we could get to see him. And of course we all sat round and listened to him snore, it was pretty grim, we knew he wouldn't live—the puzzle was why he was still alive—and we'd all liked him. But then we had to go, and by the time we'd gone a hundred yards we were laughing and joking as if nothing had happened." He looked at her averted face. "Sorry, I know it sounds harsh, but there's not a lot of point grieving when you know you're going to be next."

He couldn't tell what she thought. She was looking down at the dregs of wine in her glass, swishing them from side to side. "Can I get you another?"

She came to stand beside him while he poured. As he handed her the glass his hand touched hers and he felt her shiver. Gently, he ran his forefinger up her arm, tracking the groove between radius and ulna, pressing hard enough to produce a wave-like motion in her flesh. She didn't pull away. He took the glass from her, set it down on the table, and, cradling her face between his hands, began to kiss her, gently at first, barely brushing his lips against hers, letting their breaths mingle, afraid that any sudden movement would send her scurrying away. But then, she began to kiss him back. Soon their arms were twined around each other and he could feel the edge of her rib cage pressing into his chest; he was more aware of that than of her breasts. Her dry skin rubbed against his, as thirsty as sand. His hands slid down to her hips, tilting her pelvis toward him, his mouth found the hollow at the base of her throat . . .

Instantly, she pushed him away. "No."

"Why not?"

"I can't. Don't ask me, I just can't."

"All right." He had to force the words out, producing in the process a hard, scratchy little laugh that shaded uncertainly into tenderness. "But at least let's sit together, you seem terribly far away over there."

She came and curled up beside him on the sofa. Perhaps that's what she wanted: a brother's love. The comfort of long familiarity, without any of the thrill and danger of sex. But no, there'd been real passion in that kiss, and it hadn't all come from him. She would let him make love to her, if not tonight, then tomorrow. They'd gone beyond the point where either of them wanted to turn back. But it would be completely wrong—and stupid—to go on pressing her now. So he was patient, stroking her arm, talking softly, pleased when he made her laugh.

When it was time for bed, they went upstairs together, passing the tall mirrors that faced each other across the half-landing. Briefly, they became a million couples, their linked reflections stretching away into an unimaginable distance. Even now, he was full of hope. But outside her bedroom door, she stopped and looked up at him, and her face in the lamp-light was pinched and old.

"Well then, good night," he said, deliberately flattening his voice on the final word to stop it becoming a question.

"I've been sleeping in Toby's room, I'm afraid I haven't even got round to changing the sheets."

"We've slept in the same sheets before."

He tried to prevent this remark sounding sharp, but he didn't succeed, and the slight pressure hardened her against him, as he'd known it would.

"Just go down and make yourself a cup of coffee in the morning," she said. "Though I'll probably be up."

She slipped into her bedroom and the door clicked shut behind her. He rested his hand, briefly, on the cold wood, before walking the few yards farther along the corridor to Toby's room.

———

It took him only a few minutes to unpack. Apart from his drawing pads, shaving kit, and a change of underwear he'd brought next to nothing with him. Then, feeling too tense for sleep, he wandered round the room, looking at books and photographs.

It was very obviously a young man's room. If Elinor had been sleeping here, she'd left no trace of her presence. He wished he could remember Toby more clearly, but he'd only met him once, that last weekend before the war, and all his memories of that time were of Elinor and Neville. Elinor, awkward and rebellious in her mother's presence, quite unlike the startlingly self-possessed young woman he knew at the Slade. Neville, his usual bumptious self: almost, but never quite, ridiculous. Toby had just been a fair-haired young man in the background. Paul probably wouldn't have noticed him at all, if it hadn't been for his extraordinary resemblance to Elinor. Curiously, Toby had been beautiful, whereas Elinor, even at her best, just missed beauty, though Paul found her more attractive because she didn't have that final, daunting perfection.

Apart from that, the weekend was a jumble of random recollections: newspapers on the terrace, fields of corn bending in the wind, shadows of clouds fleeing across them, Neville's pink, excited face as he came into the drawing room after dinner to announce that Russia had mobilized. Paul hadn't known what to make of it all; he'd swung between bursts of wild excitement and complete indifference. Wars were fought by professional armies. Once the novelty wore off, he couldn't see this making much difference to his life.

The photographs were mainly of cricket and rugby teams. Nothing more recent than Toby's schooldays, not even a graduation photograph, though there was one on the piano downstairs. This was a room frozen in time, and not at the moment of Toby's death. No, long before that, possibly when he left home to live in London. You got the impression that on subsequent visits he'd brought very little of himself back.

But then, that was true of Paul as well. On his rare visits to see his father and stepmother in Middlesbrough he always felt as if he were impersonating the boy he'd once been. It was impossible to feel comfortable; even in his old bed, his shoulder blades refused to fit the hollows in the mattress left by a shorter version of himself.

A row of books lined the shelf above the mantelpiece. He ran his fingers along the spines, selecting a volume here and there for a closer look. Shakespeare's Sonnets, heavily underlined throughout, little self-conscious comments written in the margins. Obviously a school prize: the name and date written in a rounded, still unformed hand. *Treasure Island.* Another prize, but much earlier. On the flyleaf, Toby had written his name and address: "Tobias Antony Brooke, Leybourne Farm, Netherton, Sussex, England, Great Britain, Europe, Northern Hemisphere, Earth, Solar System, Milky Way, the Universe."

Paul was smiling as he closed the book. That little boy was suddenly a powerful presence in the room. He picked up a photograph, the only one, as far as he could see, of Toby as an individual rather than a member of a team. The image was overexposed, so one side of his face had faded into white. Looking at it, Paul could almost believe he heard a faint echo of the explosion that had blown this laughing boy into unidentifiable gobs of flesh. The poignancy of a young life cut short. He hadn't known Toby, but at this moment he could have cried for him: the small boy who'd located himself so precisely in the world, and now was nowhere.

Thoroughly unsettled, Paul got into bed and turned off the lamp. Lying on his back, listening to the night sounds that came through the open window, he closed his eyes and tried to sleep. The sheets smelled of Elinor's hair and skin. He wondered whether they'd been changed since Toby's last leave, but yes, surely they would've been: the shrine-keeping would have started with his death. The room was a shrine, but there was nothing unusual in that: thousands of women were tending shrines to dead young men. Many of them went to seances, and were battened on by people who claimed to be able to contact the dead. There were even some who produced photographs of the dead man's spirit hovering behind his loved ones. Well, Elinor didn't need that: she had her paintings. Was there even one in which Toby didn't appear? Tomorrow, he'd ask Elinor if he could look at them again.

If tomorrow ever came. He was afraid of nightmares. He'd worked out little rituals to fend them off, routines he went through every night at bedtime, but nothing worked for long. And tonight, made restless by desire and with far too much alcohol coursing through his veins, he knew he was in for a bad time.

An owl hooted. And again. And again. Perhaps there were two, calling to each other? Some dispute over territory that would not be resolved in blood. He lay, listening. An owl's cry is such a knowing sound. As he drifted off, he found himself wondering what it was that these owls knew. Their cries pursued him through the thickets of sleep. He was stumbling over tree roots in the depths of a winter forest, so still that a solitary leaf, falling, fractured the silence. But then, from somewhere up ahead, came the sound of a branch creaking. The noise fretted his sleep until, at last, he came awake with a cry, his heart thudding against his ribs. He'd heard something. Perhaps no more than a floorboard creaking, but somehow the sound had wound its way into his dream. Then he caught the soft slur of naked feet, and, clearly visible in the violent moonlight, the knob of the door began to turn.

Elinor slipped into the room, a slight figure in a white nightdress.

It was no dream: I lay broad waking.

"Can't you sleep?" he asked.

"It's the owls, I've never heard them like this before."

Still half drowned in sleep, he shifted towards the wall and patted the counterpane, inviting her to sit down.

Instead, she slipped her nightdress off her shoulders and let it fall around her feet. His throat was too swollen to let him speak. Silently, he held the covers open and welcomed her into his arms.

12

Next morning, he woke to find her still sleeping, curled up against his side like a medieval carving of Eve, newly born of Adam—and how scathing Elinor would have been about *that*. Looking down at her, he noticed again the sharpness of her bones. He was tempted to wake her, but resisted and edged out of bed.

She woke as he reached the door.

"It's freezing," she said. "Why don't you put that on?"

She was pointing to a dark gray coat that hung on the back of the door. As he put it on, the cloth released a masculine whiff of tobacco and hair oil. She lay looking up at him as he stood there, in Toby's coat. He thought it must be painful for her to see him like that, but no, she was smiling, though her eyes were darkening as the engorged pupils swallowed the blue.

She pulled him down onto the bed and started kissing him, as hungrily as if they'd never made love. He struggled to free himself from the heavy coat, but as often as he tried to shrug it off, she pulled it on again, and, suddenly, he thought: *No.* He rolled off her, swept a kiss across her forehead to soften the rejection, and stood up.

"Coffee?"

She pouted. "That's not very flattering."

"Man cannot live on love alone."

In a hurry to be gone, he went downstairs. The coat's silk lining, warmed by his body, had produced an unpleasant clamminess, like the touch of skin on skin. He would have liked to take it off, but the kitchen was cold.

While waiting for the water to boil, he went across the yard to the barn. As he opened the door he caught ghost smells of hay and cattle, though this couldn't have been a working farm for years. Before its conversion into a studio, the barn would have housed only gardening tools and a lawn mower, certainly not cattle. The lawn mower was still there, a heap of earth-smelling sacks piled up beside it. At the center of the open space, a woodstove, crusted with rust, squatted in its own shadow.

He touched the cloth on the easel, but didn't pull it off. He hated people looking at his own uncompleted work and he wouldn't do it to her. Slowly, methodically, he worked through the finished paintings, admiring, doubting, more than once feeling a stab of envy at what she'd achieved. He was Toby-hunting. Only one landscape was genuinely empty: the fields behind the house in winter. Cropped hawthorn hedges ran across a vast expanse of snow, like lines of Hebrew script. Even here, though, a shadow between the trees revealed itself, on closer examination, to be the head and shoulders of a man. She hadn't left him out of anything.

When, eventually, he carried two cups of coffee upstairs, he found her sleeping. It was almost a relief. Quickly, he scooped up his clothes and went along to the bathroom, where he washed and shaved, avoiding, as far as possible, his own gaze in the mirror. He didn't want to think.

Downstairs again, he made a pot of tea, spread butter thinly over a crust of bread and forced it down. The house seemed to have turned against him. Even Hobbes, curled up in his basket by the dead fire, opened one bloodshot eye, only to close it again when he saw Paul. He no longer felt welcome. Images from last night clung like bats to the inside of his skull; he needed a blast of cold morning air to shake them off. He put on his coat, his own coat this time, thank God, and went out.

He chose the path through the woods. It was still dark, though on the fringes of the wood the trees were beginning to let in shafts of stronger light. Frost, everywhere. A single leaf fell to the ground and immediately he was back inside the landscape of his dream. The girl in the white nightdress belonged in that dream. Nothing that had happened between them belonged to the waking world. He went on his way, rustling through dead leaves, cracking twigs, breathing heavily, no doubt in a fug of his own hot stink. All around him, he felt small animals shrink into the shelter of the trees.

He came out into an open field enclosed by hawthorn hedges. Because he'd just been looking at Elinor's painting, he saw the place through her eyes, more clearly than he could have seen it on his own. Thorns pulled at his sleeves. He blew on his fingertips to warm them, but the real chill was in his memories of last night.

Something had been wrong from the start. He'd felt it, but pushed on anyway, he couldn't stop; and he'd thought he could make it all right. But even in the most passionate moments—and there weren't many—Elinor had seemed to pull away. Of course, she was grieving for her brother . . . And it wasn't as if he didn't know about grief; his mother had killed herself when he was fourteen. It had taken him years to get over it: if he ever had. It seemed, looking back, that he'd grown around the loss, that it had become part of him, as trees will sometimes incorporate an obstruction, so they end up living, but deformed. He certainly didn't underestimate what Elinor was going through. Only he'd felt there was something else, a shadow falling across them, cast by something he couldn't see. He'd never known lovemaking like it. It had felt like a battle, not between the two of them—there'd been no antagonism—no, more like he was struggling to pull her out of a pit and sometimes she'd wanted to come with him, and at other times she'd turned back into the dark.

Always before, even at the most difficult moments in their long, wrangling love affair, sex had never failed them. Last night, it had.

———

He'd hoped to find her downstairs waiting for him when he returned, but the kitchen was empty. No fire; only one log left in the basket. Well, however useless he'd been in bed, at least he could chop wood. He went across the yard to the fuel store, where he found a pile of logs and an ax.

The first blow sent shock waves up his arm. He freed the ax, struck again, and the two halves fell sweetly apart. A smell of raw wood, sharp on the cold air. He was reaching for another log when he realized Elinor had come up behind him. She smelled of oil paint and turps, and that smell, mingling with the more feminine scents of skin and hair, took him back to the Slade and "the wild girls." They were the best thing about the Slade, those girls. The memory softened him towards her.

"Did you have a good morning?" he asked.

"Quite good."

He sensed her excitement. "I'll just finish these, then I'll come in."

"Have you been for a walk?"

"Just up the hill there. I wish I'd had a gun, I could've got you some rabbits. Place was hopping."

"You're a town boy, aren't you? Who taught you to shoot?"

"The army," he said. Very dry.

"Oh, yes, of course. Sorry."

She was blushing. He positioned the next log and swung the ax, smiling to himself as the blade bit.

Five minutes later, he came into the kitchen carrying an armful of logs. She was by the range, heating up the remains of last night's stew. He put a hand on her shoulder and she turned round; her face was pale, but her eyes glittered with barely suppressed excitement.

"You have had a good day," he said.

"The thing is, I think I might have finished. But you never really know, do you?"

"Let it settle."

He began to build up the fire, feeling an immense, simple satisfaction as he saw the first lick of flame. Holding a sheet of old, yellowing newspaper across the fireplace, he heard the roar of the draft behind it. Columns of names curled and blackened in the heat. Worse than the Somme, people were saying, as the lists grew longer day by day. A black hole edged with sallow gold appeared at the center of the page and he whisked the paper away in a whirl of smoke and sparks. "There."

Elinor was ladling steaming stew into two big bowls. He sat at the table and reached across for the loaf. Elinor passed him the knife. They were a good team, he thought. In surprising, simple ways they made a good team.

"Do you really think it's finished?" he asked.

"Well, I don't know. I thought it was."

She looked pinched now, coming down the other side and, my God, he knew every step of the way. "Can I see it?"

"If you like. Not now, though. Let's eat."

Paul fetched a bottle from the dresser and poured them both a glass. "Congratulations."

"You haven't seen it yet."

But she clinked glasses with him and took the first sip. By the time she'd finished the glass, she'd lost that white, glittery look and was back among the living. They ate the stew, which was actually rather better than last night, and she seemed more interested in him. Or perhaps she was just being polite.

"How have you been, really, since you got back?"

He decided to tell the truth. "Pretty bad. I mean, the leg . . . well, there's nothing to be done about that, I'm lumbered with it. But I can't seem to fit back in. You know, I go to the Café Royal, I *make* myself go, and it's like I've landed on another planet. And sometimes I just drift off in the middle of a conversation and . . ."

"But you'll get past that."

"Yes, I suppose so."

As soon as they'd finished eating, she stood up. "I want to show you something."

Of course, the painting. He got to his feet.

"No, you stay there, I'll bring it down."

She was gone no more than two minutes. When she came back she was holding a piece of paper: crumpled, stained, with that unmistakable smell. Oh, God, the last letter.

"I found this in Toby's tunic, they sent the spare uniform back, the one he wasn't wearing, well they couldn't send the other one back, could they? I mean—"

She was gabbling. Gently, he took the page from her. "Would you like me to read it?"

"If you wouldn't mind."

He sat down, this time with his back to her, and quickly read the letter. Then, slowly and carefully, he went through it a second time, thinking, *What on earth am I supposed to say about this?*

"He never sent it," she said. "They must've moved forward before he finished it and then I suppose he changed his tunic and forgot all about it. It'd dropped through a hole in the lining, you see, that's why we didn't find it when the parcel came . . . I only came across it a week ago."

A week ago she'd written to Paul inviting him to stay. He had no doubt that this was why he was here; this was why she'd got in touch again after the long weeks of silence. He was starting to feel, very subtly, used. He folded the page, running his thumb and forefinger along the crease, wondering why she'd waited so long to show it to him. They'd talked about Toby last night; it would have been natural to mention the letter then. "At least you know his last thoughts were of you . . ."

"Oh, come on, Paul. *I won't be coming back this time.*"

"People do have premonitions."

"If you ever want to know more, I suggest you ask your friend Kit Neville . . . He's been no friend to me."

"One sentence, Elinor, *crossed out,* in a letter he didn't finish, let alone send. For goodness' sake."

"At the very least Kit knows something."

There was no denying that. "What do you want me to do?"

"Write to him. There's no point me writing again, I've tried twice."

"All right. But you're making far too much of it. So all right, perhaps Toby didn't get on with Kit, perhaps something happened, they had a row or something . . . I don't know, but it doesn't mean it's connected to his death. Kit's always putting people's backs up, you know he is—he's *famous* for it."

"It's more than that."

"Have you tried Kit's parents?"

"I wrote to his mother, I haven't had a reply, I think she might be out of London. You could try; I mean, you have met them." She touched his sleeve. "I don't want much, I just want to know how he died."

That was actually quite a lot.

"Who else do you think Kit might be in touch with?"

"Catherine Stein. You remember Catherine?"

Oh, yes, he remembered Catherine. He remembered how she and Elinor had walked round and round the quad, in the lunch breaks, always with their arms around each other's waist. Catherine was German, which, at the time, had seemed to be of no importance whatsoever. He wondered how she was surviving the war.

"I thought it was over. Her and Kit."

"It is, but they still write. She's back in London, you know, I thought you could go to see her."

"Why don't you go? She's your friend."

"I've already asked if she knows anything. She says no."

"Well, then . . ."

"But if Kit did say something critical about Toby she mightn't tell me. If it was something really bad . . ."

So she had thought about the possibilities. "All right, I'll see what I can do. And now, Miss Brooke . . ." Henry Tonks's acerbic voice entered the room. "I believe you have a painting to show me."

As they walked across to the studio, a few flakes of snow drifted irresolutely on the bitter wind. Once inside the barn, there was some heat from the woodstove; the frost-blind windows had circles of clear glass at the center where the ice had begun to thaw. All the same, to work all morning at this temperature . . .

Elinor went to stand in front of the easel. "Right," she said, taking a deep breath. She swept the cloth aside.

Toby. Of course, Toby. Who else? Paul stood and looked at the portrait for a long time. He couldn't make up his mind whether it was good or not; he rather suspected it wasn't, certainly not in comparison with some of the landscapes. But if it was a failure it was an interesting and disturbing one. The resemblance to Elinor—she and Toby hadn't been so alike in life, surely they hadn't?—impressed itself on him with unpleasant force.

"It's very good," he said, in a tight, little voice.

"Is it? I don't know, I just can't see it anymore."

"Perhaps you need a break. You've been here a long time, alone." He watched her examine the word, and reject it. "Why don't you come back to London with me, we can easily find you somewhere to stay a few nights; and don't say 'the dog'— you can bring him with you if you have to."

"I'll think about it."

"No, *don't* think about it. Come back with me."

"I can't. Not just yet. There's Toby's twenty-eighth to be got through first . . ."

She'd turned away from him to face the portrait again. He wanted to grab her by the arm and pull her away from it. Despite her isolation and the loss of weight, he hadn't been afraid for her till now.

"You might never know what happened to him, have you thought of that?"

"I know. I know I might have to live with that, but I'm not going to give up yet. He was my brother, for God's sake."

Blindly, she turned to him.

"All right, all right." He cupped her face in his hands, brushing his mouth against hers in a sexless, almost brotherly kiss. "I'll do anything I can to help. Promise."

13

Back in London, Paul threw himself into work. Ever since he'd left hospital he'd been aware of an increasing restlessness. He was only really calm, now, when he had a brush in his hand, so he worked very long hours, dreading the moment when the shortening days and the failing light forced him to give up and go home. Evenings were bad; nights worse. Wherever he was, was the wrong place. Partly, this was a side effect of learning to live with constant pain, but it wasn't just that.

One night after work he got his drawing pad out and tried to go on working, but he was too tired to think. Losing patience with himself, he grabbed his coat and went downstairs, hoping a walk might help to clear his head. The night was clear and cold; the moon full. He walked rapidly, head down, pushing his body as hard as the pain in his leg allowed. Shuttered windows—dead eyes—ignored him as he passed, and the blue-painted lamps gave people's faces a cyanosed look, not unlike the first darkening of the skin after death. It would be easy, in his present febrile state, to start seeing London as the City of Dreadful Night.

At the end of the street, he stopped and looked up into the sky. A searchlight fingered the underside of the clouds, like a careful housewife assessing the quality of cloth. He couldn't go back to his lodgings. He should probably go to the Café Royal, where at least there would be people he knew and could—well, almost—talk to. Any company was better than his own.

But tonight, there was another possibility. He'd written to Catherine Stein, and received a brief, friendly reply expressing a willingness to meet. No date had been suggested. Now, though, he thought he might call on her. If she was out there was no harm done; if she was busy she needn't see him. At the very least, it would provide a focus for his walk.

The streets were almost deserted. On these bright moonlit nights people hurried home, pulled the blackout curtains across and slept—if they slept at all—under the kitchen table or in the cupboard beneath the stairs. It was difficult not to despise these excessively timid civilians, when you thought what their sons and husbands were going through. No, not difficult: impossible.

He turned into Catherine's road. A girl was walking along the pavement ten or so yards ahead of him, a slight figure wearing a black coat and hat. There was something about her posture—rounded shoulders and folded arms—that gave her the look of a victim. Even as he thought this, she turned and the light from the streetlamp fell full on her face.

Catherine, he almost said, but checked himself. "Miss Stein." He'd called her Catherine when they were students but it seemed presumptuous to do so now. "I was just on my way to see you."

"Paul. Good heavens. I wrote to you."

"Yes, I got it this morning."

They were still put out by the unexpected meeting, a little awkward with each other.

"It's been a long time," she said.

"Two years?"

"More than that."

She was right, must be more like three. Yes, that was it. The last time he saw her, they'd been to the Café Royal, not long after the war broke out, and just as they were leaving a man came up and insulted her—called her a filthy German, something like that—and Kit Neville had head-butted him.

"I was thinking about you only the other day." He sensed a slight withdrawal, a wariness. "You and Elinor. I'm working at the Slade now and I was walking through the quad and . . . Oh, I don't know, getting a bit nostalgic, I suppose. Thinking about old times."

"Well, they were good."

The sadness in her voice so subtly echoed his own he knew he had to talk to her—and not merely about Neville.

"Are you going out tonight?" he asked.

"No, I was just—"

"Would you have dinner with me?"

She seemed to hesitate, but only for a second. "Yes," she said. "I'd like that."

They set off walking down the hill.

"I was very sorry to hear about your father," he said.

"Least they let him out before he died. I'd have hated him to die in that place."

Catherine's father had been interned as an enemy alien and spent the first year of the war in what had once been the Islington workhouse. Conditions there had broken his health, which, even before the war, had been giving cause for concern. He'd been released on health grounds but died not long after. Paul's sympathy was entirely genuine, and yet part of him almost jeered. An elderly man dying at home in his own bed, surrounded by people who love and care for him . . . What, exactly, is there to be upset about in that?

But he liked Catherine; he liked her a lot. He took her to

one of the few restaurants that had stayed open despite the threat of air raids. From the outside it looked closed. As they entered the dining room, a bored waiter peeled himself off the wall. The place was empty.

Facing Catherine across the table, Paul had his first chance to look at her properly. In the street, she'd been no more than a black shadow flitting by his side. Now, as she shrugged off her coat, he thought she looked beautiful, without being beautiful. Her face was full of light. Her front teeth protruded slightly and she kept pressing down her upper lip to hide them in a way he found utterly enchanting. She was far more conscious of the slight imperfection than she had reason to be.

As she read the menu, he remembered with a rush of blood that he'd seen her naked. Some of the girls at the Slade got together to pose for each other in the evenings and Elinor had produced a really exquisite drawing of Catherine lying naked on a bed. And he'd danced with her—God, how the memories came flooding back. She and Elinor had both come to the end-of-term fancy-dress party as Harlequin: identical costumes, and, of course, wearing masks. For a long time they'd danced together, the two girls, totally absorbed in each other, and every male eye in the room had been fixed on them.

"Catherine," he said. "What would you like to eat?"

There was no great choice; in the end, they settled for the game pie.

"At least you know roughly what's in it." Paul indicated the owner, who was slumped over the bar, gulping down his own wares at an alarming rate. "He goes shooting every weekend."

She giggled. "Good for him. I shoot, you know, when I'm in Scotland. I thought I'd hate it, but I don't. Only I kept bagging too many rabbits and, in the end, my aunt just refused to go on gutting them, so we started selling them to the local hotels."

Her first glass of wine brought a flush to her cheeks. She seemed excited, even reckless, but then she'd been living with grief for a long time and that did strange things to you. He remembered the relief he'd felt at getting away from Elinor. Perhaps he should be ashamed to admit it, but relief was what he had felt.

"Is your mother in London with you?"

"No, I don't think she'll ever come back. It's been . . . Well, you know. Quite hard."

It must've been. Before the war, everybody had known Catherine was German, though she had no trace of an accent. Nobody had attached any importance to it, and yet there it had been, all those years, like an unexploded bomb waiting to blow up in her face. Exiled from her home in Lowestoft— enemy aliens were not allowed within five miles of the coast— shunned by previous acquaintances, even by some so-called friends, she must have been incredibly lonely.

"Oh, by the way, it's not 'Stein' anymore," she said. "It's 'Ashby.'"

Of course she'd have changed her name; it was the obvious thing to do. "Is that your mother's maiden name?"

"No, it's a village in Suffolk."

"Well, you're in good company. The King's changed his name to 'Windsor.' Another village. Bit less of a mouthful than 'Saxe-Coburg-Gotha.'"

"It'll take more than that. I mean, to make people forget they're German."

"Oh, I don't know. We've been ruled by German grocers for centuries. Why make a fuss about it now."

"I feel sorry for Dachshunds," she said. "Apparently quite a few of them get killed."

The bored-looking waiter arrived with two plates of game pie and they spent the next few minutes stoically picking shotgun pellets out of lumps of strong-tasting and unidentifiable meat. They smiled at each other's efforts, but didn't bother to comment.

"Have you seen Elinor recently?" she asked.

"Yes, the weekend before last."

"How is she?"

"Tired. Working too hard."

"Well, at least she can work. I couldn't. I mean, after Father died. I couldn't concentrate."

"She told me once if Toby was killed she'd go back home and paint, you know, paint the places they'd grown up in together. And that's exactly what she's done—only I think she's worn herself out in the process. I'm actually quite worried about her. I wish she'd come to London."

"She'd be very welcome to stay with me, but I've told her that already."

"She's obsessed with finding out how Toby died."

Catherine went very still. "Yes, I know."

"She wrote to Kit Neville, twice in fact, and he didn't reply. Did you know they were serving together?"

"I believe Kit mentioned it once."

"So you do still hear from him?"

"Well, yes, now and then."

"It seems so out of character . . . I mean, not replying."

"I don't know. Kit can be very awkward."

"Oh, yes, but surely . . . I've been in this position and whatever you thought about the man you cobble something together for the sake of the relatives. It's just not acceptable."

She shrugged. "Kit was so kind to me when my father was interned, I find it very hard to think badly of him."

He watched her add another pellet to the heap on the side

of her plate, letting the silence pile up around them, forcing her to go on.

"You know, we were walking down Oxford Street once and it was the night of that very big raid. Do you remember?"

"I was in France."

"I don't know how many people died in the raid—too many—and there was this Zeppelin just hanging there, and that awful throbbing sound they make . . . Oxford Street was crowded, people just looking up, open-mouthed, staring. And suddenly it caught fire, a great whoosh of flame all over it, and everybody cheered. All the people in shop doorways, cheering, cheering . . . And not just in Oxford Street either. There were people cheering all over London. And I just stood there and watched it burn, and I thought what a terrible death. It could've been my cousins in there, I haven't heard from them since the war started, I don't know if they're still alive . . ." She pushed her plate away. "That was the moment I stopped being British."

"What did Kit do?"

"Put his arm round me, took me home." She laughed. "Asked me to marry him."

Did he ask every girl he knew to marry him? This was the second proposal Paul had heard about in the last ten days. "What did you say?"

"Ask me again when the war's over. I mean, it was kind of him, but . . . Kindness isn't enough, is it?"

Kind? Well, yes, but there'd have been another force at work: Neville's strange need to be an outsider. There he was: quite possibly the most famous artist of his generation—the toast of London, no less—only, being Neville, he'd have felt compelled to engineer his own rejection, and what better way of doing that than marriage to a German?

Paul realized the silence had gone on too long. "No, it's not enough."

They contemplated pudding, but decided not to risk it

and ordered coffee instead. The owner didn't mind how little they ate; he was resigned to the collapse of his business and far too drunk to care. The waiter went back to leaning against the wall and picking at his spots. Paul looked at him: too young for conscription. With any luck he might miss it altogether and spend the rest of his life wondering how he would have measured up.

"Sixteen," she said.

He looked at her.

"The waiter. Sixteen."

"Yes, about that."

He felt very comfortable with her. Always before, there'd been a slight tension between them, the unspoken knowledge that in different circumstances they might have been lovers. Now the awkwardness was gone. She was leaning towards him over the table, her hand almost touching his. A faint, musky scent clung to her dress, not the usual roses or violets, something much darker, at odds with her delicate features and fair hair. He was intensely aware of her body under the plain dress, of the breasts he'd seen, and not seen.

She was restless under his scrutiny. "Perhaps we'd better be going," she said.

As he helped her on with her coat, his mouth was only inches away from the nape of her neck, that secret groove she never saw. *Careful.* They said good night to the owner, who managed to raise his drooping eyelids long enough to acknowledge their departure. Paul opened the door and the bell chimed as they stepped out into the night.

The cold air restored a certain formality, though after a few yards of walking along the uneven pavements in virtually total darkness Catherine's hand came up and nestled in the crook of his arm. He liked that. It was a good feeling to be strolling along beside her, adjusting his stride to hers.

"Do you mind if we walk for a bit?" she asked.

"No, I'd love to."

It was getting late. The houses in the moonlight seemed insubstantial. Only the moon was real, pouring white acid onto the streets, dissolving cabs, trams, motorcars, offices, and shops in its cold stream. Its light seemed to form a brittle crust over the city, like the clear fluid that oozes from a wound. He suggested they should go for a walk on the Heath and she nodded without speaking. Once they'd left the shelter of the buildings behind, the moon emerged in its full murderous magnificence. They stood with their heads back and their mouths slightly open, drinking it in.

"Makes you wonder about the blackout, doesn't it?" she said. "I mean, if you were up there now in a Zeppelin you'd be able to see absolutely everything."

Something in her voice made him shiver. He wondered if her father's death and the prolonged isolation of her life had made her change sides: she'd said she no longer felt British. So perhaps he was walking with the enemy? Oh, what nonsense. Catherine, whom he'd known since she was, what— seventeen, eighteen? *The enemy?*

They stopped on top of the hill. He'd often visited this spot before the war, looking down on a city laid out before him in all its brilliance. He'd been so full of hope then, of vague, cloudy ambitions: the life he was going to lead, the pictures he was going to paint. He didn't despise that boy. Of course, he should've been at the Slade, hard at work, exposing himself, day by day, to the brutal gap that opens up between aspiration and reality the moment you put brush on canvas; but the dreams are necessary too.

Catherine was silent. She'd taken her hand from his arm and left a small, lonely space there. Trying to pull her back, he said, "You know, I used to love coming here, before the war. You could see all the little villages lit up like fireflies."

Somewhere in the distance whistles began to blow.

"I hate that noise," she said.

"Me too." In the trenches, whistles blowing signaled the start of an attack. "Do you remember when the raids first started, there used to be boy scouts with trumpets cycling round the streets?"

"God, yes, they were funny."

But her smile faded quickly. Looking up, he saw that a second moon had appeared. So beautiful, so ethereal, it seemed that awful drumming sound must be coming from somewhere else. A second later came the flash and roar of guns. The ground shook. He'd have liked to play the battle-hardened veteran, but couldn't stop himself flinching. Quickly bringing himself under control, he put an arm round her shoulder. "It's all right," he kept saying. "It's all right."

Her eyes were fixed on the sky. When he tried to draw her into the shelter of the trees, she followed reluctantly, stumbling a little as her feet moved from tarmac to grass. At first, when he tried to hold her, she struggled, but then suddenly relaxed against him. With his back against a tree and Catherine in his arms, Paul looked up at the floating silver oval and prayed: *Don't burn. Don't burn.*

The guns boomed again. She was very strange to him, standing there in the circle of his arms. He remembered the night of the fancy-dress party, the almost serpentine suppleness of her body as they danced, the anonymous, masked face lifted to his.

"Do you still think that? That they might be your cousins?"

"Every time."

"You must feel . . . I don't know, alienated."

"But that's exactly what I am. An alien." She flared her eyes at him. "The enemy."

"But they don't do much to women, do they?"

"I can't go home. Our house is right on the seafront—at

least, it used to be—I expect some patriotic citizen's burnt it down by now. I suppose they think we'd be flashing lights out to sea or something."

Another crash and recoil of guns. The Zeppelin vanished into a cloud.

"I think I should get you home."

He walked her back to her lodgings. She cut through a side street and, a few minutes later, they were standing outside a tall, narrow house, while she scrabbled inside her handbag for the keys. He was a little surprised when she invited him in, but told himself she'd be sharing the flat with another girl. The three of them would soon, no doubt, be drinking cocoa together, the girls giggling and chattering while he fretted and burned. What a strange evening it had been. He'd known her for years and yet, in any meaningful way, they'd only met for the first time tonight. And where was Elinor in all this? He didn't want to think about that.

"The other tenants go downstairs when there's a raid," she said, throwing her hat onto a chair. "I don't bother."

"I tend not to either."

He thought of telling her about his landlady, who kept suggesting he should take refuge with her in the understairs cupboard, but decided against it. Catherine had put the kettle on and was taking two cups from a shelf above the sink. The evening had taken an unexpected turn, but the cocoa, at least, was arriving on time.

She handed him a cup, and sat on the other side of the fireplace, slim ankles crossed, skirt pulled well down. Their situation might be unconventional, but her behavior certainly wasn't: she might have been entertaining the vicar to tea. A dreadful thought occurred to him: that she was simply indifferent to men. But no, that couldn't be true. What about Kit Neville? They mightn't have been lovers, but they'd certainly been very close. At one stage they'd been seen everywhere together. And Neville had head-butted the man who'd insulted her. He could remind her of that, surely?

He was rewarded with one of her slow, curved smiles.

"That's Kit for you."

"Do you suppose he's ever heard of the Queensberry Rules?"

"Oh, I think he might've *heard* of them." She shook her head. "He's a strange man."

That was one way of putting it.

"Do you know, he always liked me to speak German when—"

Abruptly, she stopped, and blushed. To cover her confusion, he said, quickly, "He speaks it himself, doesn't he?"

"Yes, quite fluently. That's one of the reasons he ended up nursing the German wounded—and he was very good at it too, by all accounts, but you can't get him to talk about it."

"No, well, it doesn't fit with the image of the great war artist, does it?"

God, that was sour. He wasn't surprised when she didn't reply.

"Do you think he does know something about Toby Brooke's death?" he asked, after a short silence. "And he's not telling Elinor because he doesn't want to . . . I don't know. Make things worse for her than they already are?"

"I don't think I know him well enough to say. He's changed a lot in the last few years. We all have."

He put his cup down. "I think I'd better be going, I've got an early start in the morning."

She followed him to the door. As he opened it, he turned to face her. "Do you think we might go out again sometime? A concert or something. I don't much like the music hall these days."

"No, nor me. A concert would be nice."

"Right." He nodded. "I'll be in touch."

———

He couldn't bring himself to go back to his lodgings, not yet. After dark, his restlessness increased; he didn't so much walk the streets as prowl, his senses alert for any sign of life. Even during a raid, there were always some people about. Across the road, in a shop doorway, there were two girls standing close together, huddled up against the cold. Rather bedraggled they looked, in their tawdry finery, and as skinny as a brace of ninepenny rabbits. He imagined what it would be like: their slim fingers swarming all over him, bringing his clay-cold body back to life . . .

No, definitely not. Though something about the idea of two girls together had always excited him. It was surprising how many of his memories of Elinor involved Catherine as well. He saw them walking round the quad with their arms around each other's waists, or dancing together on the night of the fancy-dress party. And then there were the letters from Elinor in the first few weeks of the war, describing how she and Catherine, wearing only their nightdresses, had turned cartwheels round and round the lawn. They'd been cartwheeling around his imagination ever since, their white nightdresses falling in bell shapes over their heads, as they continually wheeled and turned. Now there was an image to come between a man and his sleep.

It was having quite a marked effect on him even now. He could hardly believe he was taking Catherine to a concert; she'd agreed to come out with him. Possibly he should have felt slightly awkward about this, but he didn't. The last night he'd spent with Elinor had been so disastrous that, in a way, it had seemed to free both of them, to mark, not the resumption of their relationship, but its end. Of course, he couldn't be absolutely certain she felt the same, but he strongly suspected she did.

All the way back to his lodgings, he thought about Catherine. Her alienation attracted him; it seemed to echo his own difficulty in fitting in. There'd been times, recently, when he'd hated London: the hysteria over the Zeppelin raids, the spurious sense of excitement and even glamour that seemed to cling to it all. Catherine's nationality set her apart from all that, and her isolation drew him to her.

He let himself into the house just as the whistles were blowing the all-clear. His landlady, bright-eyed and sour-faced, emerged from the understairs cupboard, where she'd been left to face the might of German airpower alone. If this went on, she said, she'd have to think seriously about shutting up the house and going to live with her married sister in Worthing, and then some people, mentioning no names, but *some people* would have to find themselves somewhere else to live.

Paul disengaged himself as quickly as he could and climbed the stairs to his rooms, where he undressed and lay on the bed, exhausted, in pain from the cramping of his leg, and, for the first time since his return to England, full of hope.

14

By midafternoon Paul was too tired to go on working and went outside for a cigarette. The shadows of trees and buildings were already encroaching on the quad; soon it would be time for the men in wheelchairs to be pushed away. They felt the cold badly—in spite of the blankets wrapped round their waists many of them looked gray—but somebody, somewhere, had decreed that fresh air was essential. Perhaps there was a theory that it made amputated limbs sprout? As Paul watched, a group of nurses arrived, greeted their patients with professional good cheer, and, laughing and chattering, pushed the wheelchairs through the iron gates into Gower Street, for all the world like nursery maids pushing perambulators round the park.

Tonks had come out of the door and was standing immediately behind Paul. Together they watched the last wheelchair as it moved out of sight.

"I'm always rather glad when they go," Tonks said. "At least inside they'll be warm."

Paul expected him to say a few brisk words and walk on, as he generally did, but today he lingered.

"Kit Neville's back."

Paul struggled to take it in. "Wounded?"

"Shrapnel injuries to the face."

How did he know? There'd been nothing in the newspapers. "Is he in Queen's Hospital?"

"Yes, he was admitted a few days ago. I only found out yesterday."

"Is he well enough for visitors?"

"He doesn't want to see anybody; well, except his parents, of course. He'll come round to the idea, but he shouldn't be rushed. A lot of them don't want to see people at first."

"Well, give him my regards, won't you? If you do see him."

Tonks nodded and walked off. No sooner had he turned the corner than Paul thought of half a dozen questions he should have asked, but the news had shaken him: he couldn't think clearly. Elinor must be told; that was the first thing. And Catherine. He probably ought to tell Catherine the news in person. This wasn't a difficult decision to reach: he was longing to see her.

The Friday before last they'd gone to the Aeolian Hall to hear a Schubert Octet, almost miraculously beautiful it had seemed with Catherine sitting beside him, and then afterwards they'd gone to Spikings for tea and walked round Piccadilly arm in arm, looking in shopwindows and listening to raindrops peppering his umbrella. Its black silk canopy created a world within a world. He had felt totally at peace.

Now there was a crater in the pavement where they'd walked. Low-lying mist had made the Zeppelins miss their targets and they'd unloaded bombs at random. One of them had landed just opposite Swan & Edgar's, blowing out the windows. Next morning queues of people had been crunching over broken glass, trying to peer into the hole. Why? God knows.

Too restless to wait for the bus, he set off to walk, head down, watching his feet devour the pavement, thinking about

Neville. Shrapnel in the face. My God, he'd seen injuries like that. He shrank from trying to imagine Neville's despair and yet, even now, the old, stupid rivalry surfaced and he caught himself thinking: hmm, *he* won't be doing much painting for a while. Immediately, he cringed with self-contempt.

He arrived at Catherine's lodgings out of breath and doubting whether he should have come at all. He knocked, waited, knocked again, and was just beginning to think she must be out when the door opened and there she was, looking rather flushed and disheveled, with her hair down and the top three buttons of her blouse undone.

"Paul." She seemed so taken aback that for a moment he thought she wasn't going to ask him in, but then she stood aside. "Come in. Sorry, I was just getting changed . . ."

"My fault, I should have . . ."

"Is anything wrong?"

"No, well, yes. Kit Neville's been wounded. Tonks just told me."

She took a step back. "Is it bad?"

"Quite bad. He's in Queen's Hospital."

"Queen's . . . That's facial injuries, isn't it?"

"Yes."

"Oh, my God." She pushed her hair off her face. "You'd better come up."

He followed her upstairs and into the living room. Two cups lay side by side on the draining board. He sat on the sofa. Catherine stood with her back to the fire, twisting her fingers together, almost wringing her hands. He hadn't known people actually did that.

"Has Tonks seen him?"

A door clicked open and Paul turned to see Elinor in her gray silk dressing gown. So she'd come to London and not told him . . .

Catherine was looking over his head. "Kit's—"

"I know, I heard. How long's he been back?"

"A few days."

"So, this wound—it's not the reason he didn't write?"

"No, they ship you back pretty fast if it's a bad wound. Especially facial injuries because they just don't have the facilities out there. Everybody goes to Queen's."

Belatedly, she came across and kissed him. He felt warm flesh through the thin silk—she must be naked underneath—and her hair smelled of rosemary. It felt awkward, embracing her like that in front of Catherine; he was relieved when she pulled away.

"I've got to see him," she said.

"Tonks says he doesn't want visitors."

"Too bad, I'm going."

"Elinor, for God's sake, he's got a shrapnel wound in his face."

"I don't give a damn what he's got, I'm going."

"*No*. You can't—"

"Oh, I think you'll find I can."

She was pacing up and down the small room as she spoke. At one point she leaned against the sink, only to push herself off it again immediately. She went to the bedroom door; he thought she might be going to shut herself away, but then she turned and came back into the room. At last she came to a halt, standing by the fireplace, chafing her arms under the loose sleeves of her gown.

"Grief's bad enough at the best of times," she said. "But when you don't know . . ." Her voice hardened. "I've got a right to know."

"And Neville's got a right to privacy. Look, why don't you leave it a couple of weeks, let him settle in, and then we'll go together."

"No. Now. I owe it to Toby."

The mere mention of his name produced a paroxysm of

grief. Paul could do nothing but hold her close and wait for it to pass. He saw Catherine, who'd been reduced to a bystander in all this, watching them, and sensed her confusion. She was visibly withdrawing from him, as she realized how deeply involved he still was with her friend. He could have howled.

Instead, he went on holding Elinor, rocking her, until at last her sobs subsided into hiccups. Finally, in despair, he caught her face between his two hands and kissed her, lightly, on the forehead. "There, there. Come on, now, it's all right."

Elinor freed herself. "It's not all right, nothing's *all right*. I want to see him."

Exasperated beyond bearing, Paul went and looked out of the window, leaving the two women to whisper together. A young soldier came staggering along the street, weaving from side to side as if the pavement were the deck of a ship laboring through heavy seas. As he passed the house, he almost overbalanced, clutched at a lamppost and clung to it, his fair, foolish face dazed with drink and shame. Shame, because he'd never intended his precious leave to be anything like this.

"Paul," Catherine said.

He turned to face them. They were sitting on the sofa, their arms and legs so entwined it was difficult to see which limb belonged to which girl. There was something accusing in their joint stare. His fantasy was rapidly turning into a nightmare.

"She's going to see him, Paul. Whatever you say. Wouldn't it be better if you went with her?"

"Why don't *you* go?"

"Because he wouldn't want to see me. I'm the last person . . . But he might want to see you. You're a soldier—he knows you won't be shocked. I just think it'd be easier, that's all. Easier for *him*."

This was defeat, and he knew it. Turning to Elinor he said, "When do you want to go?"

"Now."

"Don't be silly, it's far too late."

"Tomorrow, then. First thing."

He nodded. "I'll see you at Charing Cross Station at ten o'clock. I don't know what time the trains go, but they're quite frequent, so I don't suppose we'll have long to wait."

He didn't want to stay after that. They both came to the front door to see him off. He walked away from them, conscious of his limp, feeling them all the time behind him, watching, though when, eventually, he turned round, they'd gone inside and the door was shut.

———

Next morning, the train journey to Sidcup passed in almost total silence. Elinor gazed out of the window; Paul pretended to read. It seemed they were no longer even friends.

At Sidcup Station, a pretty young girl came up to Paul, holding her hand out, begging for cigarettes. When he gave her a packet of Woodbines, she said, "Gawd bless yer, guv," and bobbed a curtsy, before running back to her mother, a tall, angular woman with an imposing bosom, floor-length skirts, and a wide-brimmed hat. She was one of three smartly dressed society ladies standing behind a trestle table collecting for the wounded soldiers at Queen's Hospital. The young girl was managing to dart flirtatious glances at Paul behind her mother's back.

Elinor looked exasperated. "If you've finished . . ."

"Shall we get the tram?" Paul said. "The porter said there's one goes straight past the gates."

"No, let's walk."

He didn't think she was up to it, but he was too tired to argue. At Charing Cross he'd exhausted his patience in a last-minute attempt to persuade her not to come at all. This unannounced visit to Neville was, at best, ill-judged; at worst, unfeeling, even cruel, but Paul was committed to seeing it through. So let her walk, if she wanted to. He didn't care.

The road took them through the village and out into open country. Blue-painted benches were set at regular intervals along the grass verges. Hospital blue. Evidently the color was intended as a warning: *Don't look this way, if you don't want to see horrors.* On one of these benches a soldier was sitting, wearing the red necktie and blue uniform of patients in military hospitals. Twenty yards or so ahead of Paul and Elinor, a dumpy little woman with a shopping bag was dragging a small child along by the hand. As soon as she saw the soldier the woman crossed, very obviously, to the other side of the road, but not all her care could prevent the child staring at the strange man on the bench. He smiled; the child screamed. Her mother bent down to smack the backs of her legs, and then yanked her—crying inconsolably—away. The soldier got stiffly to his feet and strode off down the road, back to the hospital grounds where he knew he would be safe.

The whole ugly little incident had taken no more than a minute, but it confirmed Paul in his view that they should not be here.

The hospital was approached by a long avenue of beech trees. Their dead leaves lay on the grass, reddish-brown, smelling pungently of decay. As a boy, he'd have been down on his knees scuffling through handfuls of mulch in search of stag beetles. Now, he limped soberly along, escorting a young lady, though they kept straggling apart, and not merely because of the uneven ground.

After a few minutes, the house came into view: a huge, mid-Victorian building with Italianate towers and turrets and a covering of ivy leaves that stirred as a breeze blew across the lawn. The front garden was set with beds of roses, many of the bushes still with lolling, loose-lipped blooms clinging to the stems. A solitary bee toppled from flower to flower.

Elinor was walking more slowly now. He suspected she was beginning to realize they might simply be turned away. He hoped they would. There was no sound except for their footsteps crunching over the beech mast in the drive. The silence was almost uncanny: it didn't seem like a hospital at all. Only when they had opened the front door and stepped inside did they hear the sounds of a busy office: typewriters clattering, telephones ringing, the squeak of rubber-soled shoes on black-and-white tiles. A bowl of roses stood on a table by the door, much as it would have done when this was a private house, but the smell of boiled cabbage would not have been tolerated in any well-run home. It smelled like a boys' school.

A secretary wearing a mannish tweed suit and rimless spectacles strode up to them. Paul explained their business.

"Visiting's Mondays at seven in the evening and Thursdays at two in the afternoon."

"We've come a long way," Elinor said.

The woman looked at her. "I'll have to ask."

She was gone some time, returning eventually with a nurse who rustled and crackled and asked about their relationship to Mr. Neville, and when Paul admitted they were merely friends—*close* friends, Elinor put in—seemed equally unsure.

"I'll ask him if he wants to see you," she said. "Meanwhile you'd better wait in here."

She opened a door into what might well have been a dentist's waiting room. A round table covered with copies of *Punch* occupied the center of the room. Elinor retreated to an armchair in the far corner; Paul went across to the window and looked out over the rear of the house. Once, all this land must have been set to lawns; now it was covered in row after row of huts. Some had narrow flower beds planted round them, but nothing could soften the brutal reality of raw, hastily erected wooden buildings crammed together in a waste of mud and trampled grass.

At the center of the grid stood a black-and-white timbered building with a curious octagonal roof, designed, he supposed, to let in the maximum amount of light. As he watched, the doors of this building opened and a trolley emerged, pushed by a porter, with a nurse walking alongside, trying to steady some kind of apparatus that covered the patient's nose and mouth. The trolley was wheeled rapidly along the covered path and through the doors of the next hut along. The journey had taken less than a minute.

Paul heard the creak of the door opening behind him. When he turned round, he saw that a man, not immediately recognizable as Neville, had come into the room.

"Tarrant. This is a surprise."

Something wrong about the voice; something terribly wrong. Pulling himself together, Paul went across and shook hands. "Sorry to hear about the . . ." He was thinking: *Don't look away. Don't stare.*

"Oh, there's a lot worse than this. And let's face it, Tarrant, I was always an ugly bugger. Your profile—now that *would* be a loss to mankind."

His speech was very difficult to follow.

"Sorry, I know I sound a bit odd. Like farting in soapy water, I'm afraid."

Paul realized Neville didn't know Elinor was there. She'd got to her feet and was standing motionless, arms hanging limp by her sides. Neville followed the direction of Paul's gaze and took an involuntary step back.

Elinor came towards him. "Hello, Kit."

She stretched out her hand. Neville took it as one might grasp a dead and decomposing fish. Then he retreated to an armchair as far away from her as possible and, even then, turned it a little to one side so the wing would cast a shadow over his face.

They sat down, their chairs forming an approximate triangle, and tried to think of things to say. Paul, who knew he had to take the lead, asked about Neville's treatment.

"They seem fairly optimistic. Gillies says a lot of damage was done by the surgery I had before I got here. You're meant to come straight here but I ended up in the wrong hospital and they just stitched the edges together—so, apparently, the first thing is to undo all that. Gillies says it might look a bit worse, initially."

Neville said this almost apologetically, as if well aware of their incredulity. Could anything be worse?

"Odd chap, looks a bit like a bloodhound. New Zealander. He calls the patients 'honey' and 'my dear' and sits on the beds. God knows what the army makes of him, but he's supposed to be the best there is."

Paul forced himself to ask about the food.

"Not bad, actually, not bad at all. The hospital's got its own farm so we get fresh milk, eggs . . . A lot of the chaps can't eat solid food, so it's eggnog, soup . . . Well, that's it really. Food's not as good for the men as it is for officers, of course." The red ruin turned in Paul's direction. "Apparently, their delicate systems require more nourishment than ours."

"Is that a dig at me?"

"My dear chap. Wouldn't dream of it. You're a temporary gentleman, I'm a temporary non-gentleman. That's just the way it goes."

Paul could feel Elinor itching to ask about Toby's death, but she waited until there was a natural pause in the conversation and then handled it really rather well. No reproach for Neville's not having written, no suspicion, just a dignified expression of her desire for more information.

"I think it would help my parents to know a bit more," she said. "I know it would help me."

Neville's expression was unreadable, but then all his expressions were unreadable.

"Nothing to tell, I'm afraid. Direct hit. His death was instantaneous, completely painless. He was a brave man, a wonderful doctor, everybody who came into contact with him admired and respected him." He might have been reading from a script. "I don't know what else to say."

"Did you see him die?"

A fractional hesitation? "No."

Elinor quite clearly didn't believe him—and, rather to his surprise, neither did Paul. He couldn't think of anything further to say. After a few minutes of strained silence, Elinor stood up. "Do you know, I think I might have a walk round the garden."

"Are you all right?" Paul said.

"Fine, I just need a bit of fresh air. Anyway. I'm sure you two have lots to catch up on." She shook hands again with Neville, not looking at him, and turned to Paul. "I'll be outside when you're ready."

After she'd gone, Paul said, "Sorry about this, we shouldn't have come."

"So why did you?"

"Because I couldn't stop her coming, and I thought it would be worse if I wasn't here."

Neville shrugged. "Well, it's done now. I suppose I have Tonks to thank?"

"Not really, no, he told me you were here, but he made it perfectly clear you didn't want visitors. It's my fault, I should've stood up to her."

"You were never good at that."

Paul was still inclined to hope that Neville might speak more freely—and more honestly—now Elinor was gone. If there was anything more to say about Toby's death, Neville would tell a man rather than a woman, a serving soldier rather than a civilian—a relative least of all. But instead, he began to talk about old times, before the war, before the trauma. He talked about the years immediately after he left the Slade, his discovery of Futurism, the excitement of scraping away the dead layers of the past. And he talked about girls, the models at the Slade whom he'd painted because he had to, and slept with because he wanted to. He had an old man's hunger for the past. Paul joined in easily enough, though he knew he'd have to raise the subject of Toby's death again before he left. He owed Elinor that, at least.

At last, Neville's stream of reminiscences seemed to be trickling to an end. Paul sat gazing into the fire, waiting for the right moment. He was tired; he hadn't slept very well last night. Once or twice he caught Neville looking sideways at him; he was expecting the question. *All right . . .*

"Is there anything else to say about Brooke?"

"Nothing it would do her the slightest good to know."

"You could tell me."

"No, I couldn't, you'll tell her. Oh, I know you'll say you won't, but you would, you couldn't help yourself. She'd have it out of you in no time."

"So there is something?"

"You know the rules as well as I do. What happens out there stays out there." He stood up. "Along with my fucking nose."

Clearly, the conversation was over. Paul had no choice but to get to his feet and accompany Neville to the door.

With his hand on the knob, Neville turned. "Will you come again?"

"If you want me to."

"It's up to you. No, I'd like to see you."

He actually managed to make the admission sound hostile. The old Neville was still there, very much intact behind the shattered face, biting every hand that presumed to feed him.

"I'll come next week," Paul said. "Meanwhile, if there's anything you want, just let me know."

Neville nodded, tapped him briskly on the shoulder, and was gone.

15

When the door clicked shut behind Elinor, she stood for a moment listening, but no sound reached her from the room beyond. The door was solid oak. This house had belonged—perhaps still belonged—to a wealthy man. It would have been commandeered "for the duration"—or perhaps he'd volunteered to move out. Either way, he was going to get it back in very poor condition. Scratch marks, made by hundreds of heavy boots, had ruined the parquet floors.

Elinor's thoughts were skittering about like bugs on the surface of a pond while her real feelings lurked in the depths somewhere, out of reach. She looked around: she'd lost all sense of where the main entrance was.

A man with one eye came up to her. "Can I help you?"

The other eye was a moist slit with a few sparse eyelashes clinging feebly to the lid.

"No, thanks, I'm fine."

She pretended she had somewhere to get to and walked off, head down, away from him. She could feel him watching her with his one eye, and started to walk faster. A turning led into a dark passage; she was afraid she might have blundered into the kitchen area, but no, the passage opened out again onto a wider corridor. She knew she had to give Paul plenty of time to make Kit talk, so she would just go wherever this corridor took her. God, she'd have liked to shake the truth out of Kit, but it wouldn't have worked. If she'd tried to put pressure on him he'd only have clammed up more. He wasn't going to tell *her* anything.

She was walking head down when a near-collision with somebody in a blue uniform forced her to look up. The corridor, almost empty when she set off, had become crowded with people all moving in the same direction: some nurses, but mainly patients. Faces loomed up in front of her, all kinds of faces; the bodies in their garish uniforms hardly registered. Men with no eyes were being led along by men with no mouths; there was even one man with no jaw, his whole face shelving steeply away into his neck. Men, like Kit, with no noses and horribly twisted faces. And others—the ones she couldn't understand at all—with pink tubes sprouting out of their wounds and terrible cringing eyes looking out over the top of it all. Brueghel; and worse than Brueghel, because they were real.

She had to get away. She scaled along the wall, quickening her pace as the crowd began to thin. By the time the last of them had gone by she was almost running, and not looking where she was going until her nose came into violent contact with a man's chest. Slowly, she raised her eyes, braced for God knows what horrors, and found herself looking at Henry Tonks.

"Miss Brooke. Good heavens."

Her mouth opened but no sound came out.

"You don't look at all well. Come along, let's see if we can find you a cup of tea."

Still unable to speak, she fell into step beside him.

"You must be visiting Mr. Neville," Tonks said, pleasantly, as he unlocked a door.

"Yes, that's right. Paul Tarrant's still with him. I fancied a breath of fresh air."

Even that little lie made her feel uncomfortable. This was a place for truth.

Tonks ushered her into a large room that contained a desk, two chairs, and a filing cabinet. There was a screened-off recess to her right. The part of the room she could see resembled a doctor's surgery, except that at the far end, underneath the tall windows, there was an easel and a table covered with drawing pads, pens and ink and pastels. Directly underneath the window was a stool, presumably for the patient since it had been placed where the full, shadowless glare of northern light would fall directly on the face.

"I'll see about the tea. Have a seat."

He went out; she could hear his voice in the room across the corridor requesting a pot of tea and two slices of that rather nice fruit cake, do you think we could manage that? A woman's voice replied; and then a man's voice—not Tonks's—and, finally, a rumble of conversation. Clearly, Tonks had got embroiled in hospital business.

Elinor went across to the table and looked at a pen-and-ink drawing of a patient with a gaping hole in his cheek. Presumably, Tonks's medical drawings would be done in pen and ink—ironic, really, since he'd never made any secret of how much he hated that medium. In fact, he'd described it to her once as the least forgiving medium an artist could work in, calculated to expose every flaw in draftsmanship. Yet she'd have recognized this as Tonks's work from the purity of the line alone.

She wondered what lay behind the screen; probably a washbasin, something like that. But when she looked behind it she saw, instead, a whole wall full of portraits of men with hideously disfigured faces. One of them, the man with no jaw, she recognized from the corridor. Individually, each portrait would have been remarkable; displayed together like this, row upon row, they were overwhelming. She took her time, pausing in front of first one portrait, then another. Were they portraits, or were they medical illustrations? Portraits celebrate the identity of the sitter. Everything—the clothes they've chosen to wear, the background, the objects on a table by the chair—leads the eye back to the face. And the face is the person. Here, in these portraits, the wound was central. She found her gaze shifting continuously between torn flesh and splintered bone and the eyes of the man who had to suffer it. There was no point of rest; no pleasure in the exploration of a unique individual. Instead you were left with a question: How can any human being endure this?

Tonks came back into the room. "Ah, I see you've found my Rogues' Gallery."

She thought she detected reserve, even disapproval, in his voice. "I'm sorry, I—I realize they're not on display."

"No, don't worry, you'd be amazed how many people see them. Though I like to think they're mainly surgeons." A pause. "I'd be quite interested to hear what you think."

Tonks wanted her opinion of his work? That was bad enough, but the awful truth was she didn't have one. She didn't know how to react to images which seemed to call for several different kinds of response. In the end she just said, simply: "I don't know how to look at them."

"Well, they are—"

"No, I don't mean I can't bear to look at them; I mean, I don't know *how*. I don't know what I'm looking at—a man or a wound."

"Both, I hope. You know, even when I was a very young doctor going round the wards I always saw them like that. On the one hand there's a patient with a problem you have to solve, or at least try to solve, but there's also the person." He stood back, looking along the row of faces. "I can't not see both."

Somebody knocked on the door.

"That'll be tea, I expect. You do look rather pale. Is there anything else I can get you?"

"No, I'm all right, thank you." She pointed to one of the portraits. "How on earth do you repair that?"

"Actually, that's not too difficult because basically it's a flesh wound. This one. Well, I'm not sure even Gillies can do much for him." He touched her shoulder. "Come on, tea."

"How do you find the time to do all this?" she said, when they were settled in chairs on opposite sides of his desk.

"Not easily. I do one day a week, two if I can manage it, but it's not nearly enough. You have to do drawings when they first arrive, then you're in theater during the operations, and then there are the post-op drawings. And the portraits." He reached for a file. "Of course we take photographs as well. Look at this, this is a really good result. There's a little bit of puckering, but Gillies thinks he can get rid of that. And when you think what the poor devil came in with . . ." He handed her another photograph.

"My God. That's amazing."

"He'd been very badly stitched up at another hospital. I'm afraid that's what happened to Mr. Neville." He offered her a slice of cake. "Probably stale, I'm afraid. How did you find him?"

"Same old Kit. You know, he served in France with my brother. Kit was one of his stretcher bearers. I was hoping he'd be able to give me some more information. You see, Toby was posted 'Missing, Believed Killed' and that's really hard. I mean, I look at one of the men there, that one . . . He couldn't tell anybody who he was."

"He could write—"

"It makes me wonder if it's possible for a man to just disappear into the system, never be able to identify himself."

"That's what identity disks are for."

"I know, I'm being silly."

"You've also got to ask yourself if you'd *want* your brother to be alive in that state. A lot of these men are real heroes—but I look at some of them, the worst cases, and I know if it was me I'd rather be dead."

"Yes, you're right, of course. I'd only want him back if he could be the person he used to be before it all started."

"I'm not sure any of us can manage that."

"I used to think I could."

"Did you?"

"Yes, for a long time. I was determined I was going to ignore the whole thing."

"Was?"

She shook her head. "It gets you in the end."

"Have you ever thought about using your skills to . . . Well, do what I'm doing, I suppose?"

She almost laughed.

"I mean, here. With these men."

"I'd be completely useless."

"You did anatomy before the war. Dissection."

"You're a surgeon."

"Most of the artists here have no medical training. Though I suppose you might find the operations distressing . . ."

"No, I don't think I would. Actually, I know I wouldn't, I'd be absolutely fascinated."

"So then, why not?"

Unconsciously, Elinor sighed. This was the usual question everybody asked her but it was coming now from the one person she felt she had to answer. "I'm trying not to have anything to do with the war."

Tonks waited for the silence to thicken. "Because . . . ?"

"Because it's evil. Total destruction. Of everything. Not just lives, even. It's like one of those combine harvester things, you know? Only it's not cutting wheat . . ."

"I doubt if you hate it more than I do."

"It's like the pacifists. You know, some of them, the majority, take on work of 'national importance'—bit of a joke sometimes, but never mind—and they go and work on a farm or in a hospital. But the others—the absolutists—won't do that. They'd rather go to prison than contribute anything, anything at all, to the war. And I just think that's a stronger position, it's more logical, because the others are just pouring their little bits of oil onto the combine harvester and telling themselves there's no blood on their hands because they're not actually driving the wretched thing. And I know none of this applies to women but actually I think some of it does. So anyway that's why I don't contribute and . . . and I don't paint anything to do with it. Because the war sucks that in too. And I don't think it should be about that, I think painting should be about . . . celebration. Praise."

She came to an abrupt halt, realizing that she was lecturing Tonks—*Tonks*—on the subject of art.

He was smiling at her, rather kindly she thought. "I wouldn't disagree with you, I think a very large part of art is about celebration, but then you also have to paint what's in front of you, don't you? And your generation hasn't been very lucky in that respect."

"Well, no, nor yours either. What could be worse than losing adult children?"

"Mercifully I'm not at any personal risk there. One thing it might help you to think about . . . The men here, the process of rebuilding their faces takes so long, I don't think many of them are going back to the front. If any. What we're doing here is simply trying to get them back into civilian life with some hope of . . . being happy. That's all. So you wouldn't be pouring oil onto the combine harvester."

Reluctantly, she started to smile. "Yes, I know, sorry, it's ridiculous. I'm just not good at explaining things." She took a deep breath. "Do you mind if I think about it?"

"No, take as long as you like. Well, not quite. Why don't you come in on Thursday and I'll show you round? See what you think."

"All right."

"Early start, I'm afraid. Eight o'clock?"

"Yes, of course, I'm up anyway. And now I think I'd better be getting back to Paul, he'll wonder what's happened to me."

At the door, Tonks held out his hand. "Sure you can find the way back? Just turn left at the end of the corridor and then it's straight down till you get to the main entrance."

So where had that sense of a labyrinth come from? The waking nightmare, where now there was only sunshine slanting into a perfectly ordinary corridor. People in white coats came and went, and yes, once or twice she passed patients with terrible disfigurements, but not the Brueghel-like horde she'd seen advancing on her an hour or so ago. On her left, an imposing door led to what might once, she supposed, have been the library, or perhaps even a ballroom. A roar of laughter reached her, followed by a ripple of titters. Somebody was thumping away on a piano, while a trio of wobbly falsetto voices sang "Three Little Maids from School." The song came to an end with another burst of laughter and applause.

Paul was waiting for her in the garden, pacing angrily up and down. "Where on earth have you been?"

"Sorry, I got talking. Where's Kit?"

"Back on the ward. Long since."

"Did you get anything out of him?"

"No, and I'm not sure there's anything *to* get."

"Yes there is. And you know it."

"This isn't helping you, you know. It just stops you—"

"Go on. Stops me what?"

He shook his head.

"No, go on. I'm interested."

"Moving on with your life."

"I am. Moving on."

"No, you're not."

"Well, if you really want to know I just spent the last half hour talking to Tonks and he's offered me a job."

"What sort of job?"

"Medical illustration."

"Here?"

"Ye-es?"

"I wasn't . . . I mean, I think you'd be very good at it." He waited. "Will you take it?"

"I'm coming in on Thursday, I'll know more then."

They set off down the drive. Up till now Elinor hadn't seriously considered taking the job. In fact, she'd been trying to work out ways of refusing it without appearing to Tonks—whose opinion she valued more than anybody else's—as egotistical, silly, uncaring, and trivial. She thought she was quite possibly all these things, but she didn't want Tonks thinking so. But then, Paul's advice to "move on with her life" had been incredibly irritating—not to mention trite—and, almost simultaneously, she'd realized that working at the hospital would give her unfettered access to Kit.

"I probably will take it."

"Good."

They walked the rest of the way in silence.

16

The following morning, after a sleepless night, Neville underwent his first operation.

He came round to find himself alone in a small cubicle, not on the main ward as he'd been last night. *Couldn't move his hands.* He pulled against the restraints and, when that didn't work, let out a great bellow of rage.

A face appeared above him.

"Now, now, we mustn't get ourselves upset, must we?"

"Good God, woman, I've lost half my fucking face, why wouldn't I be upset?"

"Lang-*widge*!"

He wanted to ask for water, but she went away and he was left crying big, fat baby tears of anguish and despair.

He squinted down, trying to see if he had one of those tube things attached to the stump of his nose, and sure enough, there it was. Couldn't remember what it was for, what it was supposed to do. He wanted to demand that they come back, explain, answer questions, give him a drink of water. There was water, in a jug on the bedside table, but he had no way of reaching it. He groaned with frustration.

"They'll give you some more morphine soon."

Knew that voice. Looking up, he saw an unfeasibly tall man preparing to jackknife himself into a chair. Tonks. My God, Henry Tonks.

"Now I know I'm in hell."

Tonks laughed—which at least established he was real. All sorts of shadowy figures crowded the suburbs of Neville's mind, or crept out of the darkness and pressed in on him. He coughed to scatter them.

"What on earth are you doing here?"

"I'm going to draw you."

"Oh, please, God, let me wake up."

Through the miasma of morphine, Neville was aware of the cadaverous figure leaning in close to get a better view.

"Somebody," he said, as clearly and distinctly as he could manage, "has given me a trunk."

Tonks looked puzzled. "Oh, the pedicle."

"The what?"

"The pedicle."

"That's a chair leg, you idiot."

"I don't think it is."

He flicked his swollen tongue across his lips. "How long do I have to be like this?"

"Three weeks? Something like that."

"Fucking Elephant Man."

"I knew him," Tonks said, unexpectedly.

"Who?"

"Joseph Merrick. The Elephant Man. I was working at the London Hospital when he was living there. He didn't look anything like that—and unfortunately, poor man, the flesh was rotting on him so there was the most appalling smell." He looked from Neville to his drawing pad and back again. "In spite of which, he was a great favorite with the ladies."

"Hope for me, then."

For a few minutes Tonks went on drawing in silence. Neville endured his gaze, hunched up, brooding bitterly over the fate that had brought him here.

"All we need you to do is stay cheerful," Tonks said. "It's a different sort of courage from what you need out there . . ."

"I was never very brave out there."

"We-ell, you must've been facing the enemy when you got that."

"Pity, really, I could've spared a chunk of arse."

"There, that's it, I'm done."

Neville was aware of the long frame unfolding itself. In a minute he'd be gone, and though he couldn't bear to ask Tonks for help, he knew he must.

"Would you mind giving me some water, please?"

Tonks poured a glass and held it to his lips. Neville slurped it in, cringing with shame. He hated himself for being weak, though not nearly as much as he hated Tonks for witnessing it.

"More?"

Gulped, swallowed, gulped again. Blessed water dribbling down his chin, running into the creases on his neck.

"Now try to sleep," Tonks said.

His lids flickered shut, as if the word "sleep" had been a hypnotist's command. When he opened them again, Tonks was gone.

"Do you know," he said to the nurse who came to wash him down, "I keep having these really weird dreams. I dreamt my old drawing teacher was here."

Not long after, the morphine began to wear off and for the next hour or so he could think of nothing but pain: pain in his chest, pain in his face, pain in the bloody tube where there wasn't supposed to be pain. The injection went in just as he felt he might start to scream. Tube, trunk. Elephant. Darkness.

When he came round, a tall, straight-backed woman with white hair was standing at the foot of his bed. Gillies was there too: Gillies, the surgeon, the elephant-maker, smiling obsequiously, inclining his droopy eyes and droopier mustache towards her. Their voices mingled: clipped, aristocratic English salted with Gillies's Antipodean twang. Fellow sat on your bed, called you "honey," called you "dear," stuck a trunk on the end of your nose, and tied you up so you couldn't pull it off. Bloody good mind to tell him what he thought of him. He opened his mouth to protest, words bubbling up like sewage out of a blocked drain, and immediately the straight-backed lady was whisked away, and Sister Lang-*widge*! took her place.

"Clench your fist for me now, there's a good boy," she said. "Just a little, tiny prick . . ."

Insult to injury. *Bollocks like a bull,* he wanted to say, but then, before he could speak, the darkness rushed in and the waters closed over his head.

————

The bed started moving. He was traveling, seasick, train sick, didn't know what sort of sick, sick anyway. There was a smell of engine oil. The officers had colonized all the best spaces: the lounge bar, the dining room. High-ranking officers had cabins; junior officers played cards in the bar. The men, other ranks, privates, the poor bloody fucking infantry—of whom he was one, a source of mingled pride and shame— slept in the corridors. There were puddles on the floor where rainwater had dripped off their capes as they settled in. Then the engines started up, everything shook, and the noise restored him, briefly, to his sweaty bed. Bound hands, the shadowy figures of nurses all around, Gillies's face looming in. A crackle of speech, some of it addressed to him, but it faded and he was back on the ship, trying to make himself comfortable with his kitbag for a pillow and a buckle scraping his neck.

Had to get up, get out of bed, get free. And he managed it, he did, he stood up, he flexed his fingers and the next minute he was walking down the heaving corridor and climbing the stairs onto the deck.

Cold air on his face. The stars formed clusters like apple blossoms. He stood at the rail and opened his mouth to catch the salt spray: he seemed to be drinking stars. The ship was traveling without lights. Half a mile away, lean, predatory, gray destroyers loped along, almost invisible except where starlight caught the white foam of their wakes. Gradually, the wind off the sea cooled his hot flesh. He couldn't go back down there, with the smells of engine oil and wet rubber and sweaty bodies; he'd find somewhere out of sight and stay on deck all night.

Crouching in the shadow of a lifeboat, he felt sufficiently safe to drift off to sleep, though women's voices kept snagging him awake.

I don't think he'll need any more tonight, do you?

No, he's out for the count.

Women on board? There must be a group of nurses going out. He rolled up his coat to form a pillow and slipped into a deeper sleep, from which he woke, jolted half out of his wits, because some blithering idiot had fallen over him.

"Look where you're going, you—" Too late he registered the peaked cap. "Sorry, sir."

"Good God, it's Neville, isn't it?"

Didn't know the bloke from Adam. But then he took off the cap and there, impossibly, in army uniform with the caduceus badge of the RAMC on her chest, stood Elinor Brooke.

Of course it bloody wasn't. Fighting off the last vestiges of sleep, he said, "Captain Brooke, sir."

Brooke sat down on the deck beside him and offered him a cigarette. In civilian life, this would not have been remarkable—they did, after all, know each other through Elinor, though not very well—but here, where men were not supposed to address officers except in the presence of an NCO, it was unusual, to say the least. All Kit's ambivalent feelings about not being an officer rose to the surface; he compensated by boasting about the extent of his experience with the Belgian Red Cross. He'd been in France in 1914, well before anybody else got there. French medical services on the verge of collapse, wounded sleeping on pissy straw, half a dozen orderlies to five hundred men, no supplies, that was the situation he'd found, and only three months later he'd been a dresser in a properly run hospital. And, though he said it as shouldn't, a bloody good one too.

Brooke nodded, asked questions, taking it all in. What an extraordinary coincidence, Elinor wrote, when he told her he was serving with her brother. Wasn't a bloody coincidence at all. *He asked for me.* Oh, he didn't flatter himself for a minute that Brooke had any particular interest in him personally, he just wanted an experienced dresser for his team and he made bloody certain he got one.

———

And slowly, with the bitterness of that realization, the hut took shape around him. While he slept, they'd moved him from his cubicle onto the main ward. In the next bed, Trotter was struggling to ingest the regulation amount of gruel. The nurse who was feeding him looked across at Kit. "You're awake, then."

People's willingness to state the absolutely bleeding obvious never ceased to amaze him. "Yes."

"That's nice."

Mousey brown hair; eyes like currants stuck in dough. Good pair of tits on her, though. It humiliated him: this melancholy, all-pervading lust.

"You going to the concert?"

"Not allowed out of bed."

"Oh, what a shame. I always think it breaks up the day."

The day was feeling pretty bloody broken, yes. He turned on his side to indicate that the conversation was over, but the sounds of Trotter being fed went on and on. Couldn't screen them out. He knew every stage of the process that produced these chokings and gurglings and regurgitations, the oohings and aahings and cooings, the "just one more mouthful now, there's a good boy." If he stayed in this place much longer he really would go mad.

Somehow or other the morning passed. Just before lunch, Gillies, attended by Sister Lang-*widge*! and surrounded by white-coated acolytes, appeared at the foot of his bed. They stared at him. He stared back. Gillies examined the trunk, which he appeared to think was a very good sort of trunk, and then they all retreated to the foot of the bed and began talking to one another in low voices. Mouths opening and shutting, drooling strings of words. It was a relief when they moved on. He was feeling drowsy; he wanted to sleep, though he knew the moment he closed his eyes he'd find Brooke waiting for him on the inside of the lids.

For God's sake. He was tired, so tired. *Bloody well bugger off, can't you, and leave me alone.*

17

When Elinor met her father in his favorite restaurant on George Street she was shocked by the change in his appearance. Toby's death had aged him ten years, though he greeted her cheerfully. An elderly waiter doddered across to their table and Father addressed him by name. He loved this place, mainly, she suspected, because it served exactly the same kind of food he ate in his club. They ordered Brown Windsor soup and steak-and-kidney pie: God alone knew what would be in it, probably neither steak nor kidney. She watched him lovingly as he chased globules of grease around his soup. "So how have you been keeping?" he said.

"Not too bad, I'm spending more time in London now, staying with Catherine. You remember Catherine?"

"Yes, of course."

It was quite clear he didn't.

"What about you?" she asked.

"Oh, you know, work. And more work."

"I don't really know whether it's worth my getting a flat in London, I still spend quite a bit of time at home."

He pushed his plate away. "That's really what I want to talk to you about."

But he didn't talk. He simply sat, staring down at his hands. She could feel tension gathering behind the silence and it made her nervous. "Yes?"

"The thing is, I don't think your mother's going back. She seems very settled at Rachel's."

"Well, I suppose it's a bit soon."

"No, I don't think she's ever going back."

"Has she said so?"

He nodded.

"I think that's a mistake. And she shouldn't be taking a big decision like that anyway. It's too soon."

"But she has."

"What does Rachel think? I mean, I know they get on really well, but . . ."

"There's a cottage in the village. Only half a mile away, she could see the children every day. Alex, you know, he's the spit of Toby at that age."

Elinor didn't know what more to say. She thought it was a mistake, but in the end it was her mother's decision. How different people were. She'd clung to the house and the memories it contained; her mother, apparently, couldn't wait to see the back of them.

"The thing is . . ." Father was toying with his knife, not looking at her. "She's made up her mind."

"What does Rachel say?"

"She thinks it's a good idea."

"A good idea for Mother to buy the cottage or a good idea for Mother to get out of her house?"

"Elinor—"

"Oh, I know. I'm not being nasty, really I'm not. Rachel's borne the brunt of all this, I haven't done anything."

"Well, the answer's a bit of both, I think. I know she finds your mother . . . Well, the word she used was 'draining.' And you can hardly blame her. Those two boys are absolute little tearaways, and there's another on the way."

"Really?"

"Nothing's been said, but your mother thinks so and I'd back your mother's judgment on that any day."

Rachel had been tense lately. The last time they'd met she'd really lashed out at Elinor. *You're behaving like a widow, for God's sake. Surely you can see how offensive that is?* Startled by the ferocity of the attack, Elinor had tried to explain that she always wore black because it was easy: you didn't have to think what to put on. But she knew Rachel's accusation had nothing to do with clothes. There it was again: the shadow under the water that none of them ever admitted seeing.

"So what happens now?"

"I'll put the house up for sale."

Elinor froze.

"I don't see any alternative. Your mother's not going back. I certainly don't want to live there."

"You never did."

That was too sharp, though he showed no sign of having heard.

"I'm afraid it's got to go. I'm sorry, but I can't afford to keep it on just for you."

"No, of course not." Her heart twisted. It felt like losing Toby all over again. "I'll start looking for somewhere in town."

"You'll need a bigger place. I'm quite happy to give you the same allowance I gave Toby."

"No, you mustn't—"

"Why not? There's nothing else to spend it on."

She'd need storage space for the paintings. He was right, she would need a bigger flat . . .

"So how do you feel?" he said.

"It's very generous of you."

"You know I didn't mean that."

"How do I feel? Well. As if something just broke." She smiled. "Too many broken things."

"There'll always be a bed for you in the cottage. Whenever you want one."

Which would be never. "What about you, Dad? Will there be a bed for you in the cottage?"

He straightened his knife and fork. "I spend most of my time in London anyway."

So this was the moment when, finally, the breakdown of the marriage was going to be acknowledged. The loss of Toby hadn't brought his parents together; if anything, it had driven them further apart.

The steak-and-kidney pie arrived, looking rather wan and sad, flanked by boiled potatoes and anemic cabbage. They ate in silence for a while; then Elinor, searching for another, less painful, topic of conversation, hit on her recent meeting with Tonks.

"And he's asked me to work there."

"What does it involve?"

"Drawing."

"No, I mean, how many hours?"

"Don't know, didn't ask. Frankly, I'm—"

"You're not going to turn it down, are you?"

"I don't know."

"Elinor, you really ought to take this, you know. It'll help you . . . help you—"

"Move on?"

"Or back, or in a circle. I don't know. *Move,* anyway."

She hadn't realized till now how stagnant her life must seem to him. "I do work, you know."

"I know you do."

Only she hadn't been, not recently. Whenever she went

back home, she got her brushes out and tried to paint, but it didn't happen. And Toby's portrait, draped in its white cloth, was still unfinished.

"What do you suppose Toby would say?"

"Dad, that is completely and utterly below the belt."

"Perfectly reasonable question."

"Well, he's not here to answer it."

"No, that's true."

He was looking away from her across the wet street, and that gave her a chance to study his face more closely. The washed-out blue corneas of his eyes were ringed with circles of opaque gray. The *arcus senilis*. Had it been there the last time she looked? She couldn't remember.

"Anyway, I haven't decided yet. I'll know more tomorrow after I've seen Tonks."

———

It was raining when she left the restaurant so she decided to take the Underground back to Catherine's lodgings. She stood on the deserted platform, listening to the rumble of distant trains, her hair and skirt ruffled by the dead wind that blew out of the tunnels.

What *would* Toby say? Not a difficult question to answer. On his last leave, they'd lain out on the lawn, side by side, close enough to smell each other's skin, but not touching. Never touching. He'd said, then, how much he wished she'd do something for the war effort. They'd wasted hours of their last days together arguing about it. Which, as she tried to explain to him, was precisely what the war did: leached time and energy away from all the things that really mattered. "I'm not going to feed it," she'd said.

He'd been exasperated. "I *think* I see what you mean but isn't it all a bit theoretical when people are suffering so much? I don't see how you can ignore that."

"But there's nothing I can do about it."

"Of course there is, lots of things."

"Such as? I haven't got what it takes to be a nurse . . ."

"I think you have."

"Oh, Toby, I'm hard as nails."

"Precisely." He lifted himself onto his elbow to look at her. "Are you proud of that?"

"No, it frightens the life out of me."

He lay down again. "You could always knit."

"Oh, yes, socks for you, I suppose? Don't think so."

"Just as well, probably. Nothing gives you blisters faster than a badly knitted sock."

They lay in silence, soaking up the sun, peaceful on the surface, but with a bead of tension between them that made her miserable. "Can't we just agree to disagree?"

"I thought we had. Do you see that bird over there? I'm sure it's a buzzard."

The bird was no more than a shadow in a ripple of green leaves. "No, it's a sparrowhawk."

"Buzzard. Definitely."

"Sparrowhawk."

"Good God, woman, are you blind? BUZZARD."

Standing on the edge of the platform, listening to the roar of an approaching train, she began to smile. The dead wind blew in her face, but she was back on the lawn, Toby alive beside her, his arm an inch away from hers. She felt the prickle of grass on her bare skin.

Oh, Toby, why did you have to die?

18

Towards evening Neville's temperature rose. A doctor he hadn't seen before came and examined him. He leaned into Neville, speaking slowly and clearly, as if to a small child. "Try to sleep."

Sleep? In this hellhole? The ward at night was never quiet, not for a second: squeaky footsteps, creaking mattresses, snores, groans, farts, the scream of a man struggling to escape from a nightmare, followed by the flap-flap of rushing feet, voices, half scolding, half reassuring, cajoling or bullying the dreamer back to sleep.

Neville fought off sleep as long as he could, but when, for the third time, the night nurse passed his bed and found him awake, she gave him a sleeping draft and stood over him while he drank it. After she'd gone he lay looking at the lamp on the nurses' table. It shifted and blurred as lights sometimes seem to do in a high wind. It was raining too, great bursts of it hurled against the windows of the hut. How was anybody meant to sleep in this? But then, gradually, his eyes closed.

He was traveling again, the train bumping over points. His consciousness, the fine point that was left of it, still bright and sharp, like a needle tacking darkness . . .

———

Cattle trucks? He hadn't expected that. He was used to columns of marching men, mud-colored against a muddy road, dodging the sprays of slush and gravel that motor lorries flung up in their wake. But now, the carriages loomed up on his left as he stood with the others: indistinguishable, expressionless blobs, all of them, enduring the long wait with no more impatience than cows. So perhaps the trucks were appropriate after all.

The pressure of men behind moved the line forward. A group of officers, Toby Brooke among them, stood and watched. The trucks had white letters on the side: HOMMES 40; CHEVAUX 9. A damn sight more than forty men were clambering up the ramp into the dark interior. Was it French or simple arithmetic they couldn't manage? He was being jostled and pushed, carried along against his will. A nail paring of a moon appeared between banks of black cloud. Not enough light to see faces by, just a silver gleam on the railway lines as they snaked away into the darkness.

He was about to set foot on the ramp when an officer shouted, "That's enough!" and so they had to march farther along the track until they reached the next truck. He was among the first to enter, which meant he ended up in the far corner, a long way from the door. Shapes of men crowded in after him: miserable, grumbling hulks encased in cloth that the drenching rain had made as stiff as cardboard. Sighs and groans of relief as they took off their packs. He made the mistake of trying to sit down with his still on his back, toppled over, and lay there waving his legs feebly, like a fucking stag beetle. No straw on the floor, nothing, but at least in this truck they weren't too badly packed in: there was room to move. Men began to set out their possessions, form circles, talk in hoarse voices that had been bellowing songs all day, though towards the end, as the rain pelted down on helmets and capes, they'd marched in silence. Some of them lit candles. The stumps were precious, had to be preserved, but crouched here like this, heading for the front, they felt the need for light. Card games were begun and bitterly argued over, people fanning the disputes to distract themselves from the immense, straining darkness outside.

Neville lit his own candle, settled down with his back to the side of the wagon, and sketched. They were used to him now, him and his endless drawing. It didn't impress them, except when he drew portraits; then, they all gathered round and watched, amazed by his ability to get a likeness in a few quick strokes. The rest of the time, they were tolerant; they left him alone.

He looked around, imprinting the sight on his memory. Raw, red hands shielding guttering points of flame, the shadows cast on faces as they bent over the cards. Water cans were swigged, mouths wiped, hard biscuits bitten into with disgust. Somebody started a song—"Tipperary," predictably—and the sound bounced off the walls of the truck until it seemed to vibrate like a communal rib cage.

The sweetest girl I know . . .

It was Elinor that he saw, not because she was the sweetest girl he knew, or even very sweet at all, but he'd just met her brother and that brought her, particularly, to mind. Her face floated in front of him, laughing and chattering, as he'd first seen her in the Antiques Room at the Slade. At that stage he'd only spoken to the men; contact between male and female students was discouraged. But he'd been aware of her, all the time. She was wearing a paint-daubed smock that fell straight to her ankles, a shapeless garment that nevertheless managed to hint at the firm, young body underneath. Pigeon toes poked out from beneath the hem. She stuck her tongue out when she drew. Elegant, she was not, and all the time, chatter, chatter, chatter . . . He'd assumed, then, that she was one of the young ladies who attended the Slade as part of their finishing, girls whose interest in art would fade as soon as the duties of marriage and motherhood claimed them. Quite a few of the women were merely filling in time till the right man came along. Not Elinor, though. He couldn't have been more wrong about that.

The train lurched forward. As it gathered speed, drafts crept in through gaps in the sides and blew the few remaining candles out. Narrow bands of moonlight striped the floor. Many of the men were sleeping now, sprawled out, heavy limbs straining against wet cloth, sullen, cold, slack-mouthed faces pressed against kitbags and rolled-up coats. The air was full of snores, coughs, snuffly breaths: the same sounds horses or cattle would have made. Neville felt he'd begun to behave like a bullock, putting his nose to a gap in the wall, smelling, beyond the grit and smoke, moist green air, sucking it in, bloody great lungfuls of it. Cattle don't know about the slaughterhouse, at least not until they smell blood. Only men have foreknowledge, and the thought of what was facing them kept him and others like him awake. Looking round, he could see, here and there among all the blank and shuttered faces, a glint where sleepless eyes caught the light.

Somebody said: "No, he's dead to the world. I don't think he needs any more."

The face of a middle-aged woman in a nurse's cap bent over him. He opened his mouth to ask her what the bloody hell she was doing here, but then the clackety-clack of the train reasserted itself and he couldn't speak. The train juddered and shuddered and shook and rumbled through the night, displacing darkness that thickened again in its wake. Now, only one other man was awake: Mason—"Boiler" Mason—though why so called Neville didn't know. Boiler looked raw, underdone. Sunburnt skin stretched tightly over his cheekbones gave him a hyperawake look, like a bird of prey. His eyes were china blue, doll's eyes, hard and cheap. Neville had taken a dislike to him, and that was unfortunate since Boiler was another of Brooke's stretcher bearers. SBs, they were called. Silly buggers, they called themselves.

Towards morning he slept and woke to find the train still limping along. At this rate the war might be over before they got to the front. There were frequent stops: you could jump down onto the tracks and stretch your legs a bit. During these breaks the men sometimes sat back to back, leaning on each other, and passed round copies of the *Daily Mail*. They were free, one to every ten men. Neville was rather amused. Here he was at the front—well, more or less—reading about the war in the *Daily Mail*, and not believing a word of it either. He walked the length of the train and saw the officers' accommodation: four to a carriage. As every reader of the *Daily Mail* knows, there are no class distinctions at the front.

Once, the train stopped just before dawn, after an unusually long stretch without a break, and everybody clambered down onto the track to relieve themselves. Steam from three hundred jets of piss rose into the cold, clear air. What a sight. Remembering it, he felt his own bladder start to leak, his piss pleasantly warm at first, then cold and wet. A hand went down and fumbled with his cock, then, finding it moist and sticky, drew back with a little *tsk* of disgust. A moment later the hand was back, small, cool, cramming his prick unceremoniously into the neck of a bottle. In or out? Bugger it, had to let go. A satisfying warmth spread over his groin.

"Oh, God," a girl's voice said. "Now I'm going to have to change the sheets."

———

The train had stopped again. Neville pressed his muzzle to the gap between the slats, sniffing the dawn wind, and found himself looking straight at Brooke. He was standing at a distance from the other officers and smoking a cigarette. At that moment, as if he felt himself being observed, Brooke turned and looked straight at Neville, an unresponsive stare that struck a slight chill. It felt like a rebuff, until Neville realized he was invisible inside the darkness of the truck. A second later Brooke dropped the stub of his cigarette and ground it out under the toe of his boot.

Gray skies, darkening. It was raining when, at last, the door at the end was thrown open and they jumped down onto the track. One man fell because his legs had gone to sleep; others walked up and down stamping their feet to get the circulation going. Neville was quickly off to one side, trying to imprint it all on his brain: lumbering figures in the gloomy light, water streaming down rain capes, round helmets gleaming. Running a little way up the slope, he looked down on metal mushroom-heads and ached to draw them. Too late. The command "Form Fours!" ran along the track. They'd arrived, then, though this place looked no different from any of the other places they'd stopped.

They marched off, heads lowered into the wind that threatened to snatch the breath from their mouths. Neville was second from the right, shielded, therefore, from the worst gusts of rain that swept across the column. Soon the fitful singing fell away and they trudged in silence, except for the swish and rustle of capes and the slushing of boots on muddy ground. In one place the steep banks on either side had produced a river. They splashed through and emerged drenched to their knees. "*Bloody hell!*" he heard somebody say, but for the most part they saved their breath.

At either end of the column, lanterns on poles threw shadows of marching men over hedges and fields and the gable ends of farmhouses. Shadow-giants sixteen feet tall leapt over walls into the nothingness beyond. Once they passed through a wood where overhanging branches dripped water onto the backs of their necks, another small discomfort added to the general misery. Intimate misery. Neville hadn't been able to wipe himself properly after his last shit and his arsehole was getting sorer by the mile. And then when they arrived, hoping for decent billets, there were only barns with bales of straw and the roofs had holes in them and most of the straw was wet.

Miraculously, it seemed, hot stew was produced and served on tin plates. In civilian life, he'd have sent it back to the kitchen with a few choice words; now he not only scraped his plate clean, but sucked his teeth afterwards, savoring every last lingering morsel.

Afterwards they pulled straw out of the bales and made themselves nests. Nobody had the energy to say much, so overwhelming was the longing for sleep. Neville found a space between two bales where he felt safe. As he settled down, he became aware of a desire to scratch himself. At first he attributed this to the sharp ends of the straw, but then realized he'd been invaded by lice. For ten minutes he itched and clawed, thinking he'd never get to sleep, but then fell, abruptly, into a sleep so deep and dreamless that when he woke no time at all seemed to have passed, though it was beginning to get light. A silver wall of rain fell steadily beyond the open barn door.

He wouldn't get to sleep again now—not with this bloody itching starting up again—and anyway he needed a fag. Clambering over recumbent figures, he made his way to the barn door. Hollyhocks and foxgloves still grew in the farmhouse garden though the people who'd owned it were gone. A cockerel and three hens, disgruntled by the downpour, fluffed out their feathers and throatily, morosely, clucked. *They* wouldn't last long. Foraging was strictly forbidden, but it was amazing how many chickens fell victim to enemy shelling even this far behind the line. Roast chicken for the officers; soup for the stretcher bearers, if they were lucky. Stopping by the water butts, he lit a cigarette, then crossed the yard and wandered down a narrow lane to where scrubby willows fringed a small pond.

Out in the middle, beneath the scum of dead leaves and weeds, some kind of disturbance was going on. The water suddenly boiled and broke around a wet head and glistening shoulders. Mad, whoever he was, swimming in all that muck. Green turds of duck shit lined the edges of the pond; you'd need to walk through that just to get in. Something about the figure—he was wading out now, wiping water from his eyes—compelled Neville's imagination. Perhaps it was the silence and the dim light. The farthest ripples were only now beginning to break against the reeds. Neville backed away into the shadows, watching as the naked, gleaming man teetered across the duck shit and began scraping his feet clean on the grass. Elinor Brooke's brother, emerging from a farmyard pond with duckweed in his hair.

19

As the hospital came into view, Elinor heard a rumble of engines and saw two motor ambulances turning into the drive. She stepped onto the grass verge and watched them go past, before following along behind them in a fug of petrol fumes.

By the time she reached the main building, their doors were open and a cluster of white-coated doctors and nurses were supervising the unloading of the wounded. One young nurse was struggling to support a patient who had bandages wound round the lower part of his face and some kind of metal contraption on his legs.

"YOU!"

Elinor realized this was addressed to her.

"Help Nurse Wilson take that man to the ward."

"But I'm not—"

The sister had already turned away. Elinor threaded her way through groups of men to where Nurse Wilson was holding on to the man with callipers. He seemed to be asleep on his feet. There was oil in his hair, and the blood that had seeped through his bandages was as black as the oil. On his chest was a label: "Queen's Hospital, Sidcup, Kent."

"Can't we get him a stretcher?" Elinor said. "Or a wheel-chair?"

"They've all gone, I think."

Elinor took the man's other arm and draped it across her shoulder. "Where are we taking him?"

"Ward One. Admissions."

They set off. The man kept tripping over his feet, and every time his head jerked forward the area of blood on the bandages increased. Elinor made soothing noises, got only grunts in reply. Nurse Wilson's childishly round face was rigid with effort. At last, they turned the corner of the building and Elinor saw before her row after row of huts: raw, almost brutal, in their uncompromisingly square functional-ity. This, she realized, not the graceful building behind her, was the real hospital.

They staggered along a covered walkway that linked the huts, their footsteps clumping along wooden boards. Every-thing smelled of creosote. "Not far now," Nurse Wilson kept saying. Somewhere nearby a gramophone was playing. *Your nose, your mouth, your cheeks, your hair, / Are in a class beyond compare. / ... You're the loveliest thing I ever knew ...* Elinor fought back a desire to laugh. Her arm had gone numb. At this rate, she might easily topple over and bring him down with her.

At last they reached Ward One. Nurse Wilson shouldered the door open and a blast of institutional smells met them: car-bolic, custard, disinfectant, sweaty socks. Toby's school used to smell like that. A sister met them at the door and pointed to a bed at the far end. It looked miles away. By the time they got there Elinor was gasping for breath. She attempted to steer the grunting man towards the bed, but Nurse Wilson seemed to be pulling the other way.

"Chair," she said. "They're not supposed to lie on—"

"Oh, bugger that."

Elinor caught a startled glance, but Nurse Wilson was too well trained—too resigned to being bullied—to argue. They heaved him into a sitting position on the bed. He sat there, swaying, for a long moment and then slowly toppled over onto his side. It was easy, then, to lift his legs, straighten them out, and pull a pillow down under his head. The bandages were now a sodden mass of red and black. The face above them, the eyes especially, looked vaguely surprised, as if he couldn't believe what was happening to him.

"Right then," Elinor said. "I've got to go." She touched the man's arm. "You'll be all right now, they'll look after you."

His head turned in her direction, but he gave no other sign of having heard.

———

Tonks was waiting outside his room, carrying a bundle of files under one arm.

"I'm so sorry, Professor Tonks. I got a bit caught up with the new arrivals."

"That's the third big intake this week, God knows what's going on out there. Oh, and by the way, it's Harry."

Harry? "Henry" she might just about have managed, but "Harry"? Harry was five stones overweight and sporting a codpiece.

"Harry," she said.

They set off to walk to the huts.

"I didn't realize how big it was," she said. "You don't get much of an idea from the front."

"There'll be a thousand beds when it's finished. We're not far off that now."

So: a thousand young men with gouged-out eyes, blown-off jaws, gaping holes where their noses had been, crammed in here to be patched up and sent on their way with whatever the surgeons had managed to supply in the way of a face.

Tonks opened the door to the third hut along. "Well then," he said, in a chirpy medical tone she didn't recognize. "Shall we get started?"

A nurse was feeding the first patient on the list. She stood up when she saw Tonks.

"No, you go on. We're a bit early anyway."

She was holding a tube linked to a small duck-head-shaped container into which she spooned some gloopy grayish stuff: gruel or thin porridge. As she raised the duck-head there was a gurgling sound, then choking, a lot of dabbing and wiping. An awful lot of it seemed to be coming back up.

While they waited, Elinor made herself look round the hut. This was the postoperative ward and many of the men were asleep. The few who were awake looked at her and then quickly away. She turned her attention back to the bed where the nurse was now clearing away the feeding apparatus. As soon as she'd gone, Tonks pulled the curtains farther open and bent over the patient, whose face was now in full light. Very gently, Tonks began to ask him questions, more to establish a connection, Elinor thought, than because the answers were relevant to the task in hand. How had he got this? Couldn't remember, it was all a bit of a blur. As he spoke, you could see his tongue through the hole in his cheek, muscular and hideously long, threshing up and down as he struggled to form the words.

Tonks started to draw. Elinor forced herself to keep looking from the face to the drawing and back again, but she found meeting the man's left eye difficult, not because it was damaged but because it was intact and full of fear. This was a complete waste of time: she already knew she couldn't do it. Confronted by this mess of torn muscle and splintered bone, nothing she'd learned about anatomy, whether at the Slade or in the Dissecting Room, was the slightest use. "Drawing," as *Professor* Tonks never tired of telling his students, "is an explication of the form." Well, you can't explicate what you don't understand.

The next one wasn't so bad. He had been a remarkably handsome man; still was, on one side of his face. If anything, his injuries threw the beauty of his remaining features into sharper relief. He reminded her of some of the "fragments" they used to draw at the Slade, where so often a chipped nose or broken lip seemed to give the face a poignancy that the undamaged original might have lacked. It disturbed her, this aesthetic response to wounds that should have inspired nothing but pity.

"It's worrying, isn't it?" Tonks said. "When it makes them more beautiful."

She was surprised he'd detected her uneasiness, particularly since it had been partly sexual. Sex was inescapable here. All the patients were young, some hardly more than boys. You knew, just looking at them, that they lay awake at night wondering what their chances of getting a girl were, now, in their altered state. Tonks, they trusted. He was gentle with them, fatherly, all the things Tonks was never given any credit for being. They didn't trust her: she was dangerous.

By midmorning, she was exhausted. Tonks took her back to his room and started to explain the filing system. Some of the patients' files were almost book length. It wasn't unusual, Tonks said, for the number of operations to reach double figures. Twenty, thirty sometimes.

"A life sentence," she said.

"Well, not quite."

"You know, there were times in there when I—I just couldn't understand what I was looking at."

"I can help you with that." He waited for a reply. "I wasn't disappointed, you know. Not in the least. In fact, I think you did remarkably well."

"My drawings were rubbish."

"There's some room for improvement, but they certainly weren't rubbish."

Praise from Tonks was so rare she felt a gush of school-girlish pleasure. Only later, walking down the main corridor, did she realize how bizarrely inappropriate that response was. Drawing, here, was not about self-expression; there was no room for vanity. No room for individual style, even. But no, that wasn't quite true. However subordinated to the surgeons' need for precision and accuracy Tonks's drawings might be, they were nevertheless unmistakably his.

She felt exposed walking down the corridor alone. It was a relief to reach the dining room, where a pot of weak tea and two slices of bread and jam did something to revive her, though chewing and swallowing seemed to have become hard work, as if she too lacked the basic equipment for the task.

Two nurses were talking at the next table: pink-faced, excited, bursting into giggles—it was something about a party they'd been to last weekend. The banging and clattering of pans in the kitchen cut off more than half the words, but she was fascinated by their faces and, above all, their eyes, the way the speaker glanced at her friend, checking she had her full attention, and then effortlessly, unselfconsciously looked away. The listener looked at her friend more directly and for longer periods, now and then she made interested noises, but it was mainly that steady gaze that said: Yes, go on. Then it was the other girl's turn to speak and the complex pas de deux of glances began again, but with the roles reversed.

That was what you forgot on the wards: how to look at people. To begin with, Elinor had made the mistake of gazing at the patients almost unblinkingly, afraid that any turning away might be interpreted as revulsion. But nobody stares at another person like that: it's a threat. And so she'd tried to work out a more natural way of looking. No movement of the eyes was innocent here. Watching the two nurses, she realized how fatuous the attempt had been. Even if you worked out exactly what those girls were doing it wouldn't help you in the least, because the interplay of glances had to be spontaneous, and on these wards you left spontaneity behind you at the door.

Before going back to the wards, she went to the small cloakroom next door, bit her lips and patted her cheeks to give herself a little color, before running a comb through her hair. Even this small amount of prinking and preening seemed obscene. But she needed to summon up her courage and these small, familiar routines did help a little. She was going to see Kit. From the beginning, she'd intended to see him again as soon as she was free, but now the moment had arrived she felt nervous.

Ward Nineteen, they told her in reception. It took her five minutes of clumping along wooden walkways to get there. Two nurses who were busy filling water jugs looked up as she entered. Rather warily, Elinor thought; probably afraid she was about to have hysterics at the sight of the man she'd promised to marry.

"I'm looking for Mr. Neville," she said. "I'm sorry, I know it's not visiting time yet, but I'm working with Mr. Tonks and this is really the only time I can get away. And Mr. Neville . . . well, he's an old family friend. He served with my brother."

That did the trick.

"He's along at the end there. Don't stay too long though, will you, he's not so good today."

Kit was propped up on three pillows. The fact that he'd been allowed to stay in bed at all meant he must be quite seriously ill. She sat down beside the bed. There was plenty of time to look at him, because his eyes were closed; he seemed to be unaware of her presence.

"Kit." She touched his hand. His skin was clammy; she

was tempted to wipe her fingers clean on the sheet. Beads of sweat had gathered on his forehead and in the creases of his neck. Every breath rasped. She watched his chest rise and fall, rise and fall, pleading silently: *Don't die, you're not allowed to die. Yet.*

He was muttering to himself. She'd leaned forward till she could feel each laboring breath on her face, but the words made very little sense. "Padre"—she got that; and she was almost sure the next word was "precious."

"What's precious?" she asked.

And then there was a flood of words. She made out "arsenic," "bedbugs," "beetroot."

Beetroot?

"Don't be too hard on them," he said, clearly.

"Kit, I don't understand."

He opened his eyes. "I'm so glad you could come," he said, in the fluting tones of Lady Bracknell welcoming guests to her garden party. A second later the muttering started again. There was something about baths and . . . fumigation, was it? Then, very clearly again, "Direct hit, sir. Four chickens dead."

He started to giggle, but then suddenly frowned and turned away. "Water."

He was trying to reach a jug on the other side of the bed. Elinor walked round, poured a glass, and held it to his lips, feeling a queasy mixture of pity and revulsion as he drank. He seemed to be drifting off, but then, just as she felt she'd lost him altogether, he roused himself and saw her, probably for the first time.

He said, coldly, "Oh, Elinor, it's you."

"How are you?"

"Been traveling all day. Never seem to get anywhere, though. I think we're going round in circles half the time."

Nothing after that. He was either unconscious or asleep. She went on sitting by the bed, a lump of disappointment stuck in the middle of her chest.

"Elinor. It is Elinor, isn't it?"

She looked up. "Mrs. Neville."

"Oh, I'm so pleased you've come to see him."

They touched cheeks. "I work here now," Elinor said. That decision seemed to have been taken; she couldn't remember when. "I wasn't sure if he'd want visitors . . ."

"No, well, he says he doesn't, but I think it's better for him to see people, don't you?"

Mrs. Neville couldn't take her eyes off Kit's face. As soon as Elinor stepped to one side, she went and stood beside him, kissing his brow and stroking his cheek and chest. What must it be like to have your son reduced to this?

"I've asked Catherine to come. She's having supper with us tomorrow night. Such a nice girl . . ."

Kit was tossing his head on the pillow. Perhaps he'd recognized his mother's voice and was trying to wake up.

"There but for the grace of God and all that bollocks."

The words slurred, became a river of sludge, and then, unexpectedly, two words: "Doc" and, a second later, "Brooke." Kit was working his mouth in a curious circular movement, as if he were chewing. "It wasn't my fault, he knew the risks."

It was tantalizing; he seemed to be on the verge of saying something about Toby, and yet she had to leave. His mother needed time alone with her son.

"Good-bye, Kit," she said. "See you again soon."

His sour breath reached her. "Drawn by bloody Tonks. What a fate."

He started to laugh, coughed, and went into such a paroxysm of coughing that he began to choke. A nurse came running over and together she and Mrs. Neville hauled him into a sitting position. The nurse thumped him on the back. His eyes were streaming; he was sucking in great shuddering breaths. When they were sure the fit had passed, they lowered him, gently, onto the pillows.

"You his sister?"

"Friend. He seems to have a very bad infection."

"Yes, well, they do tend to get them, when everything's wide open like that. Don't you worry, though, he'll pull through."

Elinor had reached the door of the hut when she almost collided with a man who was hurrying in. Kit's father. She wouldn't have detained him, but he seemed to want to talk. Perhaps he dreaded these meetings with his son almost as much as he longed for them.

"One good thing, we got the letter confirming Kit's been commissioned as a war artist. I mean, we knew he had, but . . ."

"He'll be pleased."

"Mind, I can't think why it took them so long. Far less talented people—"

He stopped abruptly; she realized he was thinking of Paul.

"Well, I'd better be getting on," she said. "I've got to get back to work."

"You work here now?"

"Yes, not as a nurse, I'm an illustrator. Well, hardly even that really, I've only just started."

"You'll be able to look in on him, then."

"Yes, well, I hope so."

"It's going to be a long job."

He was so stiff, so stoical in his bearing, it came as a shock to see tears in his eyes.

"He's been so brave, nobody knows how brave he's been."

Ashamed of witnessing his tears, she patted him clumsily

on the arm, and said good-bye. She watched him walk the length of the ward and stand at the foot of Kit's bed, twirling his hat round and round in his hands, looking lost, abandoned, as if he, rather than the new patients, needed a luggage label to tell him where he was.

20

Catherine stood at the window with her back turned to Paul. "I went home, you know. The other week."

"Home?" For a moment his mind was blank.

"Lowestoft. I walked along the beach and fortunately it was really foul weather so I wrapped a scarf round my face and pulled my hat down—and nobody recognized me. I'd have liked to go and see the house, look in the windows, but . . . I didn't dare. I was frightened the whole time."

"You should have asked me. I'd have gone with you."

"No, I needed to go alone. It's extraordinary, the whole town seems to be surrounded by barbed wire, all the bridges were guarded but of course it's the nearest point in England to the Continent so it's bound to be like that, I suppose."

Paul handed her a cup of tea. He still didn't know why she'd come. They sat on the sofa with a plate of biscuits between them.

"Mrs. Neville's asked me to go and see Kit."

"Why don't you? I'm sure he'd love to see you."

"I'm not sure it's coming from him. Oh, she means well, but, you know, she's frantic with worry and I think she's trying to push him to see people when perhaps he's not ready. What do you think?"

Paul shrugged. "He certainly wasn't ready to see Elinor. Or me. But then . . ."

"Yes?"

"You were closer to him than we were."

"For a time. No, at one point we were very close."

"What do you *want* to do?"

"I'd like to see him before I leave London."

"You're leaving?"

"I thought I might go back to Scotland."

She was looking at him, waiting for a response. "You've got work here," he said. "And friends." He didn't know what he felt, except that relief was part of it.

"It's easier up there. You don't feel the same . . . hatred." She laughed. "Probably because we don't see anybody."

"Is it really as bad as that?"

"I think so. Do you know Olive Schreiner?"

"Not personally, no. Of her."

"Well, she was staying at Durrant's Hotel, in George Street, you know? And they asked her to leave—not because they thought she was German, they knew she was South African, but because the other guests might *think* she was German. You get little pinpricks like that all the time."

He remained silent.

"Paul? What are you thinking?"

"I'm thinking there are worse things than being chucked out of a hotel. Like ending up in a hole in the ground with your guts draped round your neck."

"It's not a contest, though, is it? The suffering."

"Do you know, I sometimes think it is."

A long silence. Then she said, "I don't think I could bear not to be friends with you." She reached out and took hold of his hand.

"Only it's never going to be more than that, is it?"

"There's Elinor . . ."

"And Kit. Don't forget Kit. As if any of us could."

This was why she'd come: to end something that had barely begun. And he was in danger of trying to pull her back, but without really believing that their incipient love affair stood a chance. At the back of his mind was the image of the two girls entwined on the sofa, impossibly conjoined: Siamese twins, though there was no doubt which twin was dominant. Elinor, every time.

He reached a decision. "I think you should go to see him."

"Do you?" she said, withdrawing her hand. "I'll think about it. And now I think I should go."

At the door she turned. There might have been a kiss—he was hoping there would be—but at the last moment she smiled and shook her head.

———

Elinor traveled back to London on a jolting train full of vacant-eyed passengers staring at advertisements. A ruddy-faced young soldier stood up and offered her his seat. She thanked him, aware of his admiration, of his body, even, as she had not been aware of any man, including Paul, for a long time.

She really needed to talk to Paul, but it was difficult. After their joint visit to Kit, they hadn't parted friends. But he wouldn't turn her away; he never had. She'd go to see him now, she decided; chance his not being in.

It was a weary climb up the hill to his lodgings. She knocked loudly several times, and was about to peer through the letter box when the door was suddenly flung open and a dark woman with spots of hectic color on her cheeks stood there, her arms folded aggressively across her chest.

"What do *you* want?"

"I'd like to speak to Mr. Tarrant, please."

"Oh, I expect you would, you and half a dozen others."

She marched across the hall and yelled up the stairs, "Tarrant, there's another one!" She turned to Elinor. "No doubt he'll be down in a minute, he's keen enough, God knows."

With a sniff and a flounce she went back inside her own living room and slammed the door. For a moment the house was silent, though not peaceful. Even the dust motes, visible in the circle of light round a lamp, seemed to seethe with suppressed anger. Elinor looked around. The house was shabby and not particularly clean. The stair rods were speckled brown; some of them were missing altogether, so the carpet bulged dangerously over the treads. Somewhere in the shadows at the back of the hall, a clock ticked.

At last, she heard a door open and shortly afterwards Paul came limping down the stairs.

He stopped dead when he saw her. "Elinor."

"Were you expecting somebody else?"

"No. What makes you think that?"

"Just something your landlady said."

From behind the landlady's door came the sound of a tenor voice, swelling: *You are the cutest thing* . . . "Oh, for God's sake, if I hear that bloody song one more time today . . ." She looked at Paul. "Do you mind if I come up?"

"No, of course not, though . . ." He jerked his head towards the music. "It's not popular."

"She's in quite a state, isn't she?"

He mouthed: "I think I might have to leave."

Something was wrong, she could feel it, and it wasn't his landlady's mood. Following him up the stairs, she said, "How are you?"

"Oh, you know . . ."

"Work going all right?"

"Yes, in fact I think I might have turned a corner. Mind you, I've thought that before." He was opening his door. "You must've been to the hospital."

"All day. I didn't realize it was going to be like that."

"Threw you in at the deep end?"

"You know Tonks."

"How was it?"

"Hard, really hard."

"Do you think you're going to do it?"

"I'm not sure I *can* do it. But yes, I'll give it a go. Tonks says he'll help, he says I can go back to the Slade, one day a week, if I want. Feels a bit like flying backwards . . ."

"Well, I'm back there. Perhaps there's a bit of elastic round our middles . . ."

"I really hated being on the wards."

"So why do it? You don't have to."

She pulled a face. "You've changed your tune."

"No, really. Why put yourself through it if you don't have to?"

"Can't say no to Tonks?"

She was taking in the room as she spoke. The walls were covered in a dingy yellow paper with an intricate paisley pattern that would have driven her mad in a week. The sofa sagged; he hadn't bothered to add cushions or do anything to soften the bulging disgrace. How on earth could somebody with Paul's eye for line and color live like this?

He took her coat. "Can I get you anything?"

"No, I'm all right, thanks." She smoothed an imaginary crease in her skirt. "I saw Kit today."

"You haven't been pestering him, have you?"

"I don't think he even knew I was there. Thing is, he's developed a chest infection, it doesn't look good."

"But he's not . . . ?"

"I don't know."

"Did you talk to him?"

"I tried, he wasn't making a lot of sense." Quickly, she ran through as many of Kit's ramblings as she could remember.

"There was one moment, he said, 'It wasn't my fault, he knew the risks.' So he does obviously feel guilty about something."

" 'He'? Not 'Toby'?"

She shrugged.

"So you don't know who he was talking about."

"Toby. Who else?"

"Anybody else. Half the bloody army, more or less."

"No, you're not listening. You don't say, 'It wasn't my fault' unless you've got a pretty good reason to think it might be."

He was shaking his head. "Elinor, we all feel guilty. Everybody who survives."

"Do you?"

"Every minute of every day."

A dragging silence.

"You don't understand," he said, patting his pockets in search of a cigarette. "And it's not your fault, I'm not blaming you. But the fact that he feels guilty—*if* he does—means absolutely nothing. And anyway you shouldn't be listening to what he says when he's off his head."

"I didn't go on purpose. I was drawing somebody on the ward. What am I supposed to do? Walk past?"

Now she was lying. But only because he made her feel she was in the wrong, when she wasn't.

"I don't know about you," he said. "But I could do with a drink."

He was drinking a lot more than he used to. It was only a couple of days since she'd last seen him, but he looked different. Older. Harder. Or perhaps she hadn't noticed the changes before. Still, in every way that mattered, the same old Paul. She thought: *I've missed you.*

"What's the matter with your landlady?"

"Doesn't approve of lady guests." He produced a small bottle of whiskey from a cupboard under the sink. "Oh, and . . ." He contemplated the end of the sentence and evidently decided against it. "I don't know."

"How many are there? Lady guests?"

"Catherine was here earlier, that's all."

"Two young ladies in one day." She was smiling as she took a sip from her glass. "Bluebeard."

"Oh, hardly that."

"What's going on? Between you and Catherine?"

"Nothing's going on."

"You like her, though, don't you?"

"Yes, I do, I've always liked her."

"Come on, Paul."

"I don't know what you want me to say. After that weekend, you know, there didn't seem to be a lot left between us. So when I bumped into Catherine I asked her if she'd like to go out with me. We went, I enjoyed it, I think she did too, and then . . . Well. Basically she thinks I'm not over you."

"And are you?"

"Does it matter?"

She forced the last of the whiskey down. "I think I should be going. Is that the only reason your landlady's fed up?"

He shrugged. "It's a long story."

"And you don't want to boast."

He insisted on coming with her to the front door, though she wished he hadn't. She needed to get away from him now. In the hall, they stood facing each other. The question: To kiss or not to kiss? In the end, they brushed each other's cheeks with closed lips. Wrong choice. Worse than a handshake; worse than nothing. The awkwardness was almost unbearable.

"Well . . ." she started to say.

At that moment, the landlady's door was thrown open.

"You'd better get off, if you're going. It's not a station waiting room, you know."

"We are going," Paul said.

He pulled Elinor out of the house onto the pavement. A strangled sound, half sob, half derisive laugh, and then the door banged shut behind them.

"How do you put up with it?" Elinor said. "It's like living in Wuthering Heights."

He didn't smile, just went on looking concerned. "Will you be all right?"

"Good heavens, *yes*." The slight irritation she felt freed her to go and she turned to walk away.

He caught hold of her arm. "Look, you don't want this, I don't want it, what are we doing?"

"You want Catherine."

"No, I don't, honestly, I don't. If anything I want the two of you together."

"*What?* Paul, I can't believe you said that."

If his expression was anything to go by, neither could he. "At least, let me walk you home. I can't go back in there anyway."

"'Fraid she'll gobble you up?" Her expression softened. "You're going to get soaked."

It was starting to rain. They linked arms; she felt him shivering through his thin shirt.

"Come on," he said. "If we walk quickly . . ."

By the end of the street, the rain had thickened to a downpour and was bouncing off the pavements. Flitting along between the streetlamps, they were blotched into a single shadow. His trousers, her skirt, were quickly soaked to the knee. Outside Catherine's door, they looked up at the light, at the silver lines that slanted away into the darkness.

"Why don't you come up?"

"Catherine might be in."

"And that bothers you?" She seemed to regret the sharpness. "No, please, I'd like to talk to you."

"I thought we had."

"No, properly. About the hospital. I promise I won't mention Kit."

A heavier squall of rain settled the matter. It would be madness to walk back in this. He stood shivering and wiping his eyes as she unlocked the door to let them in.

21

Rain beating down on Queen's Hospital, peppering the rhododendrons in the formal gardens, shaking the last petals from a rose.

A nurse emerges from one of the huts, peers up into the lowering sky, and runs, stiff-legged, splashing through puddles, to the shelter of the main building.

The windows of the hut are blind with rain. "Bloody hell, will you look at that," somebody says, but though several men glance up from their card game, nobody bothers to comment.

Neville, in bed, dozing, is only half aware of the gust of wind that slams doors shut and blows dead leaves along the slippery walkways. His eyes flicker behind his closed lids.

Rain gleams on the capes of a party of stretcher bearers preparing to go out, drips from their helmets, drives pale furrows in their mud-daubed skin. Their eyeballs, in the darkness of the trench, appear unnaturally big and bright.

Brooke's voice, echoing around the hut, along the covered walkway, and into the formal garden where a pale mulch of rose petals half covers the wet soil, says:

"Right, then. Off we go."

———

He was lying naked on the side of a shell hole when they got to him. The blast had blown off almost all his clothes. He was curled up, comma-shaped, like a newborn baby who hasn't yet cast off the constriction of the womb. Deep, black night. A prickle of stars; no moon. They'd been crawling on their bellies through mud for a hundred years and were close, now, to the German trenches. The bottom of the crater was flooded: oily, iridescent swirls catching the faint light of the stars. Then, for a long, long moment, the whole scene was brilliantly illuminated as a Very light went up and hung, trembling, in the black sky. Like a rich jewel in an Ethiop's ear. Odd little tatters of words and phrases blew through his brain, nothing to do with anything that was happening here.

They slipped and slithered over the rim down to where Warren lay, coiled in his fetal dream. Neville noticed that Brooke didn't bother to check for a pulse. They rolled Warren onto his back. Rain fell steadily onto his face, but he didn't blink or turn his head away. It was strange to crouch beside him, watching the Very lights bloom and die in his dead eyes.

They were going to have to drag him all the way. The fighting had been too fierce to allow chivalrous gestures to the stretcher bearers of either side. The rain became heavier, bouncing on the black surface of the water. They tried to get a grip on him, but their numbed hands slid across his naked flesh and they had to fasten a rope round his waist before they could begin dragging him, against gravity, away from the stinking water and up to the crater's edge. They crouched there for a moment, waiting for another Very light to die. Neville could see Brooke's cheekbones gleaming like a skull.

"Come on," Brooke said. "If they fire, they fire."

Slowly, infinitely slowly, they started to drag Warren back to their own lines. It must have taken thirty minutes or more, but though firing continued, causing every muscle to jerk, nobody seemed to be firing specifically at them. They crawled through the gap in their wire, with a further delay when the few remaining shreds of Warren's tunic snagged on one of the barbs. Boiler reached behind and tore it free. And then they were clambering, falling rather, into the trench in a great gush splother cascade of mud and water and for a minute Neville just sat there, wiping mud out of his eyes, but then he couldn't be bothered to do even that, he just let it drip.

Brooke was already on his feet.

"Come on," he said, sharply. They heaved Warren onto the stretcher and set off along the crowded trench, Boiler at the front calling out "*Beep-beep!*" to secure a passage. He seemed to have no nerves, Boiler. No nerves, no manners, no eyelashes, no bloody nothing, but still he survived. Stuck a tab end in his mouth, squinted through the smoke, foul-mouthed, fond of dirty jokes, laughed among the dying without a care in the world, apparently. Sentimental, though, about horses and mules.

At the back of the stretcher, Neville's hands were rubbed raw, his thoughts scattered like pins. All he could think was: *I mustn't let him drop.* And then he wanted to laugh, because what the hell did it matter whether they dropped him or not? Warren was past caring. Out of the front line they trudged, down the communication trenches, jam-packed with men crowding up for the counterattack, bulky figures they were in the darkness, stamping and steaming like horses. Cigarettes everywhere, illuminating a mouth, a hand, an eye.

One more corner and they'd reached the regimental first-aid post. Tarpaulin had been rigged up over the entrance; the walking wounded queued underneath it, teeth chattering in blue faces, blackened wounds oozing blood. The slight wounds attempted jokes, but jerked like the others as a shell whizzed over.

Boiler pushed through the crowd, down the steps to the dugout, where they set the stretcher down. Neville flexed his raw fingers and then, suddenly, in a great explosion of rage, kicked Warren in the ribs. The shock as his boot made contact traveled all the way up his body and reverberated inside his brain.

Brooke turned on him. "What the hell do you think you're doing?"

"What do I think I'm doing? You just risked four men's lives for a corpse."

"Orders. We were ordered to get him back and we did." He glanced at the other stretcher bearers and lowered his voice. "Look, I know you're having a rough time but it's no easier for the rest of us."

Pointless saying anything. Anyway, all he wanted to do was sleep. The others were hunkered down against a wall, their hands hanging between their knees.

"Right," Brooke said. "I want you to go across to C Company. They could do with a bit of help."

He was gone before anybody could speak. Boiler began swearing steadily, inventively, under his breath. He was a great big bullyboy on the surface, but too used to doing what his betters told him to *really* protest. Not Neville. He pushed through the crowd into the back room, the operating theater, if you could call it that. The low ceiling was hung with lamps, and despite the stench of blood, the place had a curious seedy glamour about it, halfway between a nightclub and an abattoir. Brooke was scrubbing his hands while two orderlies heaved a bleeding lump of meat onto the table.

"Captain Brooke, sir."

He was always correct, even formal, in front of the others. Brooke wiped his face on his sleeve, looking at Neville with smears of blood around his eyes.

"You can't just lend them out like that. They're absolutely bloody knackered. Look at Wilkie, he's dead on his feet."

"That was an order."

They stared at each other. For a moment the prospect of head-on collision loomed, then Neville turned on his heel and went back into the other room. "Come on, lads." He dragged Wilkie to his feet, pushed the gas curtain aside, and went out into the night.

———

Somewhere a tenor voice was singing: *They didn't believe me, they didn't believe me . . .*

Well, no, Neville thought, struggling to sit up in bed. Who the fuck would?

He could kill for a cigarette. Instead, he lay with his eyes closed, his mind ranging back through the furthest reaches of his dream. Lending them to another company when they were on their knees with exhaustion. Even now, looking back, he didn't believe it.

That was the moment, he thought. After that, Brooke was the enemy.

———

Gillies settled one buttock on the edge of his bed. "You're looking a lot better."

"Oh. Grown back, has it?"

"Now then."

Why did everybody in this fucking hospital talk to you as if you were three years old? "I just need to get out of this place. It's driving me insane."

"You are allowed out, you know. It's not a prison."

"Could I go into London?"

"I'd try a walk round the grounds first."

"And the operation?"

"Well, that was a very nasty infection you had. I'm afraid the first thing I'm going to have to do is remove the pedicle . . ."

"*Remove* it?"

"It hasn't taken. In fact it'll slough off by itself in a few days—"

"You mean, you have to start again?"

"Afraid so. Things might look a bit worse initially . . ."

"You keep saying that."

"I know, I'm sorry."

"Ah, well."

After Gillies had gone, Neville sat looking round the ward, from face to face to face. Once, he and Brooke had watched some young officers, newly arrived from England, using beetroots on poles for target practice. Shouts of "How-zat?" when somebody smashed the beetroot head to pieces. "Idiots," he'd said. But Brooke shook his head. "Don't be too hard on them. They'll learn, soon enough."

Suddenly Neville pushed back the bedclothes and swung his feet onto the floor. When he first tried to stand he went dizzy and toppled back onto the bed. Getting dressed took the best part of an hour, but he managed it at last.

Staggering down the ward, he encountered his nemesis, Sister Lang-*widge!* Wasn't really called that, of course, but so far he'd managed not to learn her name.

"Where do you think you're going, Mr. Neville?"

"Mr. Gillies says I have to have fresh air."

And besides, you fucking ugly cow, he mouthed at her retreating back, *I need a cigarette.*

22

They're letting me out, Neville's note had said:

Just for one evening but it's a start. There's nobody I
would rather spend my first evening of freedom with
than you, my dear fellow. So, if you're agreeable, I
could pick you up from the Slade this Thursday at
half past six. I believe you still work office hours? Of
course if you'd prefer not to be seen with me, I shall
quite understand . . .

———

Since when had he been Neville's "dear fellow"? Neville
must have many friends closer than Paul whom he could have
arranged to meet, but there again, perhaps not. His capacity
for offending people was legendary. *And* he'd chosen to have
no visitors.

Refusing to be niggled by that sly dig about office hours,
Paul finished work precisely at six, cleaned himself up, and
changed into the uniform he'd brought with him. Even with
a stick and a limp it wasn't wise to be seen on the streets in
civilian dress. He wasn't much looking forward to the evening, but it was the kind—the decent—thing to keep Neville

company on his first venture into London. They'd find some back room in a pub somewhere and talk, he supposed, about painting. Now that Neville had been commissioned as a war artist, painting was, once again, a safe topic. And then, duty done, he could pour Neville onto the Sidcup train, and go home.

Neville was waiting near the reception desk. He was not in uniform, which surprised Paul a little, until he reflected that Neville had his face to vouch for him. Standing there in the shadows, like that, he became a figure of menace. Paul wished he would move, look round, say something, and yet, as Neville turned towards him, he had to brace himself for his second sight of that face.

Nothing. That was the first impression. A featureless, silvery oval hovering in the half-darkness, as if a deranged, wandering moon had somehow strayed into the building. Then he understood: Neville was wearing a mask.

"My God."

"Yes, my son?" Neville came across and shook hands. "Oh, come on, Tarrant, how often do you say that and get an answer?"

"I'm sorry, it's . . . a bit of a shock."

Paul was still struggling to take it in. The mask was beautifully made, expressionless, of course, except for a faint, archaic smile. It reminded him of a kouros, except that they had no individuality, and this most definitely did, though it wasn't a portrait of Neville as he'd once been.

"I borrowed it," Neville said. "It's not mine."

"Well. I'm impressed."

"So you should be. It's an original Ward Muir." He might have been explaining the provenance of some recently acquired painting. "Chap it belongs to—well, no face at all, basically; I don't think even Gillies could do much for him. So off he went to the tin-noses department. The last resort."

"It's beautiful."

"Bloody should be, it's Rupert Brooke."

God, yes, so it was. Now he'd been told, it was obvious.

"Very popular, apparently. The Rupert Brooke."

"But why? Why would you want to look like somebody else?"

Neville shrugged. "Why not? Why not aim for something better? You've got to admit he was absolutely stunning."

"I'm afraid I never met him."

"No, I suppose not . . ."

It was hard to relate to Neville wearing that thing. And though it hid the ruin of the face it also directed the imagination towards it. Paul struggled to find something sufficiently neutral to say. "Is it comfortable?"

"Not really. Fact, if you had to wear it all the time it would be absolutely bloody intolerable." The eyeholes turned towards him. "And if you try to see it from a woman's point of view, what would be the point of kissing *this*?"

Too raw, too intimate. "I don't know."

"No bloody point at all. Better the gargoyle underneath. Well, I'd have thought so, wouldn't you?"

His voice was shaking with anger and pain. Suddenly, Paul realized that behind the mask anything was possible: Neville could say—and quite possibly do—*anything*. Immediately, Paul's nervousness about the evening increased; he compensated by trying to get the conversation back onto more mundane topics. "How do you drink through it?"

"Straw." Neville produced one from his inside pocket. "Bet you've never drunk whiskey through a straw, have you?"

"No, I don't believe I have."

They walked to the Rose and Crown and sat in the back room, attracting sidelong glances, though Neville kept his hat on and pulled the scarf well up to his chin. As he drank, snuffles and slobbering came from behind the mask, but it certainly didn't impede his intake: whiskey was running up the straw like lemonade on a hot day.

"Hey, take it easy. We've got all night."

"I have absolutely no bloody fucking intention whatsobloodyever of 'taking it easy.' A brass monkey would drink if it had my life."

A moment later, though, he settled back into his chair and looked around the room. Nobody returned his gaze.

"I've been meaning to congratulate you," Paul said.

"What on, exactly?"

"Becoming a war artist."

"Been one for years. Didn't need a bloody government committee to . . ."

"Will you be able to paint?"

"Not if I stay in that dump, no. I could if they let me out."

Another brooding silence. Paul said, quickly, "Elinor says she went to see you."

"So I believe. Mother said she'd been, but I don't remember. Probably talked a whole load of bloody rubbish . . ."

Paul felt his tension through the mask. "She said you were talking about something precious, but she couldn't make out what it was."

" 'Precious'?" He shook his head. "Oh, wait a minute, yes, the Padre was Precious. I mean, his name was Precious. He certainly wasn't—perfectly dreadful little man. Brooke hated him. And for once Brooke was right."

"Why?"

"Why did he hate him? Oh, I don't know, they kept having stupid arguments. About—well, one of the things was books. We had a stock of books we used to hand out to the men. You know, penny dreadfuls, shilling shockers, that kind of thing, nothing that would raise an eyebrow really. But oh, my God, you should have heard Precious on the subject, you'd have thought we were passing round dirty postcards.

And then there was syphilis. 'The Bad Disorder,' Precious insisted on calling it. He thought the solution was for the men to find Jesus, tie a knot in it, basically. Brooke thought the answer was this stuff you were supposed to paint on your willy if you'd been a naughty boy. Dyed it bright blue." He put his glass down. "Not much of a choice really, is it? Bible-thumping or a blue dick."

"And Brooke . . . couldn't leave it alone?"

"Brooke couldn't leave anything alone."

He was looking towards the bar as he spoke. Paul drained his glass. "Do you want another or shall we move on?"

"Move on, for God's sake, let's get out of here."

Standing up, Neville knocked over a chair and set it clumsily to rights. Paul heard him breathing heavily as they walked across the room. As they reached the door, an old man with muculent blue eyes stood up and solemnly shook Neville's hand. As if this had been a prearranged signal, a ripple of applause spread around the room.

"Christ, that was embarrassing," Neville said, as the door swung shut behind them.

"People want to show their respect, that's all."

"No, they don't, they want us out of sight. You should hear Gillies on the subject. And Tonks. When they were in Aldershot there used to be a weekly parade, patients in uniform, brass band, flags, whole bloody works . . . It was supposed to give a grateful nation the chance to say thank you. Three bars of 'Tipperary' and the streets were empty."

They'd set off to walk, but now, unexpectedly, Neville veered out into the road and hailed a cab.

"Where are we going?" Paul asked.

"The Café Royal."

"Is that a—?"

But Neville was already inside the cab. Paul followed him in and gave the address. A sharp intake of breath from the driver as he turned and saw the mask, but his response was calm, if unpredictable.

"I had him in my cab once."

"Who?" Neville asked.

"Rupert Brooke. He was good, him. 'There's some corner of a foreign field / That is for ever England.'"

"That would be the bit with my nose under it; just fucking drive, will you?"

Conversation was at an end. Shoulders stiff with offense, the driver turned his attention to the road ahead.

"Christ," Neville said. "If there's one thing I hate it's cab-drivers who think they have to be characters."

"Yes, but let's face it, Neville, there aren't many people you don't hate."

Paul leaned back and closed his eyes. He dreaded walking into the Café Royal with Neville in this state, but there seemed to be no hope of deflecting him.

"I'm having second thoughts about this," Neville said.

"What?"

He tapped his metal cheek. "This. The mask."

"Looks all right."

"Doesn't bloody feel all right."

Outside the Café Royal, Neville insisted on paying the fare, but ended by scattering coins all over the pavement. An elderly man who bent down to help pick them up got the mask thrust full into his face, and hurried away, with a final incredulous glance over his shoulder.

"I'll get it," Paul said, reaching for his wallet. As he paid, he saw Neville bracing himself to enter the building. It moved him, that small, private act of courage. He reached out and touched Neville's shoulder. "You'll be all right, you know. They're all friends."

"I have no friends."

Outside the Domino Room, Neville hung back; it was

Paul who pushed open the door and walked in. Treading on his heels, Neville stumbled and almost fell. Paul found a table near the entrance and ordered whiskeys, but it was a minute or two before he felt able to look around. Once again they were the center of attention, though nobody openly stared.

Despite Neville's frequent, self-pitying assertions that he was finished as an artist, overlooked, forgotten, yesterday's man, his return to London had been reported in all the papers, though nothing had been said about the nature or severity of his wounds. But he was known to be at Queen's Hospital, so the injuries had to be facial. The rumors had begun almost at once. Some people said he was so hideously disfigured his own mother had run screaming from the room; others that his brain was affected too, that he was either mad or a cabbage. And now here he was, or here somebody was. Neville's thickset figure and truculent bearing were almost enough to identify him, but not quite. People glanced at the mask and quickly away. Was it him? It had to be, but nobody was confident enough to come forward and speak to him. The mask didn't help: Rupert Brooke's face gazing around a room where he'd so often lorded it in the flesh. Enough to give you the shivers.

Neville was on his fifth whiskey. Paul expected him to become even more aggressive, but instead he sank into a morose stupor, peering through the slits in the mask at scenes of former triumph. Two or three years ago, he'd have walked into this room as if he owned it. Paul remembered meeting him here: Neville, the famous war artist, whose latest exhibition was on everybody's lips, and he felt a flicker of shameful pleasure at the reversal of their fortunes; a mean, filthy emotion, quickly suppressed.

The silence had gone on too long. He tried to find a topic of conversation that would rouse Neville from his stupor, but nothing worked. He either couldn't, or wouldn't, speak.

Instead, he sat staring round the room, the silver face of the dead poet turning from group to group. Gradually, uncertainly, a few people began to respond, raising their glasses, smiling ghost smiles at what must have seemed, to most of them, a ghost. Suddenly, Paul realized they weren't sure Neville or whoever it was behind the mask could see them. Nothing was visible behind the slits in the mask and he'd stumbled when he first came into the room. A large group at a nearby table fell silent for a time, but then, slowly, the conversation started up again. They were talking about an exhibition that included three of Paul's paintings. Some at least of the group must have recognized him, but nobody spoke; the cordon sanitaire round Neville obviously included him too. They were still, covertly, the focus for every eye in the room.

The mask went on smiling its faint, archaic smile. Behind it, an eye like a dying sun sank beneath the rim of a shattered cheekbone, the hole where the nose had been gaped wide and the mouth endlessly, tirelessly snarled. Neville was clenching and unclenching his fists. "Bastards, I'll bury the whole fucking lot of them."

"Calm down . . ."

"Why? Why should I calm down? Two years ago they were queuing up to lick my arse and now look at them . . ."

"They don't know what to say, that's all."

He didn't know what to say. More important, he didn't know what to do, how to get them out of this situation. He turned to Neville. "Look, why don't we—"

Suddenly, without any warning, Neville began to roar, the bellow of a wounded bull with the full force of his lungs behind it. Paul tried to grab his arm, but he was too late: Neville was on his feet. He waited till every eye in the room was fixed on him, and then he took off the mask.

One or two people cried out. Others were blank with shock. Instinctively, Paul stepped in front of Neville, though whether to shield him from their reactions or them from the sight of him, he didn't know. He thought nothing could have been more terrible than that roaring, but then Neville started to cry, a puppy howl of abandonment and loss. Paul put an arm round his shoulders and managed to turn him towards the door. "Come on," he kept saying, "it's all right, come on," the way he would have spoken to a distraught child or a frightened horse.

Neville let himself be led from the room. By the time they reached the pavement he'd stopped crying, though his chest still shook. And then, to Paul's utter bewilderment, he started to laugh.

"Did you see their faces? Oh, my God . . ."

Paul didn't know how to respond to this. He knew—if he knew anything at all, he knew this—that every part of Neville's anger and distress had been genuine. The brooding, the resentment, the rage, the "*Look at me!*" of the abandoned child or the slighted artist, the tears, the sobbing . . . It had all been real. Surely it had? And yet Neville's laughter, now, seemed to deny that. He realized Neville was already hard at work reshaping the events of the evening, carving out for himself, if only in retrospect, a position of authority and control. That was Neville all over: a fat, moist silkworm perpetually spinning the legend of himself.

And it worked. It worked. Paul had already started to edit his own memories of the evening. Perhaps Neville had always intended that dramatic sweeping aside of the mask; perhaps he'd got drunk in order to be able to do it. Perhaps. But none of that justified his behavior.

"Well, that was pretty grim," Paul said, tight-lipped.

"My dear fellow, blame the mask. This is a mask of known bad character. Chap who owns it goes on the Underground, waits till there's a few girls sitting nearby, and then takes it off. Comes back to the ward, holds up his fingers." Neville held up his own hand to demonstrate. "How many screamed. How many fainted. There aren't many faints, but he has had two." He seemed to sense Paul's disapproval. "Oh, for God's sake, Tarrant, it's a *game*."

"It's a terrible game."

"You get your laughs where you can." He walked on a few steps. Turned back. "Do you know, Tarrant, you're no fun at all tonight."

"Sorry about that."

"I'm making the most of it, I won't be able to wear it after the next op. Trunk gets in the way. Pedicle, sorry."

"Well count me out next time."

Paul could feel Neville's anger, which up to now had been directed impartially at everybody they met, narrowing to a point and focusing on him.

"You're going out with Catherine, aren't you?" he said.

"No."

"What's the point of denying it? Mother told me. And Catherine told her."

"We had supper once and went to a concert."

"Hmm."

"What does 'hmm' mean?"

"Elinor. Catherine."

"Yes?"

"My girlfriends first, then yours. You seem to have some sort of morbid desire to slide in on my leavings."

This was so offensive, and in so many different ways, that Paul was speechless. Neville had *not* had an affair with Elinor. Catherine . . . ? Well, yes, possibly, he didn't know. But Elinor, definitely not.

He said, evenly, "This is where I punch you on the nose, isn't it? Oops, sorry, you haven't got one."

The words opened a gap between them that it seemed

nothing could ever fill, and yet, a second later, Neville laughed and threw a heavy arm across Paul's shoulder.

"You know I don't mean it."

"No, I don't know."

"We should be friends."

"Yeah, well, you don't make it easy."

"I know." He patted Paul awkwardly on the arm. "Come on, I'd better be getting back. If I'm late they mightn't let me out again."

Please, God.

There were no cabs in sight so they started to walk. After the way Neville had behaved that evening, Paul felt justified in saying anything he wanted to say. "Why didn't you reply to Elinor's letters? You did get them, didn't you?"

"Nothing I could say."

"That bad?"

"I think so."

They walked on, pausing now and then to look for cabs, but none appeared. Neville was setting a cracking pace. Paul was quickly out of breath and his leg had started to bother him.

"I will tell you," Neville said. "Just don't push me—I've got enough on my plate at the moment. Another bloody operation for starters . . ."

This was so obviously true that Paul couldn't bring himself to argue. A few yards farther on, Neville succeeded in flagging down a cab. The driver was mercifully free of poetic associations and so they traveled to Charing Cross in virtual silence.

As the train to Sidcup left, Paul stood on the platform watching its blue-tinged lights disappear into the darkness. After it had gone, he sat on one of the benches, massaging the muscles of his injured leg. Memories of the evening: the mask, the Café Royal, the shocked faces turning towards them, buzzed around his head until he was too exhausted to think anymore. Then he simply sat, staring at the humming lines, blank and motionless, as if a piece had been cut out of his brain.

23

The northern light flooding in through the high windows was pitiless, but not more so than Tonks's gaze. He was still at the table selecting pastels from a tray, but now and then he stopped to look at Neville, who felt his injuries had never been more cruelly exposed than in this glaring light.

Partly to distract attention from himself, Neville nodded at the wall of portraits behind Tonks's chair.

"I suppose I'm joining the Rogues' Gallery, am I?"

"That's the general idea."

"Do I have to?"

"I'm sorry, I—"

"I mean, can I refuse?"

"You're in the army, Mr. Neville. What do you think?"

Neville shrugged. "What's it for, anyway?"

"It's to help Gillies work out how to restore an aesthetically pleasing appearance—"

"*Restore?* Huh. Not sure I ever had one."

"I've known people say they come out looking better than when they went in. One or two of the portraits—"

"Do you mind if I have a look?"

"Not at all."

Neville went across to the wall of framed portraits, his eye moving from one disfigured face to the next. "Very powerful," he said, at last. "Mind, with subjects like that, you could hardly fail, could you? Who sees them?"

"Gillies, the other surgeons. Visitors."

"Visitors?"

"They've become something of a curiosity, I'm afraid. I think it's a bit . . ." He waved a hand in the air.

"Voyeuristic?"

"Distasteful."

"So why do you let it happen?"

"They don't belong to me."

"Pity. They're probably the best things you've done."

"It hardly matters, does it? They can never be shown."

"Mark my words, somebody's going to want to."

"The War Office did ask, I told them I didn't think it was appropriate. There's not much else I can do. As I say, they're not mine."

"Can't imagine why the War Office wants them, anyway. I mean, they're hardly recruiting posters, are they?"

Ignoring Tonks's obvious desire to get on, Neville went on looking at the portraits. The hospital had no looking glasses, no shaving mirrors, even. If you cut yourself, too bloody bad. It was nothing to what the surgeons had in mind. Even the water in the ornamental fountain had been drained, in case some poor deluded Narcissus decided to risk a peep. Of course, people did try to see themselves: in puddles, windows at night, polished taps—even in dessert spoons, though that was a quick route to hell. And yet here, all the time, were these portraits, by the Slade Professor of Fine Art, no less.

"Do *they* see them? The sitters?"

"Patients? No."

"Well, I think that tells us all we need to know."

Neville went back to the window and sat down facing Tonks. "So why am I allowed to see them?"

"Because you're an artist."

"I seem to remember you expressing some doubts about that. Not so very long ago."

No response from Tonks; he'd selected a number of flesh-tinted pastels and was ready to begin.

"Who else is doing this?" Neville asked.

"Daryl Lindsey. Do you know him? Watercolorist. Oh, and Lady Scott. You know, Scott's widow." He peered at Neville's face. "Interesting woman. She was saying how sometimes the injury makes them more beautiful."

"More beautiful?"

"You know, like an Antique sculpture with bits missing."

"No wonder the poor bugger froze to death."

Tonks stopped drawing. "That really is an incredibly offensive remark."

"Is it? Dunno, past caring."

For a moment, Neville was back in the Antiques Room, where his insistence on the pointlessness of copying Classical sculpture had very nearly got him expelled from the Slade. He wondered in passing what he could say or do that would be bad enough to get him thrown out of here. Nothing, probably. He was stuck.

"I went out the other night," he said. "Wearing Tyler's mask. You know about his mask?"

"Yes, there's not a lot they can do for him, so they sent him off to the tin-noses department."

"That's where you go, isn't it, when they've given up?"

"How was it?"

"Interesting. You know, I look round the ward and some of them . . . The number of operations, there's one chap coming up to his twenty-third. Can you imagine that? Twenty-three operations. I used to think: *Bloody hell, why not just cover it up and have done with it?*"

"And now?"

"Don't know. I was talking—well, mainly to Tarrant—and I could see him struggling, because obviously behind the mask there are all kinds of expressions going on, and you forget nobody can see them. As far as other people are concerned, it's like talking to a brick wall." Neville felt himself becoming more and more agitated. The light from the window seemed to be burning his skin. And Tonks's stare, his silence . . . "I kept trying to see it from a girl's point of view and of course it's impossible. Any lump of meat would be better than that—even if it does look like Rupert Brooke."

Tonks was looking down at his drawing.

"Did you know people ask to look like Rupert Brooke?" asked Neville.

"Well, he was very beautiful."

"I find that Greek-god look in men rather repellent."

No reply from Tonks; just the continual needle prick of his glances.

"Well, don't you?"

"Not really, no. I'm afraid I find beauty in either sex very attractive."

"But not in the same way?"

Tonks was openly smiling. "No, not in the same way."

Silence except for the whisper and slur of pastels on paper. Neville was trying to twist his head to see the image, but whenever he tried Tonks stopped drawing, waiting for him to resume the pose.

"We went to the Café Royal."

"I know, I heard."

"Oh, Tarrant blabbed, did he?"

"No, as a matter of fact he didn't. There were quite a few people from the Slade there. Somebody's birthday, I think.

Tarrant didn't say anything. Fact, I don't often see him. I think it's better if he's just left to get on with it—without his old teacher looking over his shoulder. Not that I'd presume to comment."

"How's it going?"

"This?"

"No, Tarrant's . . . whatever."

"As I say, I rarely see him."

Neville turned his head to look at the portraits again.

"What are you thinking?" Tonks asked.

"Nothing special. Churned-up flesh; churned-up earth. If you take the other features away, the wound becomes a landscape."

"Well, I've always thought landscape's the only way of telling the truth about this war."

Neville jerked his head at the portraits. "They don't do badly."

"They can't be shown."

"Like Goya's engravings. *The Disasters of War.*"

Tonks burst out laughing. "Oh, Mr. Neville, you flatter me."

"Do you think I was wrong?"

"What about?"

"Taking off the mask. Do you think it was wrong?"

"Not if it was uncomfortable."

"You know what I mean."

A groan of indecision. "I get angry too, you know. One of the convalescent homes we use—the neighbors have asked for the men to be kept indoors, so they don't have to look at them. Of course that makes me angry. So no, I don't think you were wrong, but I also think a lot of the people there would have been entirely sympathetic. It's just, they don't know what to do. They're afraid their own faces will . . . I don't know. Show something."

"Revulsion. Yes. And they're absolutely bloody right. They do."

Neville looked away for a moment, the muscles of his face and neck working with distress. "What's going to happen next?"

"The next operation? You'll have the pedicle reattached."

"Just the one?"

"Yes, I think so; you'd have to check with Gillies."

"One of the chaps in the next hut has three. I don't mind looking like an elephant but I draw the line at squids." He watched Tonks work for a while. "Will you be there?"

"In the operating theater? Yes."

Neville was cursing himself for revealing a need for reassurance from a man he'd always disliked. "Not that I'll know who's there and who isn't, I'll be well out of it."

"And there'll be morphine afterwards."

"I think I dread that almost more than the pain. You have such terrible dreams. Dreams? More like hallucinations."

A few minutes later Tonks said, "Well, that's me finished." He stood up and put his pastels to one side. "Would you like to see it?"

"Not if the others can't." Neville was already on his feet, itching to leave. "Do you know I've been made a war artist?"

"Yes, I heard."

"The thing is, I can't paint here. And I can't paint in that overcrowded loony bin up the hill either."

"You mean, the convalescent home?"

"Whatever. I need to get away."

"I've been thinking about that. I had a word with Gillies and of course he's sympathetic. We'll see what we can do."

Neville had been prepared for a fight and felt rather deflated to find it wasn't necessary. He held out his hand, startled, not for the first time, by how cool Tonks's skin was. Of course his hands were miles away from his heart.

"Thanks."

"No need, I'm only too pleased to help. If you find Radcliffe waiting outside would you send him in?"

————

After lunch, Neville asked permission to leave the grounds and set off across the fields, carrying a sketch pad and pencils. After half an hour's walking, he reached the brow of a hill. All around him were gorse and hawthorn bushes so deformed by the prevailing wind they seemed to be frozen in the act of running away. Below him, a shallow valley striated by hedges stretched up to a wooded ridge. It amazed him that Tarrant could still find pleasure in painting the English countryside, as apparently he did, when not working office hours at the Slade. Neville saw only potential battlefields. Nameless English woods became, in the blinking of an eye, Devil Wood, High Wood, Sanctuary Wood. It took no time at all to blast craters into these fields, splinter the trees, and blow up the farmhouse over there. And as for trying to take that ridge . . .

Plod, plod, on he went, putting one foot in front of the other, numbed, almost hypnotized, by the sight of his moving feet. He was remembering the preparations for the battle. Two solid weeks of training over ground dug out to look like the German trenches they were supposed to take. Drums beating, hour after hour, to simulate the sounds of a bombardment, as if drums could begin to suggest what it was like to endure sound breaking in blast waves on your skin.

As a stretcher bearer he'd been spared most of these mock attacks. Instead, he washed iron bedsteads in an arsenic solution designed to discourage bed bugs (it didn't); and he organized Brooke's sick parades, which were always well attended. "Old soldiers" hoping for a day off, men suffering from trench foot—not nearly as many of those as there used to be—and, of course, malingerers. Old soldiers and malingerers are very different people. Brooke prided himself on being able to spot a malingerer half a mile away. Invariably, they were given a dose of No. 9 and sent straight back to duty. Laxatives: a strange remedy for men who were shitting themselves. Of whom Neville had been most definitely one.

In the few minutes he'd been standing there, the sky had begun to clear. Fitful sunshine chased cloud shadows across the land. But, despite the improvement in the weather, he decided to turn back, though he'd meant to walk a lot farther than this. The truth was, he didn't know where he wanted to be. Nowhere was the right place.

By the time he reached the hospital, he was almost running in his eagerness to get back, though he knew he couldn't face the hut, where that bloody gramophone playing the same songs over and over again jangled his nerves. Instead, he went to sit in the conservatory at the back of the house. This was easily the quietest place in the whole hospital, and it had become his favorite refuge.

He was all the more dismayed, therefore, to open the French doors and find that Trotter had got there before him. They nodded to each other, before Neville picked up a newspaper and went to sit some distance away. Trotter had a tray on his knees and was playing one of his endless games of patience. Sunlight cast faint shadows on the floor. It was warmer in here and there was no sound except for the slippery whisper of cards sliding under cards. Neville tried to concentrate on his paper, but his eyes were heavy. He was on the verge of nodding off to sleep like some pathetic old man in front of the fire. Trotter's absorption in the game fascinated him. That ray of light on the side of his face . . .

"Where's Doc?" somebody said. Nobody ever called Gillies that, but then, after a moment's reflection, he realized they must mean Brooke. It was dark outside, an immense yawning darkness unbroken by any gleam of light. From miles away you could hear the rumble and thud-thud of the guns. They were gathered round a table in what had once been the farmhouse kitchen, playing cards. Candlelight, reflected up into their faces, made the undersides of their eyes bulge like lids. Boiler, with red, shining skin stretched tight across his cheekbones. Hen Man—so called because he was good at finding chickens that had fallen victim to enemy action; many a bowl of chicken broth the patients owed to him. Evans, the Welshman, a blatherskite if ever there was one, talked so fast the spit flew. Wilkie, a strange, lopsided, big-eyed, uncoordinated sort of boy, given to sudden collapses when his knees went from under him. Bit of a shock if you were on the other end of the stretcher; even more of a shock if you were on it. A more ill-favored crew it would have been hard to find, and yet this light made them beautiful.

"So," Hen Man said. "What do you think he gets up to?"

"Brothel-creeping," said Boiler, who did a fair bit of creeping of his own.

"Nah," Wilkie said. "He's in love with his horse."

Evans called them to order. "Is anybody actually interested in playing this game?"

A door banged; a moment later Brooke came into the room, setting the candle flame guttering. You could smell rain on his skin, and his eyes were dilated from the dark . . .

Jerking awake, Neville realized his paper had slid onto the floor. Couldn't be bothered to pick it up. His mind traced the fading outline of his dream. Of the five men playing cards at that table Evans and Wilkie were dead; Hen Man, he didn't know; Boiler had been wounded, but survived. And he was here.

He drew a deep breath and looked around. Trotter was still absorbed in his game. All the cards were placed in a circle, except for the Kings, who were lined up, one by one, in the middle of the clock face. How harsh their faces were. Strange; all the card games he'd played—must be hundreds, in the last few years—and he'd never noticed that before. The aim, as far as Neville could tell, was to complete the outer circle before the last King joined his brothers. But if that was true, then Trotter must be doing something wrong, because in all the time Neville had watched him play the game, he'd never once completed the circle. Hours of effort, total concentration, and it counted for nothing: the four cruel Kings always won.

24

28 November 1917

Just back from a weekend in Garsington. All the way to Oxford on the train I was wondering whether the garden in winter would still be as beautiful as I remember it. The last time I was there was the second week in May. Toby was still alive.

Well, anyway, the answer to the question: Yes. As soon as I got there I went out and stood on the terrace looking down to the swimming pool. A sheet of silver water surrounded by strong dark shapes of box and yew. That's why it's still beautiful of course. It's really a sculptor's garden.

But. *The garden's still beautiful, but in this weather people don't spend nearly as much time in it and what I noticed on this visit particularly was how much Garsington needs its lungs. Being cooped up inside on long dark evenings intensifies the atmosphere of gossip and intrigue. And I don't think I've ever noticed before how* red *everything is. A very practical shade, of course, when the knives come out, as I think they often do.*

I used to love it. Well, not Garsington, I used to love Ottoline's parties in Bedford Square. For one thing it was the only place—is that an exaggeration? No, I don't think it is—

*where Catherine was welcome. People could be incredibly
hostile. And there was a time before the war when a couple of
"Sladettes," tastefully arranged on the lawn or by the fire, was
an essential part of Bloomsbury decor. I've been one of that
pair many a time, and I shouldn't grumble because I learned
a lot. But we all move on, I suppose. Now, when I think about
being a "Sladette," I'm reminded of Ottoline's pug dogs trotting
behind her wherever she goes.*

*Anyway, there I was, the ghost of my former self, wearing
my brown taffeta evening dress (also a ghost of its former self),
coming down to dinner far too early because I didn't want to
sit alone in my room. After mooching around the Red Room
for a few minutes, I decided I might as well go for a walk. I
went all the way down the garden but the wind was so cold I
ended up taking refuge under the yew hedge that runs alongside
the swimming pool. I was watching the reflections of clouds in
the water, wondering how you'd paint them—how I'd paint
them, rather; a lot of people wouldn't have any problems—when
round the corner of the hedge came a peacock, running towards
me. I suppose he thought I was a rival, or a peahen perhaps—
God knows I looked dowdy enough—because he immediately
went into full display, his tiny, crested head darting from
side to side, tail feathers quivering, with that curious, silvery,
death-rattle hiss. It was terrifying. I backed away, he followed;
I backed away again—and again—until I could feel yew twigs
sticking into the back of my head. And then suddenly, just as
I was about to scream or something, Ottoline appeared, skirts
kilted up like a scullery maid, and shooed him away. Off he
went, trailing all that feathered glory over the wet grass, and we
stood and watched him go.*

*That's what I like about Lady O. Underneath all the
vapors, all the nonsense, there's this very practical, shrewd,
hardworking woman. How she puts up with the pacifists
who're supposed to be working the farm I just don't know, for*

a lazier and more incompetent bunch it would be hard to find anywhere.

We walked slowly back to the house, Ottoline trying very hard to put me at my ease, and by the time we got there the gong had sounded for dinner. So in we trooped. Little red caps shading the candles—there you are, you see, red again—giving a livid tinge to the faces of the people round the table.

The talk was all of Ottoline's recent trip to Edinburgh to see Siegfried Sassoon, who's apparently decided to abandon his protest against the war and return to the front. He does seem to have treated her rather badly—he'd asked her to come, after all—but he refused to talk about his reasons for going back, and was generally offhand—and of course she was hurt and can't understand why he's given in. Since then he's written, so it's been patched up a bit, but she still can't understand why he'd want to go back and look after his men. I can actually and I said so. Everybody seemed surprised. I suppose I don't normally say very much. It's a hangover from being a Sladette: look pretty, keep your mouth shut. I said I admired people like Tonks, who hates the war as much as anybody but nevertheless spends hour after hour drawing ruined faces, because it's the only thing he can do to help. And perhaps looking after a particular group of men is the only thing Sassoon can do.

After dinner we went into the Red Room for coffee. And then the pianola started up—playing very loud, dramatic Hungarian dances—the dressing-up chest was pulled into the hall, everybody donned various hats and scarves and wraps and feather boas and began leaping about in time with the music. And oh, my God, I sympathized with Sassoon, who's spent months in a madhouse keeping his sanity (well, as far as anybody knows), and here I was after only one evening— crumbling.

In the end I just stood against the wall and watched. The music was absolutely deafening and yet all the time I could hear

*the death-rattle hiss of the peacock's feathers as he paraded up
and down in front of me.*

*My only real contact with Ottoline (apart from the great
peacock rescue) came after tea next day. We sat by the fire and
talked rather comfortably about this and that. She wanted to
know what I've been up to since Toby was killed. I talked about
going back home to paint the places we'd grown up in, and she
told me about Katherine Mansfield, who, after her brother was
killed, started to write stories about their childhood in New
Zealand. Best things she's ever done, apparently—according to
Ottoline.*

*I suppose I should have been flattered by the implied
comparison, but I wasn't. In fact the whole conversation made
me feel uneasy. Something about that use of her dead brother
as a muse—because that's what we're talking about, really—
seemed, I don't know, not quite right. I've never liked the
word "muse" anyway, always makes me think of seedy old men
groping young girls. But grief is a strange and savage thing. I'm
thinking about the Ancient Britons—or the ancient somebody,
I'm not sure—who used to eat their father's liver because that's
where his courage was, and his sons had to make it part of
themselves.*

*All very primitive, nothing to do with us. But is it? I'm
aware of something happening in me that I can't explain. It's
almost as if I'm turning into Toby. It's not just me thinking it
either, other people have commented. As if you cope with loss by
ingesting the dead person . . .*

*God, what a morbid thought. And it's left me feeling rather
doubtful about those paintings, the ones I did immediately after
he died. It's no use, I'll have to go back and look at them again.*

29 November 1917

*First day back at the hospital. Woke up dreading it,
butterflies with boots on all the way to Sidcup, but then,*

walking down the main corridor, I suddenly felt I belonged.
Probably just because one or two of the patients stopped to say
hello. There's no doubt it makes a huge difference when you
get to know the men as individuals, rather than just wounds
and case histories. And I'm starting to do that now. There's
one chap, Maddison, used to play pool before the war, and he
was really good, he used to play for his "beer money," he said.
Handed over his pay packet to his wife unopened—*he was very*
proud of that—and all his spending money came from winning
at pool. His wife and daughter came to see him three days ago—
and he'd been looking forward to this visit—and dreading it—
for weeks. And when the day came the little girl walked straight
over to him and kissed him. I think I was almost as relieved as
he was! Because you hear so many dreadful stories of children
who just say flatly, "That's not my daddy." Or run out of the
room. He doesn't think he'll be able to play pool again though—
his left eye's so much lower than his right.

For some reason I keep thinking of Paul and Kit, the way
they were when I first knew them. I think each of them felt at
a disadvantage in comparison with the other, and in a way
they were both right. Paul envied Kit that public-school self-
confidence of his. It was very much a surface thing, Kit was
anything but self-confident underneath, but it opens doors,
that kind of thing, and I think Paul was very aware of it. On
the other hand, Kit always looked like a sack of potatoes in his
expensive suits, whereas Paul, in that ludicrously long, shabby,
black overcoat he used to wear, looked like the Prince in Act
Two, thinly disguised as a swineherd.

30 November 1917

One day good, the next . . . Yesterday, I really did think I
was starting to get the hang of it. But today was my first day
in the operating theater. Scrubbing up reminded me of the
Dissecting Room, same smells, same feel of rubber on the skin.

Only difference is, the body we're all clustering round can still feel pain.

It hadn't occurred to me till I was actually there, surrounded by people in masks and gowns, that anesthesia's a major problem. The ether tube goes down the throat, but the surgeon's always operating in the same area, and that makes things difficult, to say the least. Sometimes a patient comes round and they end up having to hold him down while the surgeon finishes off. Sometimes when they pull the tube out they spray ether in people's faces and then you're left with a groggy surgeon or a theater sister who's ceased to take any interest in the proceedings.

Tonks went in with me and stayed close the whole time. The first three operations were nose repairs. I don't know whether that's typical, I forgot to ask. Tonks has developed a standard system for recording nose operations, so provided I follow that I can't go wrong. Well, that's the theory, anyway.

I didn't find it as hard as I thought I might. You're not actually drawing; it's more a question of taking notes. I had a few horrible minutes when my mind went completely blank, but after that I was all right. In fact, by the end of the morning I was almost euphoric because I hadn't passed out, or done something else equally stupid. I hadn't let Tonks down. That was what kept me going, really, the fear of letting Tonks down. I suppose beforehand I'd been dreading the sights, but I didn't mind that so much, because I was so fascinated by the process. But the smells made me feel sick, after a while.

And then, just as we were starting to think about lunch, another patient was wheeled in, added to the list at the last minute. Tonks didn't know; I'm sure he didn't, he'd have warned me. Kit. I couldn't see his face, it was his voice I recognized. I went across and looked down at him and his eyes widened. He seemed really startled, I couldn't think why till I remembered the mask I was wearing, and of course he wouldn't be expecting to see me there, anyway. But it was a nasty moment.

2 December 1917

Catherine and I don't get on as well as we used to do and in a flat this size that really matters.

Of course it's not bad all the time. Sometimes in the evening when we're sitting by the fire in our nightgowns it's exactly the way it used to be. But we talk too much about old times. We're living off the past because, in the present, there are just too many things that can't be mentioned. I think she's attracted to Paul, I know he's attracted to her, and I can't work out what I feel about it. A few weeks ago I'd have said it wouldn't matter if Paul found somebody else. Now, I'm not so sure. For one thing, I never thought the "somebody else" would be my best friend. And part of me thinks he's attracted to her for that very reason. He almost said as much.

They'd suit each other, probably. Paul needs somebody who'll put his work first, deal with the domestic side so he doesn't have to think about it, believe in his talent, forget about her own. Catherine's got talent, but she's not ambitious. She'd slot into that role perfectly well—and it'd kill me. I don't blame Paul for wanting it. I know if somebody offered me that kind of support I'd jump at it, but I don't think women are offered it, not very often anyway.

So I go round and round in circles. A lot of this is because I'm not painting. I'm never any good when I'm not painting, but you need some stability to be able to do it, and I haven't got that. Probably I should just focus on finding a place of my own. Forget everything else.

25

You had to lie on a stretcher to be taken to the operating theater. He hated that: the helplessness. Why not let him walk while he still could? But no, you had to be turned into an object to be fetched and carried because that helped the people who were going to slice into you. He lay, fuming, staring at the ceiling of the hut, shut off from the voices around him. "Good luck," somebody called out. He raised his hand in acknowledgment, but didn't turn his head.

Outside, a brisk wind blew a mist of fine rain onto exposed areas of skin. They trundled him along, wheels squeaking and hissing on the wet walkway. Familiar smells of creosote and starched linen. A nurse, her face screwed up against the rain, marched along beside him, sensible shoes clumping on the boards.

Boots thump-thumping on duckboards, the misery of wet clothes. If he closed his eyes, he might be back there. What a luxury a wheeled stretcher would have been . . . By the time they'd finished carrying the wounded back he'd felt as though his arms had been wrenched out of their sockets; he was trailing his knuckles along the ground like a baboon. The nurse's hair was stringy with wet. He raised his hand to his face and touched a crater that no amount of rainwater would fill.

A blast of heat as the swing doors burst open. Bright light, his eyes hurt, he's afraid now, horribly afraid, then Gillies's eyes above the mask, crinkled at the corners, he must be smiling. "It's all right," he says. "It's all right." A long struggle to get the ether tube down his throat, he's choking, gagging. It's Brooke's eyes now above the mask. Enormous eyes, that curious pale translucent blue, Elinor's eyes. It could be Elinor standing there. But it's Brooke's voice he hears. "You did this to yourself, didn't you?"

Gillies's face, not smiling now.

YOU DID THIS TO YOURSELF, DIDN'T YOU?

"No," he tries to say. "No, I didn't."

But the words gurgle down a plughole and all of him flows after.

———

For one mad moment he'd thought Brooke was talking to him.

"You did this to yourself, didn't you?"

Not a trace of compassion. But he couldn't dose this lad on laxatives and send him back. His left arm was shattered, with splinters of bone sticking through the mangled flesh.

"You may as well tell me, I know anyway."

How did he know? *Oh, yes, of course.* Burn marks round the bullet hole. Unless there'd been a German in the funk-hole with him, this had to be a self-inflicted wound.

The boy was—how old? Seventeen? His teeth were chattering with shock, he could barely speak. "Can't stand it, it's no use going on at me, I can't, I can't . . ."

Brooke turned away. "Give him some rum, for God's sake."

"What are you going to do?"

"Cut the burn out, of course." He caught Neville's expression. "What else can I do? Can't let the miserable little bugger get shot."

They worked alone: the fewer people who knew about this the better. Technically, Brooke was aiding and abetting a deserter; he could get into a lot of trouble for this. When the pain got too bad, Neville held the boy down, stuffed a roll of bandages into his mouth, ended up with one knee on his chest. Brooke scraped and scooped the burnt flesh from around the wound, poured iodine into the hole, and applied a dressing.

"Right, that should do it."

The boy was crying for his mother. The whimpering grated on Neville's nerves. "For Christ's sake, shut up, you should be bloody grateful."

Brooke turned away. "You might like some rum yourself," he said, over his shoulder, as he started to scrub his hands.

Was that a reference to the state of Neville's nerves? It couldn't have escaped Brooke's notice that he jumped and flinched at the sound of every shell or that he'd developed a persistent tremor that made him almost useless as a dresser. He spent more time now as a stretcher bearer in the front line than in the Casualty Clearing Station behind it.

That night, Neville lay on his bunk, exhausted, but too tense to sleep. He kept thinking about the boy who'd put a rifle against his arm at point-blank range, and fired. Not the easiest thing to do with a rifle . . . Unless, of course, he'd managed to get his hands on a revolver. And Brooke: so callous, so unfeeling, on the surface, and yet prepared to take that risk. It only needed the boy to start blabbing—and he might easily do it too.

Where was Brooke? The bunk opposite was empty, as it

often was around this time. Boiler and Hen Man were snoring and muttering in their sleep. Evans was in the next room, not asleep yet, reading, and Wilkie was along the corridor, on night duty, tending to a burly Scotsman who had pneumonia and wasn't responding to treatment. So where was Brooke?

He might have walked up into the front line. He often did that, couldn't seem to keep away from the place. He'd spend a couple of hours talking to the men, spotting the ones who were struggling with illness but wouldn't give in till they collapsed. Sometimes a couple of days' rest was all it took to keep a man in the line. Take more than that to keep me in it, Neville thought, as he drifted off to sleep.

He was jerked awake by somebody saying, "Right then. Let's get him on the stretcher."

Wounded coming in. Get up, get up . . .

"Calm down, we're just taking you back to the ward."

A burst of shellfire close at hand. Every object on the table jumped; the bunk underneath him shook. He put up a hand to his face . . . Something seemed to be sticking out of it.

"Naughty, *naughty*." He felt the back of his hand being slapped. "You mustn't touch that."

My God, Nanny Barnes. How did she get in?

He was being wheeled along; either that or the bunk was floating. When he opened his eyes, he saw Brooke, sitting beside the table in shirt and braces, taking his boots off. He sat for a moment, wiggling his toes, reveling, as they all did behind the lines, in the sheer pleasure of being able to take his boots off. In the next room the gramophone had started playing. Evans was beyond a bloody joke: same bloody song over and over.

And when I told them how beautiful you are,
They didn't believe me. They didn't believe me.

Briefly, Neville registered that he was back in the hut with the screens round his bed. The noises of the daytime ward were muffled, except for the wretched gramophone, which cut through everything.

Your lips, your eyes, your cheeks, your hair,
Are in a class beyond compare.

Tossing and turning on his chicken-wire bunk, Neville fell into a deep, but far from dreamless, sleep. He woke with a cry, afraid that he might have been heard, and the nature of the cry recognized. His eyes fell on Brooke's sleeping face. So he was back, but where had he been?

And the dream . . . My God, whatever next? But it was only because Brooke looked so much like Elinor. It had been Elinor, really, in the dream.

———

He woke again to find Gillies perched on the side of his bed.

"Well, that went well," he said.

"Did it?" He was tied to the bed again. In his sleep, when he'd struggled, the leather straps had cut into his wrists. "When can I get my hands free?"

"Today, I'll do it for you now, if you like. But you'll have to put them on again tonight." He was unbuckling the straps as he spoke. "We daren't risk another infection."

"And when can I go out? I've got to paint."

"I'm sure we can find you a room . . ."

"No, not here. I can't—"

"Tonks mentioned it, actually. I'll see what I can do."

After Gillies had gone, Neville rubbed his wrists and stared round the ward. Every time, it was like returning from the dead. An orderly, pushing a squeaking trolley, was dispensing tea: two slices of gray bread and a blob of plum-and-apple jam. His mouth flooded with saliva: he was famished. He could hardly wait for the food to get to him. And what was more, what was better than anything, he was going to get out of here.

Even at night, with the restraints back on his wrists and a bitter-tasting sleeping draft winding its way through his veins, he still felt the same fierce joy. It was almost indistinguishable from anger. The night nurse sat at her table in an island of light. Snuffles, snores, creaks, groans: the usual cattle noises, but at least the gramophone was quiet. Though that blasted song followed him into sleep.

And when they ask us, how dangerous it was,
Oh, we'll never tell them, no, we'll never tell them . . .

————

Lying in his bunk, listening to the flickering rumble of the guns—very close they sounded tonight—Neville couldn't stop thinking about the boy who'd shot himself. It was becoming an obsession. How desperate he must have been to do that.

A few nights later, back in the line, they went out to bring in a wounded officer and while the others were lining up the stretcher Neville slipped his hand into the officer's holster and pulled out the revolver. Nobody saw him do it. He slipped the revolver inside his tunic, feeling the metal cold against his skin. He'd taken it without forethought, almost without volition, and he was briefly tempted to put it back, but he didn't. By the time they got back to the British lines, the revolver had become a warm bulge against his side, part of him, almost, and yet still foreign. Like a tumor.

He didn't know where to put the bloody thing. In the end he just pushed it into a sock and shoved it down to the bottom of his kitbag. He told himself he wouldn't think about it again. Only he did, all the time. It lay heavy on his mind and, especially on night duty, when there wasn't enough going on to distract him, it throbbed and ached like an infected wound.

But then, suddenly, it didn't matter. They were being pulled out of the line, going back far beyond the reach of shells, to prepare for the big attack, the one that everybody knew was coming. But you could forget about that, as you marched away from the trenches into open country where birds still sang and there were flowers, trees, streams . . . Even as far back as this, some of the buildings had holes in their roofs and there were craters in the fields, but soon they'd leave all that behind. There'd be villages where no bombs had fallen, cafés, food that didn't come out of a tin, drink. My God, yes, drink.

Increasingly, he needed a drink to take the edge off his fear. With one part of his mind he could, quite objectively, analyze his condition because he'd seen it so often before, in other men. You began by being appropriately, rationally afraid, the extent of the fear always proportionate to the danger. With luck, and a sound constitution, that stage might last for many months. But the process of erosion is unrelenting. After repeated episodes of overwhelming fear, you start to become punch-drunk. You take stupid risks, and sometimes you get away with it, but not for very long. If you're lucky you may be wounded, but don't count on it. If you're not, the third stage is just round the corner. Fear is omnipresent. Sitting in a café, with a beer in front of you, you're neither more nor less afraid than you are in the front line. Fear has become a constant companion; you can't remember what it's like not to be afraid. He was at that stage now.

And the next? Breakdown: stammering, forgetting how to do even the simplest things, shaking, shitty breeches . . . Oh, he'd seen it. And he knew it wasn't far away.

As stretcher bearers and orderlies they played little direct part in the rehearsals for the coming attack. Brooke held a sick parade at six o'clock every morning, dispensed laxatives, listened to chests, attended to blistered feet. One man, a tall, yellow-skinned, cadaverous sort of chap, older than the rest, became really quite ill with a septic throat. *How did you get that?* Neville wanted to ask. If he'd thought it was contagious he'd have climbed into bed on top of the chap and gone through the whole *Kiss me, Hardy* routine, though he probably wouldn't have got it, no matter how hard he tried. Beyond the usual coughs and sniffles, he couldn't get anything.

Many of the soldiers were young recruits fresh from home. They had no knowledge of the men whose places they were taking in the line, very little idea of what lay ahead, and the others, those who knew, who remembered names and faces, were silent.

When not actually rehearsing for the attack they played a lot of football. Neville's bulk and labored breathing kept him off the pitch, though he liked watching. Rain pelted down; the men's shirts stuck to their backs and their mouths were wet and red in muddy faces. He remembered the same men as they'd been ten days ago: pinched, gray faces, stumbling along, many of them half asleep. They'd been old men, then. And the smell: that evil yellow stench of a battalion coming out of the line. And look at them now. Yes, but in a few days they'd be back in the line, and this time, everybody said, this time they'd really be in the thick of it. Of course rumors were always flying round, but he thought there was some truth in this one. You could tell from the jumping-off points in the rehearsals that they were going to bear the brunt of it.

All this time, whether drunk or sober, Neville was aware of the revolver lying at the bottom of his kitbag. Knowing it was there both disturbed and comforted him. Two days before they were due to start the long march away from safety, he went and sat by himself in the barn where the men slept at night and took it out of its wrapping. Hardly knowing what he was doing, he put the muzzle against the skin of his bare arm, trying to imagine what it would be like to squeeze the trigger: the agony of torn muscles and shattered bone.

An act of cowardice, people said. And he didn't dare do it. So what did that make him? His fingers as they stroked the cold metal left prints that quickly faded. If only he could get wounded, a slight wound, nothing too serious, just enough to make sure he got sent home.

An illness would do. Trench fever: that was a good one. Oh, for God's sake, he didn't need to get ill, he *was* ill. He'd had rheumatic fever as a child; there'd been a question mark over his heart ever since. He'd been excused rugby for a whole year. And the symptoms he'd been experiencing recently: racing pulse, indigestion—ah yes, but was it indigestion? Skipped beats . . . His heart skipped so many beats it was a wonder the bugger kept going at all. Even now, this minute, he could feel his heart thudding: skipping beats, every vein in his body pulsing and throbbing, as if he'd suddenly become transparent. Honest to God, if he stripped to the waist now, you'd be able to see it beating. Nobody could say that was normal . . .

Brooke was the problem. Why couldn't he stay in the Casualty Clearing Station like every other MO and wait for the wounded to be brought to him? There'd be no disgrace in that, none whatsoever. In fact, it was the way the system was meant to work. But no, Brooke had to be in the front line, or preferably in front of it, crawling around on his belly in the dark. Sometimes, after the wounded and dead had been brought in, he'd go out again, searching for identity disks. Anything, he said, to bring down the terribly long list of "Missing, Believed Killed." How could people grieve, he said, when they didn't know? And Neville had to go with him; there was no choice. That was the crux of it, really: Brooke had a choice; he didn't. He was ordered to go, and so he went, crawling about in bright moonlight over what felt like the eyeball of the world, searching through a mess of decomposing body parts to find the little scraps of metal.

Six: that was the score from their last excursion into hell. Ah, yes, Brooke said, but that was six families rescued from the pain of not knowing. You couldn't fault him: not on that, not on anything. Only, if he went on like this, he was going to get them all killed. For one brief moment, Neville let himself imagine the unthinkable, pointing the revolver away from himself. Leveling it. Then, quickly, he pushed it back inside the sock and returned it to his bag.

Next evening, after a particularly bad day, Neville decided he couldn't put off talking to Brooke any longer. He went round to the farmhouse where the first-aid post was currently located, but found it empty except for Evans and Wilkie, who were rolling bandages and grumbling over a smoky fire.

"Where's Doc?" he asked.

"Where do you think?"

He set off to the stables. As soon as he opened the door he heard Brooke's voice and followed it, between lines of tossing heads and manes, to a box at the far end where he found Brooke kneeling down, peering at a horse's hoof that one of the stable lads was holding between his knees.

"Can't see anything," he said, straightening up, "but she's definitely limping on that side."

He jumped as Neville came up behind him. So perhaps even Brooke's nerves weren't perfect? "Do you think I could have a word, sir, if you're not too busy?"

"Yes, of course, I'm nearly finished here."

Neville went back to the farmhouse, sat on his bunk,

and waited. He was trying to work himself up into a state of desperation, but couldn't manage even that. After a while Brooke came in, wiping his hands on his breeches.

"Did you have a good ride?"

"Huh, not really, she went lame on the way back. I think I might have to rest her a day or two." He looked more closely at Neville. "What's the matter?"

"I'd like you to have a look at my chest."

"Why, what's wrong?"

"Dunno, really. My heartbeat's irregular, feels as if I'm choking, sometimes I can't breathe . . ."

"All right, get your tunic off." Brooke's tone was cold. He went to the table, poured water into a bowl, soaped his hands, and dried them on a towel, managing, somehow, to imbue each of these simple actions with deep skepticism. "Let's have a look at you, then." The stethoscope moved across the pallid flesh. "Breathe. And again. Again. Deep breaths . . ."

When, finally, he took the stethoscope away he remained unnervingly silent.

"The thing is I had rheumatic fever when I was a child, I couldn't play games for a year, and then when I went to enlist I was told my heart wasn't up to it, and—"

"Who told you?"

"Bryson. He's a good man. Harley Street."

"So it wasn't the army that rejected you?"

"No, Bryson told me not to bother trying to enlist."

"I see."

"I did volunteer for the Belgian Red Cross instead."

"Well, I can't find anything wrong with you. You do have a few skipped beats but they're quite common—doesn't mean there's anything wrong with your heart. You tend to get them with worry, tension, tiredness . . . Too much coffee. Too much alcohol. All of which is true of you."

You cold-blooded little prick. He wasn't going to plead—

he'd see Brooke in hell first—but then something went wrong, something slipped, and he heard himself pleading anyway. That awful whining, so familiar from sick parades, now coming out of his own mouth; the humiliation.

"I just can't take it anymore. You can call me a coward if you like, I don't bloody well care. I've reached the end of the road. I cannot go on."

"You can't say that. It ends when it ends." He went to the door, obviously wanting the conversation to be over, but then turned back. "What do you want me to do? Send you back to base with a heart problem that doesn't exist? I can't do that."

"You won't."

"There's no quick exit. And please don't do anything stupid . . ."

"Like crawling round no-man's-land rescuing dead bodies? God forbid."

"We're all frightened, every single one of us. It's what you do with it that counts."

"And what do you do? Drink too much? Slope off to a brothel when you think nobody's looking?"

"I ride. Horses."

"'Course you do."

Suddenly losing patience, Brooke seized Neville's tunic from the back of the chair and threw it at him.

"Time to get back to work, I'm afraid. It's your night duty or had you forgotten?" He turned on his heel and was about to leave when he said, "Oh, and keep an eye on Kent, will you? Wake me up if he gets any worse."

Slowly, Neville put on his tunic and buttoned it up, before walking along the corridor to the large parlor that served as a temporary hospital.

Hen Man looked up from his crossword.

"You all right?"

"Fine. More to the point, how's he?" He nodded towards

Kent, who was propped up in bed on four pillows with his head drooping to one side. He was one of the older men and had been in the sick bay with chest infections several times before this latest crisis. "No better?"

Hen Man pulled a face. "Bit worse if anything." He folded the newspaper and stood up. "Well, I *hope* you have a quiet night. But if you don't, don't wake me."

———

Night duty. On the ward, Neville's wide awake, the morphine beginning to wear off just as the other patients are settling down to sleep. Peering along the row of beds, he sees the night nurse sitting at her table. She's got her head propped up on her hands and seems to be nodding off. He tries to turn onto his side, and realizes he can't move. Of course, his hands are tied to the bed, to prevent him touching the tube that's stuck in the middle of his face. Boss-eyed, he squints down at it, but it's only a blurred shape on the periphery of his vision. He closes his eyes because that's the only way he can ignore what's been done to him. Instantly, the morphine he thought was gone reaches out clammy hands and tries to smother him.

Somewhere quite close there's a sound of tortured breathing. Where's the bloody nurse? Why doesn't she do something? The man's obviously suffering. Lazy cow. He opens his mouth to shout "Nurse? Nurse?" but other words come out.

"Calm down. Now I want you to sit forward, that's right, put your arms forward as well, like this, look, now breathe, that's right, and again. Deep as you can, and now I want you to hold the next breath and cough. Can you do that for me?"

A stream of green phlegm, enough to fill the small bowl he was holding.

Kent fell back against the pillows, a yellow doll with cavernous pits above his collarbone.

"It ought to feel a bit easier now. Try to sleep . . ."

Kent's eyes flickering upwards so that for a few seconds there was only white. *Bloody hell,* Neville thought. *I've got to get Brooke.*

When he was sure Kent was settled, or as settled as he could be, he set off down the corridor, dogged by his own pale shadow in the lamplight. Boiler muttered a protest as he felt the light on his face. Quickly, Neville passed through into the room he and Brooke shared. Brooke's bunk was empty: must've gone for a pee or something. Couldn't be anywhere else at this time, it was two o'clock in the morning. Neville waited, but he was aware, all the time, of Kent alone in the sickroom, of the urgent need to get back to him, and so when, after a few minutes, Brooke still hadn't appeared, he set off in search of him.

The lantern, held high above his head, showed slanting lines of rain disappearing into thick mud. Sploshing and slithering, he crossed the yard to the stables. Brooke was worried about his lame horse, that's where he'd be. Amazing how horses need rest, and men don't. The door was open. Inside, the noise was deafening; the wind hurled rain onto a corrugated-iron roof. No wonder the horses were restless. The darkness seemed to be full of tossing heads, stamping hooves, neighs, snorts, whinnies, here and there a glint of silver as a rolling eye caught the light. He was transfixed by the horses: huge heads, weaving bodies, smells of shit and straw. In the interval between one blast of wind and the next he thought he heard voices. Following the sound, he walked along between the rows of boxes to the last one on the left.

A tangle of limbs and labored breathing. His first thought was that a horse had fallen and was threshing about in the straw. For several long seconds, his brain went on telling his eyes that they were looking at a sick horse, but then he began to see faces in the gloom. A boy's face first, dazed and panting, and behind him Brooke's face, his mouth stretched wide in a silent scream.

Neville didn't know how long he stood there, before Brooke opened his eyes and saw him. They stared at each other. And then, suddenly, Neville was free to move. He backed away, half walking, half running between the lines of panicking horses, pushed the door open, and almost fell into the yard. He stood with his back to the wall, blankly watching raindrops plop into puddles; unable to think. He couldn't go back to the ward, not yet. Instead, he took shelter in the adjoining barn, where he lit a cigarette and stood, breathing deeply, while his brain struggled to make sense of what he'd seen.

The fool. The utter bloody fool. He couldn't believe the stupidity. In those first few seconds, his thoughts were all of concern for Brooke, who was risking everything, and for what? From his vantage point inside the barn door he saw Brooke come out of the stables and run across the yard. Neville threw his half-smoked cigarette away, watching the bright descending arc before it sizzled to a quick death in the mud. Then, slowly, he followed Brooke into the main building.

An hour later they were standing on opposite sides of the bed as Kent breathed his last. When he was certain it was over, Brooke reached across, closed Kent's eyelids, and pulled the blanket up over his face. Automatically, he reached for the file and noted the time of death.

"You can lay him out in the morning, there's no rush."

As Brooke handed him the file their eyes met. Now, Neville thought, he's got to say something now. But Brooke's face remained expressionless and almost immediately he turned away. That was it, then. There was to be no discussion, no explanation—and, after all, what explanation could there be?

Just this proud, stony silence: Brooke saying, in effect, *I'm stronger than you. You'll never hear me plead.*

Neville spent what was left of the night in the sickroom. Kent's corpse was more acceptable company than Brooke.

Towards morning, he went into the yard and held out his hand to see if it was still raining. A pinprick now and then; no more. He looked down at his palm as if he were seeing it for the first time, and then slowly, involuntarily, curled his fingers, turning his open hand into a fist.

26

Paul had been in the Domino Room for perhaps twenty minutes before Elinor arrived. At first he didn't recognize her. She was flushed, her hair and shoulders covered with a fine mist of rain. When he bent to kiss her she smelled, mysteriously, of woodsmoke. Apparently she'd spent the whole day at Kew, going there and back by river. A wonderful day, she said. Her speech was quick and passionate, her pupils still dilated from the darkness outside. She was like a wild creature glimpsed in the headlights of a motorcar; he was startled into a fresh awareness of her.

"Wasn't it very cold?"

"Freezing. It was wonderful, though, and such a change from the hospital. Do you know, even outside the huts you never really feel you're outside?"

She didn't seem to belong to this room, with its dark red plush seats and wreaths of cigar smoke, and that pleased him because with each visit his dislike of the place grew.

"Why are you smiling?" she asked.

"I was thinking about Kit. Do you remember how he used to call the Café Royal 'vile'?"

"Yes, and he practically lived here."

"I'm going to see him this weekend," Paul said. "He's invited me down to Suffolk." She was looking away from him so he couldn't read her response. "Did you know they were letting him out?"

"Yes, Tonks told me. It's only a couple of weeks till the next operation—they're hoping to fit it in before Christmas. I'm pleased he's having a break—it'll do him good."

Paul wondered how much he should say. "He says he wants to talk to me."

"About Toby?"

"I suppose so. Can't think what else it would be."

"Well, you know . . ." She brushed her hair out of her eyes, still not meeting his gaze. "I've got to leave that to you."

"I won't press him, you know, if . . ."

"No. I understand that."

They sat in silence for a moment, looking around the room. It was a while since they'd been seen here together and at several of the tables he could see people rather obviously commenting on their presence. What his father would have called a clatfart shop. God, he hated it.

"What are your plans?" he asked.

"I'm going to look for a flat. Catherine says she'll go round with me."

"How is she?"

"Getting ready to go back to Scotland. At least that's the current plan. But . . . She's going to have dinner with Kit and his parents before he goes back into hospital. So. We shall see."

"She said his mother was pressing her to go to see him."

"I don't know how much pressure would be needed."

"I just hope she doesn't get carried away by . . . Well, by pity. There's a real danger here, you know, of people thinking that Kit's like . . . That he's the way he is because of his injuries. Whereas you and I both know Kit was a very difficult man before any of this happened. I think if you want to be a real friend you'll remind her of that."

Elinor was smiling. "There wouldn't be anything personal at stake for you, I suppose?"

"No, of course not."

They lapsed into silence again, but he could feel the tension gathering in her.

"Whatever it is," she said, turning to him and looking straight into his eyes. "You will tell me, won't you?"

"Yes, of course," he said, realizing, even as he spoke, what a rash promise that was.

———

With a final petulant hiss of steam, the train stopped. Paul hauled his bags off the luggage rack, opened the door, and dropped them onto the platform. A porter appeared, but no other passengers. The train must have been empty.

Neville was standing directly under the lamp. His nose and mouth were hidden by a thick scarf that he'd wound round and round the lower part of his face. Only the eyes showed, the corners creased by some change of expression, a smile, presumably, though of course a snarl has the same effect. Paul held out his hand, registering the shock of Neville's hot skin against his own cool palm, and then Neville pulled him into an awkward, backslapping embrace.

The porter coughed. Before Paul could take action Neville had slipped a coin into his hand.

"Good journey?"

"Not bad. Certainly wasn't crowded."

"Never is, that one."

He picked up one of Paul's bags.

"No—"

"*Face,* Tarrant. Nothing wrong with the arm."

They walked side by side down the hill. They should have known each other well enough by now to chat easily in this situation, but despite the embrace there was still the awkwardness of strangers between them. It had always been like this: they greeted each other like long-lost brothers and a minute or so later remembered they didn't actually like each other very much. Paul had never had such a strange, unquantifiable relationship with anybody else. Even now, after years of admittedly intermittent contact, he'd have hesitated to call Neville a friend; and yet nobody mattered more. There was nobody whom he so persistently measured himself against.

Neville was quickly out of breath, puffing and gasping through whatever apparatus was hidden by the scarf. Ahead of them, in the darkness, the sea turned and turned, the crash and grating sigh of its retreat more imagined than heard. They came out between narrow rows of houses to find it waiting for them in the darkness. Huddled dark shapes of fishing boats were drawn up on the shingle. The roofs of the huts sparkled with frost: the last few nights had been freezing.

"Do you mind if we walk on the beach?" Paul said.

"No, go ahead. It's all shingle, mind, won't be easy on that leg."

Paul's breath plumed on the air as he slipped and slithered down the slope and half ran the last few yards to the sea. Neville followed slowly, a bulky, top-heavy shape, breathing stertorously through his mouth. At the bottom of the slope, there was a strip of firm, hard sand, but you couldn't get to it because of the tangle of barbed wire that ran along the water's edge. A gap in the wire left a space for fishing boats to come and go and presumably for the lifeboat to be launched. That, too, was hauled high onto the shingle, poised like a fish hawk about to dive. Neville joined him and for a time they were silent, looking out to sea through coils of rusting wire, thinking their own thoughts.

It had started to rain and the rain quickly turned to sleet, slanting silver rods disappearing into shining gray-brown pebbles. They turned by mutual consent and walked up the shingle slope, still not having spoken. Paul glanced sideways at Neville, who was struggling up the bank, hunched over, hands thrust deep into his pockets, the moonlight glinting on the whites of his eyes. Paul noticed that the scarf had a curious bulge on one side.

Suddenly Neville put on a burst of speed and pulled ahead. "Come on, Tarrant," he called over his shoulder. "It's bloody freezing out here, and I could do with a drink."

They climbed the last ledge onto the path, every step dislodging pebbles that peppered in their wake. The terrace facing the sea had gaps in it, missing teeth in an old man's mouth. Many of the houses had their windows boarded up, and there were sandbags piled up against the doors.

"Like the sandbags," Paul said.

"Thought you might. Lends a homely touch."

"Do you know the Department of Information wants to send me back to Ypres? They think I might need to refresh my memory."

They laughed, the secretive, inward laughter of veterans, but Neville stopped laughing first. "Will you go?"

"I'm not sure there's a choice."

After that they walked in silence, the moon accompanying them on the water. After the first fifty yards Paul stopped and looked back along the row of houses. "Does anybody actually live here?"

"Not really. It's Hampstead-on-Sea. You don't get many people coming down this time of year." A few paces farther on he stopped outside a double-fronted white house. "Here we are."

It took Neville a while to persuade the key to turn in the

lock. The woodwork was swollen and cracked and bloated and blistered from constant exposure to damp air, blown spume and quite possibly the sea itself, if the sandbags were anything to go by. At last, with a thump of Neville's shoulder, the door fell open onto darkness and a smell of burning logs.

"Can you manage to climb over?" Neville said.

He held out his hand, but Paul insisted on scrambling over the sandbags unaided, only to stumble and have to accept Neville's assistance after all. Neville followed, closing the door behind him. Total darkness, everywhere. Of course here on the coast blackout regulations would be particularly strict. After a few seconds Neville's groping hand found the switch. The bulb cast a dingy light onto a hall that was scarcely more than a passage between two rooms. Striped deck chairs and parasols stood against the wall near the stairs. Rather more realistically, perhaps, four big umbrellas hung from a hatstand near the door. Everything was faded, but the effect was pleasant nevertheless. The house didn't have the mildewed smell so many holiday homes have in the winter months.

Neville led him into the living room, which looked surprisingly well-furnished after the shabbiness of the hall. A fire blazed in the grate; a rush basket full of logs had been pulled up close to the hearth. Fat upholstered armchairs and sofas echoed the blues and reds of a Turkey carpet and on several low tables ranged round the room lamps cast a warm glow over books and scattered papers.

"This is lovely," Paul said.

"Not bad, is it? My mother loves this place. Would you like to unpack straightaway or shall we have a drink first?"

"Oh, a drink first, I think."

Paul took his greatcoat into the hall. When he came back Neville had thrown his coat and hat onto a chair and, with his back turned to Paul, was unwinding the scarf. Paul had seen head wounds that left the brain exposed, missing jaws, eyes dangling onto cheeks—the lot. And yet, when Neville finally turned to face him, his heart thumped.

Neville joked about the Elephant Man, but he didn't look anything like an elephant. He looked like a man with a penis where his nose should be: obscene, grotesque, ridiculous. Paul swallowed, trying to work out exactly what he was looking at. The lamplight cast a shadow across Neville's face, making it difficult to see where the excrescence began and ended.

"I know," Neville said. "Here, have a whiskey. Dad knocks back a fair few these days—even Mother risks a tipple now and then."

He sounded tired, rather than angry or bitter.

"What is it?"

"It's a tube pedicle. They—no, look, I'll show you." He unbuttoned his shirt. "They cut a strip of skin off the chest, here, and then they roll the edges over so it's a tube—that's to stop it getting infected—and then they stick the other end . . . Well, wherever it has to go. Nose, in my case. If they need any bone they take it from the breastbone. And because it's all coming from you, your body doesn't reject it. Well, that's the theory, anyway. Only it all went belly-up in my case because I got a cold, would you believe. A cold in the nonexistent nose." He smiled. "Sorry about the conducted tour. I'm afraid you get a bit obsessed."

"No, no, it's interesting."

Neville raised his glass. "Well. Your good health."

"I'm afraid it's a bit late for that."

"All right, then. My good looks."

They chinked glasses and the small, familiar sound restored a kind of normality.

"Sit down," Neville said.

Paul sank onto the sofa. Neville took one of the armchairs, moving the lamp a little to his right, either because the light hurt his eyes or because he wished to spare Paul the sight of his face. Instantly, Paul was reproaching himself for not having handled the situation better, though he didn't know what else he could have done or said. His perception of Neville's injuries changed constantly. A moment ago the tube had looked ludicrous: he'd been ashamed of seeing it, but that had been his first reaction. Now Neville was sitting down, it became clear that the pedicle was pulling his head down towards his chest, restricting his movement. That had to be painful. And it added to the impression of top-heaviness Paul had noticed on the beach. Suddenly, he knew what it reminded him of: Neville had become a Minotaur, a creature that was both more and less than a man.

"I'm surprised they let you out."

"Without a mask, you mean?" He waved Paul's denial away. "I threw myself on Tonks's mercy, I told him I'd go mad if I didn't paint."

"So how long have you been out?"

"Three days in London, a week here." He was swishing whiskey round his glass. "What did you do the first day you got out of hospital?"

Paul tried to remember. "Had dinner with Michael Corder, I think. Do you know him? He—"

"Bor-ing!"

"What did you do?"

"Went to a brothel. I thought at first the stupid little cow was going to refuse. I soon put a stop to that."

Paul had an unpleasantly vivid image of Neville's vast bulk pounding away at some half-starved little whore, his tube of harvested flesh an inch away from her face. "Are your parents coming down for the weekend?"

Neville gaped at him, then burst out laughing. "My God, Tarrant, what a dried-up little prude you are. No, of course my parents bloody well aren't coming, I'm here to paint."

"And have you managed to start?"

"Yes, bit of a relief really, I wasn't sure I could. It's been a long time."

Paul drained his glass and stood up.

"I'd better get the unpacking done, I think."

"I'll show you your room. Right at the top, I'm afraid."

"That's all right."

It wasn't: he found stairs extremely difficult. He hoped Neville would go first, but he hung back so every stage of Paul's struggle was observed from behind. He reached the third floor hot, sweaty, and embarrassed. Neville led him into a room on the left and he collapsed onto the bed, in too much pain even to pretend to be all right. "Sorry, I'm a bit slow these days."

"It's bad, isn't it?"

Paul shrugged. He wasn't going to complain about his leg to a man with a penis for a nose.

"I'm next door," Neville said. "Bathroom's across the landing." He continued to hover. "I suppose I could always put you in Mother's room . . ."

"No, this is fine."

"I never thought . . . Anyway, I'll leave you to it. There's some kind of stew for dinner. No idea what it is, I just warm them up. But the wine'll be good, I can promise you that."

And flow freely, no doubt. But who was he to criticize? He was drinking far more than he should.

After Neville had gone, Paul began transferring clothes from his bag to the wardrobe by the bed. The room smelled sweet, though he couldn't tell where the smell was coming from. Nothing obvious like potpourri or lavender, but it was very pleasant. In fact, the whole room was pleasant: plain, solid furniture, a white coverlet on the bed, a faded blue rug on the polished-wood floor. No, it was good. He could have been happy here, if it wasn't for the thought of what awaited him downstairs.

Talking about the prostitute like that . . . That was Neville all over. The first time Paul had met him, oh, years ago—before the war—he'd told some sort of story against himself, without appearing to realize how damaging it was. Something about a model he'd got pregnant, or somebody had got pregnant, and he was refusing to pay . . . Yes, that was it. He was refusing to support the child. What a thing to say to a complete stranger. Of course, he had no reason to look down on Neville because he'd visited a brothel. In France, after Elinor stopped writing, he'd used prostitutes himself for a time. Sheer misery; nothing else sluiced away the blood. He didn't think he'd bullied them, though . . . Ah, well. No doubt they'd get through the evening somehow.

Paul switched off the light, but before going downstairs he crossed to the window and looked out. Even on this comparatively calm night, there was a line of white foam where the sea chafed against its bonds. On the ground, you felt safe behind that ridge of shingle, but up here you could see how vulnerable the town really was.

Dropping the blackout curtain, he groped his way along the edge of the bed until he found the door. Using the banisters as a crutch, he hobbled downstairs and followed Neville's voice into the kitchen, where he saw an improbable figure with an apron tied around its waist, hunched over the range stirring a black pot.

"How now, thou secret, black and midnight hag?"

Neville glanced up. "Beef," he said. "I think."

Over dinner and a bottle of decidedly robust red wine they talked about painting and painters. Neville's opinions were always entertaining, if vituperative. At one point, Paul realized that Neville didn't believe *anybody* could paint—

except, of course, himself. Even the great painters of the past were merely hauled into the light and damned with faint praise, before being tossed, almost casually, onto the muck-heap of history. "Past, Tarrant," he kept saying. "Past. Done with. Over."

It was an extraordinary performance and one that left Paul almost gasping with disbelief.

"I'm hoping to get some reviewing soon," Neville said. "Fact, I want to do quite a bit of journalism in the future. Sort of thing I can pick up and put down, you know, because I'm going to be in and out of hospital for the best part of next year. And they'll have to let me out to go to the exhibitions."

"Sounds like a good idea."

Please, God, don't let him review me.

"What are you doing?" Neville asked.

"Painting? Landscape around Ypres."

He was braced for some gibe about the past-ness of land-scape painting, but instead, Neville lapsed into silence, and for a moment the two of them sat there, each lost in his own memories of the ruined city.

Neville roused himself. "Can I top you up?"

"Yes, all right, go on."

"So, anyway, your dinner?"

"Sorry?"

"You said you had dinner with Michael Corder."

"Oh, yes, so I did. Dried-up little prude that I am. He lost an arm, you know. Arras. Anyway, it was quite interest-ing because we were talking about whether anything posi-tive's come out of the war—apart from the fact that you can see women's legs and you couldn't before—and he said he wouldn't have missed it for the world. I just sat there and looked at his empty sleeve. But that's it, isn't it? A lot of peo-ple want to believe they've got something good out of it. That they're better people, less selfish . . ."

"I'd settle for my nose."

Back in the living room, Neville built up the fire and sat back in an armchair, but he was fidgeting all the time. In pain. Paul knew the signs.

"So what do you think you can get away with?" Neville said.

"Sorry?"

"What will you paint?"

"It's all fairly straightforward. No bodies. You can show the wounded, but only if they're receiving treatment. I think in practice that means bandages."

"So no wounds, either?"

Paul shrugged. "I don't know. It hardly applies to me."

"Well, I intend to push it as far as I can."

"Why, what's the point? If you push it too far they won't let you show it. Besides, you can get round it . . ."

"You can. Your landscapes are bodies."

"Yes, I know. Don't worry, it's intended. I know what I'm doing. It's the Fisher King. The wound in his thigh?"

"Balls."

Paul looked surprised. Even by Neville's standards that was forceful.

"That's where the wound is. Idiot. He was castrated."

"Oh, all right, then, balls. The point is, the wound and the wasteland are the same thing. They aren't metaphors for each other, it's closer than that. Anyway, you do the same thing. All those mutilated machines."

"My machines aren't mutilated, they're triumphant."

"At least you're working again."

"Yes, I suppose I have to be grateful for that."

Neville lapsed into silence. A few moments later he said, "Have you thought what you're going to do after the war?"

"No point."

"Surely you can think about it?"

"No, I can't. I take it you can?"

"Oh, God, yes. Minute it's over, I'm out of here."

"Here? You mean, London?"

"England. I want to go somewhere where you don't have the past sitting on the back of your neck like a fucking dead weight. New York, Chicago. We're a nation of fucking caryatids. It's squashing us. Can't you feel it?"

"Well," Paul said, "I'm impressed. I've never managed to see beyond it."

All these past weeks he'd been trying to fit back into civilian life. It had been like poring over a chessboard, always trying to work out the next move, the winning strategy, and now, with one great sweep of his arm, Neville had scattered the pieces. You don't have to play this game, he'd said. There are other places. Other games.

I never did fit in, he thought. He'd always been a "temporary gentleman." And as long as he remained in England he'd never be anything else. So why not move on? New York? Chicago? No, not for him. He knew immediately, without having to think about it, that he wanted the south: warmth, sunshine, lemons growing on trees. He'd never been anywhere like that. Never been anywhere at all, except France and Belgium, and even those countries he'd experienced as a succession of holes in the ground.

"You're right," he said. "I ought to think about it."

————

They went to bed, predictably drunk, an hour later. Around two in the morning Paul woke to a loud thud. For a second he was back in the trenches, shells falling all around, but then his splayed fingers encountered clean, crisp sheets and he thought: *England. Home.* He was sweating so he pushed the bedclothes down, trying to get cool. The blackout curtains were so effective he could see nothing in the room, not even shadows. His face was pressed into a smothering pelt of darkness. He lay listening, straining to identify the sound that had awoken him.

The window shook and rattled, but that wasn't the sound he'd heard. Feeling his way across the floor, he pushed the window open. He felt rain cold on his face, rain or spray, he couldn't tell; the wind was blowing straight off the sea. Far below, waves roared and crashed, white foam slavering up the last slope of shingle. The house seemed to sway and rock in the gale. He tried to close the window gently, but the wind pulled it from his grasp and slammed it shut. His chest was wet. He stood there, struggling to calm himself, and then he heard it again: a cry from the room next door, long-drawn-out, despairing . . . Desperate.

All his instincts were to rush in and help, but he knew from his own experience that no help was possible, and that Neville would be humiliated if Paul found him lying in a puddle of sweat and piss. If he was as bad as that; and Paul had known many who were. No, best let him fight it out alone.

Paul got back into bed and pulled the covers up to his chin. What must it be like, having that thing on your face? To know you looked grotesque? To know that people would find the sight of you repulsive or ridiculous, despite continually reminding themselves it was tragic?

He lay there, rigid with tension, while in the next room the cries subsided into sobs and the sobs into silence. He imagined Neville staring into the darkness, wondering if Paul had heard. He wouldn't refer to it at breakfast. They never did.

27

Not for the first time, Neville confounded his expectations. When Paul came downstairs next morning, Neville immediately said, "I hope I didn't disturb you last night?"

"No, I slept very well, thank you."

"It's just I have this recurring dream. Not about the war, it's . . . I'm walking down the central aisle of a stable, you know, with horse boxes on either side and the horses are sticking their heads over the doors, you know the way they do. There's some sort of sound going on in the background . . . Could be guns, I'm not sure. And there's something wrong. Nothing obvious, just something. It's quite dark, one oil lamp, I think. And suddenly I realize what it is, the horses are watching me and they've got human eyes. You know, white showing all the way round, not just when they're startled. And that's when I wake up." He handed Paul a cup of gray tea. "Sorry it's a bit wishy-washy. Virgin's piss."

Paul took the cup. "Long as it's hot."

"Do you think dreams mean anything?"

"Doubt it. I certainly hope mine don't."

That was strange. He felt the dream had been recounted for a reason, not merely because Neville wanted to explain, or apologize for, any disturbance in the night. "Fresh air, that's what you need," he said, bracingly. "Blow the cobwebs out."

"I've got to work."

"Work a lot better if you get some fresh air."

A few minutes later they were letting themselves out of the front door. The sea was a heaving steel-gray mass flecked here and there with white. A knot of men had gathered by the lifeboat and were staring out to sea, but though Paul followed the direction of their gaze he couldn't see anything. Couldn't hear what they were saying either, every word was snatched up and hurled away on the wind. Even breathing was difficult. But at least that meant there was no need to talk. Neville was wearing his greatcoat, had pulled his hat down and wound a scarf around his lower face, but the weather was cold enough to justify it. He looked no different from anybody else. Paul suspected his company was the last thing Neville needed or wanted, at the moment, but the situation left them with little choice.

Beyond the shelter of the houses, you felt the full force of the wind. It was still blowing almost directly off the sea. Ahead of them was a row of cottages, some obviously abandoned, their doors and windows blocked by shingle. Others had smoke coming from their chimneys, though there was no barrier to save them from the rising tide.

"How do they manage?" Paul said.

"Open the front door, let it run through."

"I can't imagine anybody living like that."

The place was called Slaughden, Neville said. It had once been a bustling fishing village, but over the generations storms had swept away most of the houses and the shingle had piled up, choking those that were left. It had become the little town's ghost twin.

"That's the awful thing, really. The sea doesn't just take away, it gives back, but what it gives is tons and tons of shingle. And that's almost equally destructive."

Paul turned and looked back across the marshes. Through some trick of the wind, the shining wet roofs of the houses seemed to appear and disappear, like a shoal of rocks at high tide. From this distance, the town might have been out at sea.

A few hundred yards farther on, Neville said, "Well, that's me done. Enough fresh air for one day. You coming?"

"No, I think I'll go a bit farther on."

After Neville had gone, Paul turned inland, hoping for some shelter from the wind. The path had recently been flooded; he slipped and slithered along until he found a sheltered spot where he could sit down and rest. All around him, the reeds whispered to one another, a papery rustle, not unlike the sound the palms of your hands make when you rub them together. Even when the wind died down, the murmuring still went on, the reeds swaying in unison, making secrets.

This place, the way water and land merged, reminded him of that other inundated landscape: the countryside around Ypres. Only there, the mud was full of death—bodies, gas, strings of bubbles popping on the surface, God knows what going on underneath. Only rats and eels flourished there. Here, the mud teemed with life. Knots and dunlins picked their way along the water's edge; he was aware of other birds too, secretive, hidden away among the reeds. Once he thought he heard the boom of a bittern. He got his sketch pad out and made a few tentative drawings, but he couldn't grasp the place, not yet, it was too new to him.

Last night's fantasy of lemon trees and sunshine seemed a long way off today. He was a quintessentially English painter, but then, he thought, rebelling, some of the best writing about place has been done in exile. Wasn't it at least possible the same might be true of painting? After all, he was painting Ypres from London . . .

Lunch was at the Cross Keys, where a log fire blazed in the grate. The locals asked cautious questions, establishing that yes, he had been to France and yes, his limp was a war wound. After that, he could easily have got drunk on the number of drinks he was offered, but managed to refuse most of them without giving offense.

The man sitting opposite had black eyebrows so bushy it looked as if two caterpillars had crawled onto his face. Paul got talking to him; he turned out to be the local doctor. His boy had been in France, he said. He'd always hoped Ian would take over the practice, but now this . . . Nothing, he said, as they parted at the door, would ever be the same again. He raised his hat, almost cheerfully, and walked off down the street.

During the time Paul had spent in the pub the weather had taken a turn for the worse. The town seemed to be hunkering down. You could see the tension in the faces of the fishermen: darting eyes, caught in nets of wrinkles, scanned the horizon or measured the progress of the tide, which had turned and was running in fast.

Neville was in the living room when he got back.

"Spring tide," he said, in that knowledgeable way of his. "They're supposed to be delivering more sandbags. I'll believe that when I see it."

"There's something going on. I noticed there's quite a little gathering round the huts."

"Trawler in trouble. Did you get any drawing done?"

"Not a lot. Fantastic place though. Oh, and I bumped into Dr. Mason, in the pub along there. He sends his regards."

"Yes, he's a good man. Shame about Ian, I used to play with him when we were boys." Neville seemed very tense;

he jumped when somebody knocked on the door. "That'll be the sandbags."

Paul heard a rumble of voices from the front door, and then Neville came back into the room.

"They've dumped them at the end of the path so I'm afraid we'll have to carry them. Are you up to it?"

"Of course," Paul said.

Outside, it was growing dark, sea and sky streaming together in a wash of gray. Even the seabirds had taken refuge inland. Every roof was covered in gulls and as they watched more came flying in, great white boomerangs of bone and sinew swooping low above their heads, before landing in a scuffle of flapping wings and jabbing beaks.

They lugged ten sandbags back to the house. Another echo of life in the trenches; the place was full of them. Now that he was getting used to the idea, Paul found the echoes almost soothing; they seemed to integrate aspects of his life that were otherwise chasms apart. Physically, though, it was hard going. Icy rain plastered their clothes against their bodies; talking was impossible, breathing difficult. They scaled along the walls, staggering when they came to one of the gaps and caught the full blast of the wind. Once Paul's knee gave way under him and he almost fell.

"Are you all right?"

"Fine!" Paul said, shouting above the wind. Their rivalry wasn't confined to painting and girls.

"That's it," Neville said, at last. "I can't do anymore and you look done in."

"I'm—"

"Yes, I know, 'fine.'"

In the hallway, Paul wiped water out of his eyes. "Do you know, I used to love rain? Now all I can think of are the poor bloody bastards out there."

Neville threw more coal onto the fire, then propped a

shovel and newspaper against the grate to draw the flames. But he was too impatient to do it properly: a singed brown patch appeared in the center of the page, deepened to orange, and began to curl back. Soon, the whole sheet was ablaze. He grabbed the poker and beat the flames down, then trod the remains of the paper into the hearth. Scraps of newsprint were sucked into the chimney; shrieking headlines whirled into the storm-tossed air.

Unable to wait any longer, Paul went to the table and poured them both a large whiskey.

"Give me your coat," Neville said. "I'll put it to dry."

Paul did as he asked, though the really uncomfortable bit was the lower part of his trousers, which chafed against his skin.

Neville came back and threw him a towel. "Here, dry yourself off. Thanks for that, I couldn't've managed on my own." He sank into the armchair and took the glass Paul handed to him. "Your knee's bad, isn't it?"

"Been better."

"I've got some stuff somewhere . . ."

"No, please—"

But Neville was already on his feet. When he returned he was holding a box of powders. "Here. You dissolve them in water and they really do work."

"I'm not leaving you short, am I?"

Neville pulled what was left of his face. "Doesn't really hurt that much. I mean, obviously it did after the operation, but it's not so bad now."

Paul dissolved one of the powders, swirling it round the glass with a pencil he found lying on a side table, and then threw it down in one gulp. "Uck."

"Takes half an hour. Meanwhile, I recommend whiskey."

"I'm drinking too much."

"Oh, for God's sake . . . How much is too much?"

The whiskey was already spreading its insidious warmth through every part of Paul's body. He stretched out his hands to the fire, which, despite Neville's ministrations, was now crackling away. The shutters banged and thumped. After one particularly loud crash Paul jumped, slopping some of his whiskey onto the back of his hand. He licked it up.

"There's plenty more," Neville said, drily.

"How do you get it?"

"Father. Dunno where he gets it. I don't ask."

Neville's painkillers were already starting to take effect. Paul's speech was becoming slurred, or sounded so to his own ears; he doubted if Neville would notice. He seemed to have become almost torpid, staring blankly across the hearth. What came next was unexpected.

"Brooke came here, you know. He sat in that chair."

"No, I didn't know. I didn't realize—"

"Oh, we weren't friends, not really friends, he just came with Elinor." A short silence. "In a way, you know, I think that might have been the trouble, part of it. He was an officer, I wasn't, and yet before the war we'd stayed in each other's houses. He could never quite . . ."

"He couldn't accept it?"

"He wasn't comfortable. One thing, he was supposed to censor our letters, but I know for a fact he never read mine. Not the done thing, old chap. He was quite conventional in a lot of ways. Surprisingly so."

"Were you with him when he got his MC?"

Paul expected Neville to back off at this point as he'd done on every previous occasion he'd been questioned about Toby, but he didn't.

"Oh, God, yes. We were told we were going forward again and there was—I don't know—a very flat feeling. Everybody was sick, sick as in 'fed up,' but also sick as in 'sick.' We had a real run of coughs and colds, stomach upsets, nothing serious, but one after the other it starts to drag you down. Oh, and I had toothache." He jabbed at his cheek. "There. One of the back molars with nice deep roots. It'd been niggling on for quite a bit and I'd been trying to ignore it, sticking cloves in, you know, rubbing it with brandy, God knows what, but then it flared up and I just had to go. Man was an absolute butcher, I ended up with a face like a football, no, literally, right out here. And I don't think he'd got it all out either. Ridiculous, isn't it? You know you can have an arm or a leg blown off any time and yet you're still frightened of the dentist. Or you can get your head blown off, for that matter, but then that would solve the problem.

"Then, well, you know, it was one of those cock-ups. We were supposed to be taken to the attack positions by guides, they never showed up, we hung about, more guides arrived, didn't know where we were going. By the time we finally got there it was less than an hour before the attack. The barrage was deafening, nobody could hear the orders, shells dropping everywhere. Massive casualties in the first minute, the stretcher bearers were just overwhelmed. The men who couldn't make it back were left out there crying for water, flies everywhere . . .

"As soon as it was dark Brooke took a party out and we started bringing in the wounded, took us the best part of three days. That's how bad it was. And then we brought in the dead. I've never been able to see the point of it; of course I can see it's a good thing to do, in itself, but not if it means risking lives, especially not my life." He glanced at Paul. "I'm telling you the truth. Brooke was a hero, I was a fat man with toothache. And then we went out looking for identity disks. Well, you can imagine, can't you, pitch black, poddling about in God knows what . . . Do you know what he did? He got a torch out and switched the bugger on."

"Did they fire?"

"'Course they bloody fired. The age of chivalry's dead, Tarrant, or hadn't you noticed. Brooke got a slight wound on the back of his hand, we had a handful of identity disks. Oh, and Brooke's MC. Eventually."

"Strange, isn't it? All that effort put into collecting identity disks and yet he ended up 'Missing, Believed Killed.'"

"Well, that's the way it goes."

They sat listening to the roar of flames. Footsteps ran past the window; farther down the path a man was shouting, though you couldn't make out the words. It seemed mad that anybody should be out on such a night.

"Can I get you something to eat?" Neville said.

"No, I'm all right."

He didn't want to risk the interruption a meal would cause. He sensed some kind of crisis in Neville; the abscess had burst and would go on leaking now till it was drained.

"Do you know what he did? Immediately afterwards? He sent us to another company to help them out. I couldn't believe it."

"What did the others think?"

"Oh, they worshipped him."

"And you?"

"Well, I worshipped him too."

This was said in a tone that Paul couldn't read. Sarcasm? No, not quite, but not unqualified admiration either. Courage like Brooke's exacts a heavy price, and not only from the man who possesses it. Neville had been, as he said himself, a fat man with toothache who didn't want to die. Brooke must have come to seem more of a menace than the German army.

"Was he ever afraid, do you think?" Paul asked.

"Oh, all the time probably. Just never acted on it."

Paul was reaching for his glass when a loud boom reverberated around the room, followed almost immediately by a second. He started to get up, but Neville raised a hand to keep him in his chair. "It's all right, it's only the lifeboat."

"*Phew!*" Paul said, wiping his brow, trying to make a joke of it, though in fact he was badly shaken. He'd only just managed not to cry out.

"Do you want to go out and watch? A lot of people do."

Paul hesitated, trying to predict the impact on the atmosphere between them, but that had been broken already. "Yes, why not."

"We'd better go round the back. I doubt if we'd get the front door open."

They went across the tiny yard and out into the lane beyond. At first the houses shielded them from the gale, but then they turned the corner and Paul realized the side street had become a funnel for wind and blown spume. The salt stung his eyes and left a foul taste on his tongue. But you couldn't keep your lips closed: you needed nose and mouth to breathe.

Heads down, they battled the few yards to the front. They came out onto the beach to find lights and a crowd of people assembled, some wearing the dark coats of ordinary townspeople, others the gleaming yellow sou'westers of a lifeboat crew.

"How the hell did they get here so fast?" Paul shouted.

Neville pointed to the pub farther along. "Never left. They've been expecting this all day."

The tide was at its peak, foaming over the last bank of shingle, slavering down side alleys, oozing through sandbags into halls and passageways. It had begun to snow, the flakes not hesitant as they'd been the night before, but whirled furiously up by the gale, mingling with spray and spume. Paul shielded his face with his arm, for this was a sea that picked up pebbles the size of pigeon eggs and hurled them against locked and bolted shutters as if they were pea gravel.

The arc lights were switched on—probably the only visible lights on the whole east coast at that moment—creating
an island of light that shaded away into blackness at the edges.
Some of the men were already in the boat, shouting down
to other men below. Paul caught the atmosphere of mingled
fear and relief. The maroon booming like that had had the
same effect as whistles blowing to signal the start of an attack.
You put your hands on the ladder, started to climb, bile gush-
ing into your mouth, bowels loosening, and yet, mixed in
with all the terror was relief because it had started, at last. He
glanced sideways at Neville, who was holding his scarf close
to his face, for the air was salt enough to sting, and in his eyes,
too, there was the same mixture of fear and exultation.

The crew were all in the boat now; some of them were
middle-aged, or even older. The young men, their sons, had
gone and so the old took up the burden again. One of them
leaned over and shouted something to the men on the ground,
but his words were snatched away on the wind. The lifeboat
was like something half imagined or dimly remembered, its
attendant figures scurrying round it like drones round a ter-
mite queen.

Just as Paul turned to speak to Neville, a stronger gust
blew, making him stagger to one side, and when he looked
round again the lifeboat was sliding down the slipway into the
sea. As it hit the water great curling plumes of foam rose up on
either side. It dipped once, twice, yawing and floundering in
the trough of a wave, struggling to free itself, before it reached
the open sea. Once there, it slipped quickly into the darkness.

It was a shock to stand there, staring at the place where
it had been, feeling how empty the beach was without it, but
then the lights were extinguished. Blackness followed, absolute, thick dark. Only gradually did Paul become aware of
knots of people dispersing, going off in small groups, some of
them, particularly the older women, alone.

Paul and Neville also turned and made for home. Paul felt numbed, mentally and physically, but excited as well, transported out of himself. Neville, too, looked and sounded different. Once inside the living room, he stripped off his coat, unwound the scarf and reached for his unfinished drink.

"That was a nasty moment, you know. I thought for a minute they were going to capsize. It's when the wind veers east, it catches them from the side."

"How long do you think they'll be out?"

"All night, probably. Go on, get yourself a drink."

Paul felt better than he'd felt for months. The soporific effect of the pain-relieving powder had worn off, but despite that mad scramble across the shingle, the pain in his knee hadn't returned. He felt a fleeting, irrational hope that it might have gone for good. He pulled his chair closer to the fire. There was an outdoor feel to the room now: a hiss of snowflakes hitting the hot coal, wind thumping doors and windows, lifting rugs, the smell of the cold, wet air they'd brought in on their skins.

He looked up and found Neville watching him. Somehow the shared experience had changed things between them: he felt they could say anything now.

"So when did you decide to get rid of him?"

Neville stared, reared back in mock astonishment, and burst out laughing. "What a taste for melodrama you do have."

"It happens."

"Does it hell. You've been reading too many penny dreadfuls, that's your trouble."

"I've heard—"

"Of course you've heard. We've all *heard*. Somebody knew somebody who knew somebody who knew for a fact that such and such . . . And so on."

"But nobody's going to come right out and say *they* did it. Are they?"

"No, because they didn't. Haven't."

Paul stared into the fire. Waited.

"I knew somebody who said he was virtually certain a platoon in his company had got rid of a junior officer. He was a bit too keen on Death or Glory and they got fed up. One patrol too many, they come back, he doesn't. I just don't believe it," Neville said. "I didn't then and I don't now."

"I think you've made that clear."

"Oh, I'm not saying it didn't occur to me. Actually, it did, for . . . Oh, I don't know . . . about three seconds? No, I'd have been far more likely to kill myself." He bent down to throw a log on the fire. "You do believe me, don't you?"

"Every word. Why would you tell lies when you can just keep quiet? It's what you've done so far."

Neville raised a hand to his face, pressing hard into his temple, as if the abnormal position of his head was causing him pain. It was the movement of a bewildered animal and it moved Paul so deeply that he had to look away.

"You must've realized by now there's nothing good to be said."

"I thought perhaps he'd . . ."

"Go on. What?"

"I thought he'd lost his nerve."

Neville made an ugly barking sound. "Brooke? He didn't have any bloody nerves."

"What, then?"

"Promise you won't tell Elinor?"

Paul shook his head.

"Well, that's up to you."

The silence went on so long Paul began to think Neville had decided to say no more, but then, staring down into his glass, seeming to talk as much to himself as Paul, he went on.

"Once we were out of the line there wasn't a lot to do. Sick parade every morning, one or two patients in sick bay, not many, and I started to notice how often Brooke slipped away. We all did. He used to ride a lot, all day sometimes, and it became a bit of a standing joke, you know: Doc's in love with his horse. And then one night, we had a patient with pneumonia—it wasn't looking too good—and Brooke told me to come and get him if he took a turn for the worse. Well, he did. Brooke wasn't in his bunk, so I went looking for him, and I found him in the stables with one of the stable boys. Lad called Duke. Big, fair-haired, rawboned carthorse of a lad, straight out of the shires, and . . . Well, I won't spell it out. I must have made a sound because Brooke looked straight at me."

"What did you do?"

"Backed off, of course. I could see it wasn't the right time for a chat."

"No, I mean, later. What did you do?"

"I didn't know what to do, I—"

"Did you tell anybody?"

Neville's voice hardened. "We're talking about a man exploiting his inferiors. Brooke was an officer. That lad couldn't have said no even if he'd wanted to."

Paul was silent for a moment. "Are you sure it was exploitation? I mean, if Brooke was just looking for . . . well, for relief—there'd be far safer ways of getting it than that. He must've felt something for him . . ."

"Oh, so it's a love story now, is it? *Tarrant . . .*"

"How do you know it wasn't?"

"I knew the boy. Total idiot, face like a pig's arse."

Was that jealousy? No, it couldn't be. "So you reported him?"

"It was the right thing to do."

"Who did you tell?"

"The Padre."

"Who couldn't stand Brooke, anyway . . . I remember

you said, didn't you, they'd had that row about venereal disease?"

"It's no use idealizing that kind of thing. It's not Greek love, you know, it's just another form of bullying. I hated it at school and I hate it now."

That was certainly true. Neville had an extreme hatred of what he described as "effeminacy" or "degeneracy," whether in life or in art.

"You knew what would happen to him though, didn't you? Court martial, ten years' hard labor, struck off the medical register . . ."

"God, yes, total waste. Tragedy. And all because he couldn't keep his dick inside his breeches. But, you know, that was his decision, not mine."

"So what happened?"

"Nothing. That was the awful thing. Brooke didn't say anything. I mean, what could he say? I started to think the Padre must've kept it to himself, though that didn't seem likely, but then Brooke was summoned to see the CO. He came back looking pretty grim. Still didn't say anything. I thought he'd be arrested. But he wasn't, and a day or two later we went back into the line. And right into the thick of it, this time. The Casualty Clearing Station was the best equipped I've ever seen—electric light, for God's sake—virtually shellproof. But no, typical Brooke, he insisted on going forward." He drank the last of his whiskey in one gulp. "It was, I think, the worst I've ever experienced. A lot of it's a blur. At one point there was a flood of German prisoners coming in, a lot of them wounded, and among them there was a German doctor and he volunteered to help—I'll always remember this— Brooke was on one side of the table, the German MO was on the other, both of them covered in blood, you couldn't tell one uniform from the other, and they were laughing their heads off. Shells dropping everywhere, the wounded screaming, and there they were, stitching up what their respective armies had blown apart. If you ever want a picture of the complete bloody insanity of the whole thing that was it. Brooke was wounded, just a gash on the side of his face, but deep, he could've gone back, nobody would have blamed him, but he didn't, of course, he went on operating. He'd have got the VC if it hadn't been for the other thing.

"There was so much confusion, nobody knew where the line was anymore, the whole area was being shelled by both sides. It took us all night to get in the wounded, but we did, every single one of them. And then, just before dawn, Brooke looked through the periscope and said he could see something moving. I looked. I couldn't see anything. But Brooke insisted, there was somebody still out there. Alive. He took me out with him. Just me this time.

"The sun was still below the horizon but the sky was getting lighter by the minute. Absolute bloody suicide, but he was determined to go, and of course I had no choice, I had to go. And he was right, there was something moving. It was just a strip of cloth caught on the wire, but it was very strange, because every time the wind blew it seemed to be beckoning. As if it were waving us to come closer. When we finally got there, it was an empty sleeve. I think he'd known all along.

"It was getting lighter all the time, I could see his face quite clearly now and there was . . . Oh, I don't know, a kind of *glitter* about him. And it suddenly dawned on me he wasn't just taking chances, not this time. He wasn't going back, he couldn't, and I think he'd made up his mind to take me with him.

"We crouched in this bloody shell hole and . . . He said the CO had offered him the chance of an honorable way out and he'd decided to take it, he knew what was waiting for him, he couldn't bear the idea of putting his family through it. Then he got a revolver out—he didn't normally carry one, some of the MOs did, but not Brooke—and as soon as I saw it I thought: *He's going to kill me.* He was pointing it straight at me, he wanted to see me shitting myself, I know he did. But then he lowered it and . . . he just stood up. I remember the first sunlight falling on his head and shoulders. And then he turned to face the German lines and started firing shots into the air. Nothing happened. Honest to God, the hell we'd been through, day and night. Where's the bloody Hun when you need him? And then I thought it was going to be all right, I thought he'd take cover, we'd wait and when it was dark we'd crawl back and . . . I don't know what I thought was going to happen then. But it was never a possibility. He just looked down at me and shrugged. Then he put the revolver in his mouth and blew the back of his head off."

Neville was struggling to go on. At last he wiped his hand across his mouth and said, "I had to go on lying there, I daren't move. And then it got dark and it was so strange, you know, his dead face looking up at the stars, not seeing them, and rain falling into his eyes. I tried to make myself close them, but I couldn't bear to touch him."

"How long were you there?"

"A whole day, half the following night. Then I managed to crawl back, only just in time too, because the bombardment started up again and the whole area was pounded."

"Did they look for him?"

"No point. Nothing would have been left."

"Wait a minute. If you saw him die, why was he posted 'Missing'?"

"Because I didn't tell anybody. I said he left me in a crater and went on alone."

They carried on sitting in the firelight, as motionless as flies in amber, until the crash of a collapsing log jolted Paul into speech. "Why couldn't you tell Elinor that?"

"The disgrace."

"I doubt if she'd see it like that."

"No, but her parents would, their friends would. Let's face it, Tarrant, everybody would—except for a few nancy boys in bloody Bloomsbury. I thought it was right to spare his family and I still think it's right. He blew his brains out to save them from it, so what do you think gives me the right to come back to London and start blabbing?"

There were hollows in the fire now. As Paul watched, a ridge of coals fell and Neville's face was plunged into shadow.

"You could have made something up."

"Lies, you mean?"

"If need be."

"You don't lie to people you respect."

"You could've told Elinor the truth."

"Are you going to tell her?"

"I don't know. Probably."

"Well, you know her better than I do." After a few seconds, he went on: "I can't make any sense of him, you know. He was one of the most compassionate—no, not 'one of '—*the* most compassionate man I've ever known. And he was also completely inhumane."

"I suspect some of the saints were a bit like that."

"Didn't go in for buggering boys in stables though, did they?" He took another swig from his glass. "Or, anyway, if they did it's not recorded."

Paul waited for more but Neville seemed to be sinking into a semicomatose state. It was late, the dead of night, and, though the shutters continued to bump, he thought the wind might be dying down. "If you don't mind," he said, "I think I'll turn in."

"No, you go on up. I won't be long."

As he left the room, Neville was leaning forward to throw another log on the fire.

———————

Paul went to bed and tossed and turned for an hour before finally slipping into a threadbare sleep. He dreamt of a desolate landscape in which nothing moved except for a black shape on the horizon, which rose and fell, rose and fell like an arm beckoning, while a bloated sun swelled to fill half the sky.

When he woke it was light. He went across to the window, pulled the blackout curtains to one side, and looked out. Sunlight and clear, cold air on his face. The lifeboat wasn't back, but the storm was over. The sea threw up huge sullen swells that petered out in little runnels and ripples of foam before they reached the first ridge of shingle.

He wanted to get out into the sunshine, forget the darkness of the previous evening. As he was getting dressed, it occurred to him that he hadn't heard Neville come upstairs last night. Well, that wasn't surprising, he'd probably stayed up drinking, Paul would have been asleep by the time he finally came to bed. All the same . . .

Before going downstairs he stood outside Neville's bedroom door and listened, but there was no sound. For a second he wondered if he should push the door open and check on him, but no, he was being ridiculous. Neville would quite rightly resent the intrusion.

Downstairs, he opened the living-room door. The room told its own story. Lamp left on, bottle empty, a glass overturned beside Neville's chair. The kitchen showed no sign that anybody had been there since the previous night. Neville was having a lie-in, and no wonder. Paul tried to remember how much had been left in the bottle when he'd gone to bed. Too much.

He buttered a slice of stale bread, took a slightly wizened russet apple from a bowl on the sideboard, and wandered out onto the path. The lifeboat was being winched up the beach. He stopped to watch and then went back into the house, increasingly concerned about Neville, who was ill, after all. When the doctors let him out to convalesce, they hadn't had drinking sessions like last night's in mind.

His bed hadn't been slept in. That left his studio, which would be, presumably, on the second floor. Paul pushed doors open till he found it. Neville wasn't there either. Paul was about to withdraw, but then his eye was caught by the painting on the easel. Normally he wouldn't have dreamt of looking at somebody else's unfinished work, but from the glimpse he'd had of this, he knew he had to see more.

No wonder Neville had seemed so preoccupied with what the censor would allow, because he'd been painting the moment of death, the only subject more strongly discouraged than corpses. The figure at the center of the composition was being blown backwards by the force of an unseen explosion, while behind him on the horizon a grotesquely fat sun, a goblin of a sun, was eating up the sky.

Paul knew he was looking at the moment of Toby Brooke's death, though not exactly as Neville had related it. There was no revolver here. Well, fair enough, Neville was under no obligation to stick to the facts. Whatever "the facts" were. Now that he was better rested and able to think more clearly, Paul wasn't sure how much of Neville's story he believed. Oh, Neville had set out to tell the truth—he didn't doubt that for a moment—but was it possible that, in the end, he'd ducked out of revealing something too dreadful to be told?

Paul backed out of the room and closed the door quietly behind him. There came a time when you simply had to let it go and accept an approximation of the truth, and he'd reached that moment now. Two men set out into no-man's-land; one man came back. That was all anybody else knew, or would ever know.

Downstairs, the front door opened. Neville was back.

"Where've you been?" Paul said.

"The doctor's. You said you'd seen him, I thought I ought to go and say how sorry I was about Ian."

Paul leaned over the banisters. Neville was standing in the hall, holding a loaf of bread and a bottle of milk. He looked surprisingly fresh. Invigorated, almost. Suddenly, Paul felt that any anxiety about this man was not merely unnecessary but stupid. Look at him; just look at him. Whoever else went under, Kit Neville would survive.

28

Paul arrived at the station early in a cold drizzle and sat down to wait for the train from Sidcup. When it drew in he got to his feet and searched for Elinor among the gray-black hurrying figures. She was wearing a lavender-colored hat; it cheered him to see her bobbing along, though the face she turned up to him was sharp, hungry for information.

All that day he'd been thinking about what Neville had said, only a few minutes before Paul had left for London.

"For God's sake, man. Brooke blew his brains out so his family didn't have to know. Do you really think he'd want you to tell Elinor? No, he made his choice, and the least *you* can do is respect it."

Paul wouldn't have dreamt of telling Brooke's parents, or his older sister, for that matter. Knowing how he'd died would only cause them additional pain and they'd already had to endure so much. But then, couldn't the same be said of Elinor? He didn't know. He took her in his arms, put his lips to her cold, damp cheek, and still he didn't know.

"We can go next door, to the hotel," he said.

She shook her head. "No, I've been stuck in a hut all day, I could do with some fresh air."

They began walking down Villiers Street towards the river. A dank stench came off the water, mingling with the sulfurous smell of the fog that had been thickening since morning.

He asked how her day had been.

"Oh, not bad. I enjoy it, you know. I never thought I would, but I do . . ."

They turned left onto Victoria Embankment.

"I've said I'll do another day. Tonks is going to France at the end of January, so they want me to do a bit more."

"Yes, he told me he was going. Doesn't seem to be looking forward to it very much. Fact, he said he'd seen enough horrors to last him the rest of his life."

"I'll miss him. I couldn't have done it without him."

Ahead of them Waterloo Bridge loomed out of the mist. The water underneath the nearest arch broke into V-shaped ripples as a boat passed through. There were flecks of crimson on the surface of the river, where the setting sun had briefly managed to free itself from a bank of cloud, but they were fading even as he watched. From the far side, almost invisible in the mist, came shouts and splashes and then, one after another, factory whistles began to blow for the start of another shift. London in winter.

"Doesn't it make you want to paint it?" she asked.

"No, it makes me want to get away from it. Oh, I can see it's beautiful, but it's not for me."

She'd slowed down and was scuffing her sleeve along the balustrade, looking at the great arc of the bridge with the hundreds of gray and black figures pattering across.

"Neville would love it. But then, he's luckier than I am." Instantly, Paul realized how crass that sounded. "I mean, as a painter, he's got all this waiting for him after the war."

"You've got the countryside."

"Well, ye-es. But landscape's starting to feel a bit old hat even to me."

She turned to face him.

"How was he?"

He started to say something bland, and stopped.

"Different. You know, before the war I used to think he was incredibly self-pitying, because, let's face it, he had it a lot easier than most. And yet there he is, no nose, quite a lot of pain . . . Not that he ever mentions it, but . . . Well, I know the signs. Facing God knows how many more operations, and there isn't a trace of self-pity. I mean, he's actually quite funny about it now and then. Is it true the last operation was a failure because he had a cold in the nose?"

"Oh, it was a bit more than that. Fact, I think he very nearly died." She took a deep breath. "Did you talk about Toby at all?"

The white face under the lavender hat took the decision for him: he couldn't lie to her, not about this. "Yes."

She tried to smile. "Well? How bad is it?"

"Bad."

"Go on."

"He killed himself."

"Why?" She was up in arms at once. "Because he was frightened? I don't believe—"

"No, nothing like that. Because . . ." He threw up his hands. "He was having an affair with a boy who looked after the horses and somehow or other the CO found out." He watched her struggling to take it in. "You've got to realize nothing could've saved him. Yes, he was well liked, he was respected, he'd got the MC—none of it would've made the slightest difference. Except, I suppose, it was why the CO took the decision he did, which was to let Toby know he'd been reported. Otherwise, the first he knew he'd have been arrested. In effect the CO gave him the chance . . . Well. To sort it out in the only way possible."

Her face was completely blank; he couldn't tell whether she was taking it in or not.

"Otherwise, you see, it would have been a court-martial, he'd have been stripped of his rank, probably got ten years with hard labor *and* he'd have been struck off the medical register—even when he came out he wouldn't have been able to practice as a doctor. So you can see, can't you, why suicide must have seemed the only way? He was trying to spare his family the disgrace."

Her mouth twitched as if she wanted to speak.

"Does that make sense?" he said.

"Oh, God, yes. Except it wouldn't be 'family'—it would be Mother. Even as a boy he was always trying to protect her." A small, hard laugh. "The wind was never allowed to blow on her."

She turned and looked over the river. Before, when he'd tried to imagine this moment, he'd dreaded her tears. Now her composure worried him more.

"Let's get you somewhere warm. It's freezing out here."

"How did he do it?"

"You're sure you want to know?"

She looked at him.

"He said he saw something moving in no-man's-land. They'd spent all night getting in the wounded, but he thought, or said he thought, that there was somebody else out there. He took Neville with him."

"So Kit *was* there?"

"Yes, he was. Just as it was getting light Toby stood up and fired at the German lines. Obviously, he thought he was going to be shot, but—God knows why—nothing happened, so he turned the revolver on himself. It was over in a second, there couldn't possibly have been any pain."

"But there would have been a body."

"Another bombardment started, not long afterwards. Every inch of the ground was shelled. Of course, they went out looking for him, but there was nothing left."

She was breathing heavily, still tearless.

"Thank you for telling me."

"Neville says he was quite exceptionally brave in the last few days. He refused to leave the line even when he was wounded. If it hadn't been for this other thing he'd have been decorated again, no question."

"No, but there was, wasn't there? This 'other thing.'"

She made as if to walk on and for a moment he hoped that might be the end of it, but then she turned back.

"Who told the CO?"

"The Padre. I don't know how he knew."

He'd set out to tell her the truth, or at least the version of the truth that Neville had told him. Instead, he'd started lying without ever taking a conscious decision.

"Will you tell your parents?"

"No, I don't think so. What's the point? It only adds to the pain."

"Perhaps I shouldn't have told you?"

"No, I needed to know."

He touched her elbow and they started to walk on again. She looked almost dazed.

"Did you know about Toby?"

"That he liked men?" She shrugged. "Yes and no. I mean, I always thought he and Andrew were lovers. But . . . It's never that simple, is it?"

"Were there ever any girls?"

She took so long to answer he was beginning to think she hadn't heard the question.

"There was a girl, once."

"What happened?"

"I don't know."

They turned away from the river, cutting up the steep lane that lead from the Embankment to the Strand. At the top of the hill, Paul looked back at the water. Here and there, dark, sketchy shapes of boats smirched the mist. Tiny figures like insects still swarmed across the bridge, while underneath the strong, brown, muscular river flowed, oblivious of the city that befouled it.

He touched her arm. "Let's have a drink, shall we?"

They went to the Savoy. Paul had never been there before, nor ever dreamt he would one day be able to afford it. The foyer seemed vast, with red-and-gold rugs covering a black-and-white marble floor. A short flight of stairs led down to a room in which groups of smartly dressed people were reflected in tall gilt mirrors. A murmur of conversation, a chink of glasses, gloved waiters bending deferentially over the tables . . .

They sat on a leather sofa several feet apart, for all the world like a Victorian courting couple. He ordered two brandies, and was pleased to see some color returning to her face as she drank. He told himself it didn't matter that he'd withheld a large part of the truth from her. Some secrets aren't meant to be told.

After a long pause, he said tentatively, "Have you thought what you might do after the war?"

He was painfully aware of how insensitive this question might seem so soon after she'd learned of Toby's suicide, but she turned to him with a smile.

"Depends who wins."

"I think that counts as Spreading Gloom and Despondency."

She nodded towards the chattering crowd. "They could do with a bit of that."

"They might look at us and think exactly the same."

"Yes, you're right, of course. Nobody wears a broken heart on their sleeve. Oh, now . . . What would I do? I don't know. I take it we're not thinking Thirty Years?"

"No point, we'd all be past it."

"I'm past it now."

"No, you're not."

"I don't know, I can't think that far. Actually, it's worse than that. The other day I realized—this is going to sound really mad—what I really think, deep down, is that the dead are only dead for the duration. When it's over they'll all come back and it'll be just the same as it was before." She glanced at him. "I told you it was mad."

"There mightn't be anything left worth coming back for."

"Now who's spreading Gloom? Anyway, presumably you have thought?"

"Something Neville said . . . I suddenly thought I want to get away from all this. Everything. I want to be somewhere where I know I could never possibly fit in . . ."

"England?"

"*No,* somewhere warm. Somewhere oranges grow on trees."

She laughed. "It does sound rather nice."

"You could come too."

No reply. He was damning himself for a fool, but then, just as the silence became unbearable, her hand crept along the expanse of leather between them and took refuge in his. Frightened, they looked into each other's eyes and tried to smile, but it wasn't possible. Not yet.

———

Now they'd decided to sell the house, it seemed to turn its face away from her, like an abandoned child rejecting the mother when she returns. No click of claws in the hallway; no bloodshot eyes raised to hers: Hobbes had gone to live with her mother. The house seemed to be giving up: there was a smell of damp, though Mrs. Robinson said she lit fires in all the downstairs rooms whenever she came in to clean.

This would be Elinor's last visit. Paul was coming tomorrow to help take her luggage to the station. Father was organizing a van to remove the furniture and the rest of their stuff. She wandered from room to room, unable to settle to anything, then forced herself to go upstairs, pack what remained of her clothes, and start on the far more difficult job of sorting out books and papers. She'd take just the one photograph of Toby, she decided; the one where his face seemed to be disappearing into a white light. All the others were of teams at school and university; this was the only one of Toby by himself.

She picked it up and looked at his face, wondering why she found it so hard to paint, when she knew every inch: the blue eyes, closed now; the ears, crammed with silence; the mouth, stopped forever. It was too painful to go on looking, so she replaced the photograph gently on the shelf.

After two hours' packing, she went across to the barn. She needed to look at her paintings again before they were sent off to be stored. As she raised the lamp, the studio's familiar shadows fled before her. One by one, she held the paintings up to the light. *Who are you?* they seemed to say. Nothing ruder, more dismissive, than a completed piece of work. But then, her eyes were drawn to the portrait waiting on the easel. She swept the white cloth aside and held the lamp close. Why didn't it work? Something about the eyes, was it? Perhaps without realizing she'd slipped into self-portraiture, producing, in the end, a composite figure, the joint person she and Toby had become. She replaced the cloth, but the eyes still followed her; she could feel them burrowing into her back as she walked to the door.

After that, she was glad to collapse onto the sofa in the

living room. She felt the pressure of Toby's empty room above her head. Wherever she was in the house, she was conscious of that emptiness. The ache of his absence was like nothing she'd ever experienced before. And knowing how he'd died had made everything worse, because now she was angry with him. He was no longer an innocent victim: his death had been a choice.

She forced herself to stand up, to go into the kitchen and look for food. Mrs. Robinson had left a stew on the stove. She started to warm it up, but couldn't bear the slow breaking up of congealed fat on its surface. Tomorrow, she told herself. She went to bed very early these days, exhausted by her work at the hospital. It drained her as nothing else ever had, except perhaps—all those years ago—dissecting poor old George. In the last few weeks George had reentered her life as she trawled through her old anatomy notes, trying to make sense of the chaos left by shrapnel wounds. Toby's textbooks too. She got them out and sat with them on her knees, discovering, as she turned over a page, that Toby had left a perfect thumbprint in the margin. She felt very close to him at such times. Almost as if, in that final moment of unthinkable tearing and rending, part of him had fled and taken refuge in her.

Slowly, she went upstairs, not bothering to switch on the lights, wanting to avoid seeing her duplicated reflection in the mirrors that faced each other across the half-landing. In the darkness of Toby's room, she undressed, feeling her way from wardrobe to chair with the assurance of long familiarity. She threw Toby's coat on the bed as an extra cover, then slipped between the sheets and buried her face in the cool silk of its lining. Beneath her own scent, she could still smell Toby's hair and skin, but fading, always fading.

Somewhere downstairs, a door creaked open. That was old houses for you; never still. She fell into a restless sleep, always aware of the square of light in the window, the shapes of objects in the room. The bedclothes seemed to be tightening round her. She flung out her arm and encountered something solid: another body lying beside her, cold and inert. The cold was spreading into her bones. She opened her eyes. God, what a dream. Rolling over, she reached for the bedside lamp meaning to turn it on, but she couldn't get to it. Something was in the way, an obstacle the size and shape of a bolster, lying along her side.

The body was still there.

This time she came properly awake, with a cry that must have sounded through the whole house. The sheets were damp; sweat had gathered in the creases of her neck. But now, at least she was free to switch on the lamp, and the light, gradually, calmed her.

It had been Toby, in her dream, and nothing Toby did could make her afraid. After twenty minutes or so she felt calm enough to go to sleep again. At the last moment, slipping beneath the surface, she heard Toby's voice say: "I can't give this up."

When she woke again, she heard him calling her name. The voice was coming from downstairs, and though the prospect made her shiver, she knew she had to go to him. She went slowly, sliding her feet carefully to the edge of each tread. Toby called her name again. She glided towards the sound of his voice, half in memory, half in dream.

And there he was: standing with his back to the window, stripped to the waist, his braces dangling round his hips, and his arms outstretched in a parody of crucifixion. The room was full of viscous, golden light; he seemed to be the source of it. His skin glowed. She walked up to him, smiling, happy, full of the wonder of his being there. "Oh, you're back," she said. His arms held her, his head bent down to kiss her. She touched his warm skin, she flowed towards him, but then a shadow fell. She thought, or said—there was no difference here—"We can't do this, you're dead." Instantly, the warmth and light began to fade. In a second, he was gone.

She knew she had to get back to bed: there was a sense of urgency in this. She walked, stiff-backed, up the stairs and into Toby's room. Bed, she thought. The owls were in full cry. Like a statue on a catafalque, she lay: legs straight, arms by her sides, wandering on the borders of sleep, until the half-light of a winter dawn restored her to the waking world.

That morning, despite her broken night, she achieved more in the way of packing and sorting out than she'd managed in the whole of the previous weekend. As she worked, she thought about her dream. She had to call it a dream, because there was no other available word, but she knew that, unlike any other dream that she'd ever had, it had been an event in the real world with the power to effect change.

Paul would be here soon. With her suitcases lined up in the hall, Elinor went upstairs to Toby's room. She stripped the bed, folded the sheets, and left them on the landing for Mrs. Robinson to find. In the process, she uncovered a small stain on the mattress, a crescent shape, like a fetus curled up in the womb, or a dolphin leaping. She pulled the blanket up to hide it, and then went across to the window.

Looking down, she saw the narrow ledge that ran the length of the house between the first and second floors. Once, when they'd been particularly naughty, she and Toby had been locked in their rooms and that night he'd crawled along the ledge to get to her. She couldn't have been more than five or six years old at the time, and yet, the following morning, looking down at the terrace below, she'd thought, with a flash of adult perception: *Yes, but you could've been killed.*

She raised her eyes, and there was Paul, bobbing along the lane, his head just visible above the hedge. At the gate, he stopped, flexing his injured leg, his face twisted by the pain he would never let her see. She was half ashamed of witnessing it and pulled back into the room so he wouldn't notice her standing there.

She waited for his knock, and then, briefly aware that she was leaving Toby's room for the last time, ran downstairs to let him in.

Author's Note

Readers who would like to see the Tonks portraits can find them online at http//www.gilliesarchives.org.uk together with photographs and case histories of many of the same patients. The original portraits are with the Royal College of Surgeons of England, 35–43 Lincoln's Inn Fields, London.

Henry Tonks: Art and Surgery by Emma Chambers, published by the College Art Collections (University College London, 2002), contains a thought-provoking examination of the aesthetic and ethical questions raised by the portraits. *Chavasse, Double VC* by Ann Clayton, published by Leo Cooper, and *Doctors in the Great War* by Ian R. Whitehead, also published by Leo Cooper, give a vivid and detailed picture of the work of medical officers in the front line. Dr. Andrew Bamji's unpublished notes on Queen Mary's Hospital, Sidcup, contain much fascinating information about the facial reconstruction carried out there.

Thanks are due to Emma Chambers; John Aiken, Slade Professor; and Dr. Andrew Bamji, Consultant Rheumatologist and Curator of the Gillies Archive, for their help during my research for the writing of this book. I would also like to thank my agent, Gillon Aitken, for his shrewd advice and unfailing support and kindness over many years.

ABOUT THE AUTHOR

Pat Barker is most recently the author of *Life Class*, as well as the highly acclaimed Regeneration Trilogy: *Regeneration*; *The Eye in the Door*, winner of the Guardian Fiction Prize; and *The Ghost Road*, winner of the Booker Prize; as well as seven other novels. She lives in the north of England.